Thistles and Thorns

A Lily Deene Novel

Annie Grace Roberts

Thistles and Thorns
A Lily Deene Novel #2
Copyright © 2021 Annie Grace Roberts
All rights reserved.

ISBN: (ebook) 978-1-953335-83-8
(print) 978-1-953335-92-0

Inkspell Publishing
207 Moonglow Circle #101
Murrells Inlet, SC 29576

Cover art by: Fantasia Frog Designs
Edited by: Yezanira Venecia

DEDICATION

For Jen, who taught all of us about courage

ANNIE GRACE ROBERTS

And fare thee well, my only Luve
And fare thee well, a while!
And I will come again, my Luve,
Tho' it were ten thousand mile.

Robert Burns
1759-1796

ANNIE GRACE ROBERTS

CHAPTER 1

26 March 1902

Dearest Mother:

As you bid, I am writing to you so that you will know that I have arrived safely. I am quite glad that the business of traveling is over. Our trip from Edinburgh was very wearisome and frightening. The northern roads are not so well maintained as we are accustomed to in Edinburgh and the carriage creaked and groaned alarmingly as we traveled along a rather precarious route to Anchoret House. We arrived on an oppressively gray afternoon on the 25th, the drizzle and damp adding to the melancholy air of the surrounding moors. I must admit that my first impression of the house of which I am to be mistress was that of a large brown toad squatting in a puddle. You will of course tell me that I must be careful of hasty judgments, but I cannot change my first impression. I suspect that adding some womanly touches to the house will soften its rather unattractive appearance. Colonel Morris has just come to tell me I must finish this letter quickly. He has arranged for the carriage driver to deliver this letter to you and the driver is preparing to leave at this moment. Please give my affection to Father, Alec, Blaire, and Isobel. I hope you will write soon as I miss you all already.

Your devoted daughter,
Mairi

***

I watched the lush green English countryside slide past my window. It had been six months since I'd last visited Brynmoor Manor, the ancestral home of my new stepfather, Sir Richard. After spending my Christmas holidays in England, I had returned to California to finish my senior year of high school. Now, newly graduated, I was back in England. Although, I wasn't entirely sure my return to Brynmoor Manor was going to be a joyful one.

I hadn't heard from Simon since April, not a text, not an email, not a phone call. Nothing. It was as if he had suddenly dropped off the face of the earth. For a long time, I kept trying to contact him, but he never responded to any of my messages. I suppose I could have asked his sister, Jenna, where he was, but my pride wouldn't let me. Eventually, I stopped trying to contact him. I decided that I would do nothing until I was back in England. Nothing, except check my messages a zillion times a day and wait and worry and fume and rage, which was what I was doing now as I sat in the car watching the green hills of Shropshire county roll past as we drove toward the village of Hexingham.

By the time Anton, my stepfather's chauffeur, turned onto the gravel drive leading to the manor house, I was a total wreck. My stomach twisted and churned anxiously as we drove past the stable. Craning my neck, I searched in vain for a glimpse of broad shoulders and copper-colored hair. The horses were out in the paddock, but Simon wasn't with them. I leaned back against the seat, gnawing worriedly on my lower lip and sighing.

To be honest, I was almost relieved that Simon wasn't at Brynmoor. I wasn't completely sure that I was ready to see him, at least not yet. I still hadn't figured out what I was going to say to him when I finally did see him again. I'd rehearsed several opening lines, currently vacillating between "You stupid idiot!" and "I missed you so much." It was hard to decide which approach was the right one, since I had no idea why I hadn't heard from him.

"Here we are, Miss," Anton said as he stopped the car in front of the manor house.

"Thank you, Anton."

I reached for the door handle to get out and was stopped abruptly by Anton's very polite but firm, "Oh, no, Miss. Please allow me."

"Sorry, I forgot," I apologized sheepishly.

It was always a bit of culture shock returning to England. My life in Los Angeles was very different from my life at Brynmoor Manor.

For the past year, I'd been living in a two-bedroom apartment with my grandmother. No chauffeur. No butler. No housekeeper. No maids. Just Grandma, me, and Boris, her obnoxious cockapoo. Now, after a long airplane ride across the Atlantic Ocean, I was back at Brynmoor Manor: eighty-seven rooms, twelve chimneys, a stable, an orangery, and more staff than I could keep track of. It made me feel sympathy for poor Cinderella. Transitioning from cleaning your own bathroom to attending fancy dress balls isn't as easy as most people assume.

I waited patiently for Anton to open the door for me, smiling my thanks when I stepped out of the car. The front door of the manor house opened.

"Lily! You're here!" my mom, a.k.a. Lady Yarlbury, called out as she hurried over to greet me.

With her blonde hair and china-blue eyes, my mother looks every inch the English aristocrat, despite the fact that she is as American as apple pie. People are always surprised to discover that we are related, mostly because I don't look anything like her. I take after my father's side of the family, tall with dark curly hair and hazel eyes.

I gave her a careful hug. "Mom, you look great."

She laughed. "You mean I look great for someone who has put on thirty-five pounds." She patted her round stomach.

I shook my head. "No. Really. You look great." She did. She looked as happy as I'd ever seen her. Her skin positively glowed. Sure, she had a belly the size of the Titanic, but that was to be expected. After all, she was almost eight months pregnant.

She put her arm around my shoulders. "How was your trip?"

I rolled my eyes and groaned. "Long."

"Oh, you poor thing. Come on inside. You'll feel better once we get you settled. If you like, you can take a nap before dinner."

I followed my mom through the heavy oak doors of Brynmoor Manor. It didn't matter how often I walked through those doors, the Great Hall still took my breath away. Oil paintings in ornate gold frames lined an elegant mahogany staircase that rose gracefully from the polished parquet floors to a second-floor landing. Tall windows illuminated the entire room, giving the apricot-colored walls a soft glow. I inhaled deeply, knowing without looking, that an arrangement of roses would be on the entry table, perfuming the air with their delicate fragrance.

"It's good to be back," I told my mother.

"It's good to have you back," my mother said, giving me a little squeeze.

Mrs. Fitzgibbon, Brynmoor's indefatigable housekeeper, bustled through a door carrying another vase of fresh flowers. "Miss Lily! Welcome home!" she said, greeting me warmly.

I gave her a quick hug. It's not really proper for the stepdaughter of an earl to hug a housekeeper, but we don't have the normal stepdaughter of the earl/housekeeper kind of relationship. Mrs. Fitzgibbon isn't just Brynmoor's housekeeper, she is also Simon and Jenna's mother.

Mrs. Fitzgibbon smiled warmly at me and cleared her throat. "We're all so happy to have you home, Miss Lily. Mr. Fitzgibbon cut these flowers for your room. I was just on my way to put them out for you."

"That's really nice of him. Thank you."

"Perhaps later, if you have time, you can stop 'round the cottage. I know Jenna is excited to see you."

"Sure. I'll do that later today," I said, nodding. I noticed that she hadn't said anything about Simon.

Mrs. Fitzgibbon pursed her lips, frowning faintly at my mother. "I hope you are not overdoing things, Lady Yarlbury," she chided gently. "The doctor said you're supposed to be resting."

"Resting?" I asked, glancing worriedly at my mom. "Is something wrong?"

"It's nothing. I'll explain later." She turned and smiled at Mrs. Fitzgibbon. "Lily and I will walk very slowly up the staircase, where I will return directly to my bed. I promise." She held up three fingers in an imitation of the boy scout salute. "Scouts honor."

Mrs. Fitzgibbon nodded, her expression properly serious though her eyes glinted with good humor. "Very well. Shall I send some light refreshments up to your room? A nice cup of herbal tea for you, perhaps?"

"Yes, thank you. That would be lovely."

Satisfied that my mom wasn't going to try and sprint up the staircase, Mrs. Fitzgibbon added, "Well then, I'll just see to Miss Lily's things and finish getting her room settled."

As soon as Mrs. Fitzgibbons left, I turned to my mother, a worried frown puckering my forehead. "Okay, so what's going on? I asked. "Why is the doctor telling you to rest?"

She shrugged. "It's really nothing. I've had a few minor twinges and my very conservative doctor wants to make sure that the next heir to Brynmoor Manor does not arrive too early."

"What! Why didn't you tell me? I would've come sooner."

"Sweetheart, I didn't tell you because there is nothing to worry about. Trust me. If there was something you needed to be concerned with, I would have mentioned it to you. Besides, you would have missed your high school graduation." She linked her arm through mine. "Now help me up the stairs before Mrs. Fitzgibbon comes back with my tea."

"Okay," I told her. "But we are going to walk very slowly and rest on the landings. I do not want to be delivering any babies."

I walked my mom to her bedroom, also known as the Queen Charlotte suite. Her room, decorated in light blue, cream, and gold, was bigger than our old apartment in LA. Soft and feminine—it was perfect for my mom.

"So, have you picked out a name yet?" I asked as I settled next to her on the bed.

She shook her head. "We're still trying to decide."

"Hmm. Aren't you the one who's always lecturing me about procrastinating?" I teased.

"Oh, we still have time. He's not due for almost two more months."

"Now you do sound like me."

She laughed. "If you have any suggestions, I'm all ears."

"Hmm. You'll want something English-sounding, of course."

"English-sounding?"

"You know. Posh."

"Oh my," my mom said. "Posh?"

"Yeah. I mean, you can't call the 10th Earl of Yarlbury Bubba or Leroy or anything like that. It just wouldn't sound right." I cleared my throat and in a deep voice intoned, "Introducing Bubba Leroy, the 10th Earl of Yarlbury."

My mom laughed.

"See," I said. "That sounds ridiculous. The baby needs a very proper English name."

"I can honestly tell you that Bubba never crossed my mind as a possibility."

"Good, because the baby needs a name that goes with his title, and Bubba definitely does not go with the title of an Earl." I laughed as another thought struck me. "What if you called him Earl? Earl the Earl."

My mother just groaned.

"See what I mean, Mom. You need to choose a name that is serious, but elegant. Posh."

"Well, what kind of 'posh' name do you think he needs?"

"Hmm. Something aristocratic, like Reginald or Percival."

"Percival?" my mother asked, one eyebrow arched in disbelief. "Do you really want to be responsible for naming your little brother Percy?"

I grinned. "Okay, maybe not Percival, but Reginald isn't too bad."

"Reggie?"

"I guess not. How about William or James?" I suggested. "Those are perfectly respectable English names."

There was a light rap on the door, interrupting our conversation.

"Come in," my mother called.

"Here's your tea, my lady. And I've brought a plate of biscuits for Miss Lily." Mrs. Fitzgibbon placed the tray carefully on the bedside table.

"Thank you."

"Will you need anything else?"

My mom shook her head. "No. Thank you, Mrs. Fitzgibbon."

I poured out the tea, wrinkling my nose, though not until I made sure that Mrs. Fitzgibbon had closed the door behind her.

"Chamomile?" I asked. "Since when have you started drinking chamomile tea?"

My mother smiled serenely at me and patted her rounded belly. "No caffeine allowed."

"Oh, right. Wow. That's rough. No coffee?"

My mom shook her head. "Not a drop. Though I do admit to going down to the kitchen at night and secretly sniffing the coffee grounds."

"You do not!" I laughed.

"Well, only every now and again," she said, hiding a smile behind her teacup.

We chatted and sipped our chamomile tea, but without an infusion of caffeine, my jetlag soon got the better of me.

"You're tired," my mom said as I yawned for the third time. "Why don't you take a nap before dinner?"

"Good idea," I agreed, stifling yet another yawn. It was five o'clock in England, but my body was still on LA time, and it was telling me it was one o'clock in the morning.

I walked along the hallway to my room. Instead of entering, I paused in front of the door. I was tired, but there was also something I needed to do, and I needed to do it before I lost my nerve.

Instead of going to bed, I went downstairs. After making a quick detour to the kitchen for sugar cubes, I headed out to the stables. I could feel an anxious knot forming in the pit of my stomach as I skirted past the white fence enclosing the paddock. What was I going to say to him? I had a dozen questions that I wanted to ask Simon tumbling around inside my head, most of them beginning with why. As in, why haven't you been answering my texts and emails? Why haven't you called me? Why are you doing this? I wasn't sure that I really wanted to know the answers, but I couldn't stand not knowing anymore.

Only Sirocco, Sir Richard's stallion, was in the paddock now. Someone had returned Wind Dancer and Posy to their stalls in the stable. The stable doors were open.

I squared my shoulders and took a deep breath. During my visit in December, Simon and I had gotten really close. At least, I thought we had. When I returned to California, we texted and talked to each other almost every day. I thought the long-distance thing was working out, but then in April, he just stopped responding to my texts. I'd managed to call him once, but the call was short and awkward, and, well, I wasn't going to embarrass myself by begging him to call me. I just decided that I could wait until I saw him again to find out what was going on. If Simon had found someone else, then he was going to have to look me in the eye and tell me. I wasn't going to let him off easy. My pride wouldn't let me. If he wanted to dump me, he was going to have to tell me to my face. I only hoped I could keep myself from crying in front of him if he did.

The horses turned to look curiously at me as I entered the stable. Posy recognized me right away. She tossed her head and nickered enthusiastically when I stopped in front of her stall.

"Hi, girl," I said to her. "Did you miss me?" I reached out to rub her muzzle.

She butted her head impatiently against my hand, making a whiffling noise by blowing air out of her nostrils, her way of telling me to hurry up.

"I know. You want your treats, don't you?" I fished the sugar cubes out of my pocket and held them out to her in the flat of my hand. Her muzzle was soft against my palm as she eagerly sought the sugar cubes.

"You know, you should at least pretend it's me your glad to see. I'm beginning to think you only love me for the sugar cubes," I chided her as I rubbed behind her ears.

She butted her head against me again. "Hey, cut that out, you greedy little thing. No more for you," I told her.

"I see yer back." A voice called out from behind me.

I turned, surprised. Old Joseph walked toward me,

limping slightly. I hadn't heard him come in.

"Now, don't yer go feeding Posy all that sugar again, Miss. It's not good for 'er teeth."

I smiled at him and tried not to look guilty. "Just saying hello, that's all."

He looked at me, an expression of disbelief on his weathered face.

"How's she been," I asked quickly.

"Posy's a good girl. She never gives me no problems except what she 'as with 'er teeth. She's got a real sweet tooth that one 'as, but it's best not to indulge 'er," he said, looking sternly at me.

I'd been busted. I shrugged apologetically. "I'll bring her an apple next time.'

"Cut up 'em up for 'er. She can't eat the 'ole ones," he warned.

"Okay. I'll do that." Glancing around the newly built stables, I added, "They did a nice job rebuilding everything."

Old Joseph shrugged. "It's not so big as the one that was 'ere afore the fire burned it down, but it'll do."

"I like it," I said. "There aren't as many stalls, but the new tack room is an improvement."

Old Joseph answered with something between a grunt and wheeze, which I took as an affirmative answer. "You're walking a lot better. How is your leg?" I asked, noticing that he was no longer using his cane.

"It'll do." He tipped his hat at me. "Got work to do. Good day, Miss," he said before turning away.

"Uhm, Joseph," I called out.

He stopped and turned around. "Yes, Miss?"

"Uhm, I was just wondering ..." I paused, my face turning hot with embarrassment. "Uhm ... I was just wondering if Simon was around today."

Old Joseph eyed me for a moment before answering. "'E's not working 'ere. 'E's taken a proper veterinary job."

"A job?"

"Yup. 'E's working at a veterinary clinic in Scotland."

I stared open-mouthed at him for a moment. "Scotland? You mean the country of Scotland?"

"That's the one." Old Joseph nodded. "G'day, Miss."

As I watched Old Joseph limp away, my thoughts were spinning. Simon was in Scotland? Why? And more importantly, why hadn't he told me he was going to Scotland? I knew he had been looking for a job, but Scotland? Why there? It was so far away. It didn't make any sense. Why would he take a job so far away when he could have easily found work closer to Brynmoor?

Then a nasty little voice inside my head whispered, *Maybe he didn't go to Scotland for the job. Maybe he went to Scotland because he wanted to get away from you.*

ANNIE GRACE ROBERTS

CHAPTER 2

15 May 1902

Dearest Mother,

I was so happy to receive your letter of Wednesday last. I must admit to feeling homesick for Edinburgh. I am frightfully bored. The countryside is not to my liking as there is not much here with which to amuse myself. I do so miss the parties and dancing. I am afraid that my gowns will not see much use at Anchoret House. You asked if I was settling into my duties and I can answer you that I am; however, there is little that needs to be done. We have no neighbors near Anchoret House and the local residents of Baliaire are rather unfriendly and not the sort of people one would invite to a dinner party. So I find I have little opportunity to entertain. I suppose that is for the best, as the cook is a rather bad-humored woman of limited intelligence. The colonel has told me that the garden is to be my responsibility and I may do as I like with it. Would you send some clematis cuttings and perhaps a rose bush? I would so like to have something beautiful to admire, as I am surrounded by nothing but the grim and melancholy moor.

As ever your affectionate daughter,

Mairi

***

"Old Joseph told me Simon took a job in Scotland," I said, trying to keep my voice casual as Jenna adjusted the saddle on Wind Dancer's withers.

"Right. You didn't know?" she asked without turning around to look at me.

We were getting the horses ready to go on a trail ride, something we had done nearly every day during my last visit to Brynmoor. "No."

Jenna kept her eyes focused on Wind Dancer's saddle and tightened the girth.

"Why didn't you tell me?" I asked, unable to keep the accusing tone out of my voice.

"I thought Simon told you," she said, adjusting the stirrups.

"Well, he didn't," I snapped.

Jenna finally turned to look at me, surprised. "What's going on? Why are you so cross?"

I took a deep breath to calm myself. "I'm not 'cross.' I just want to know why Simon took a job in Scotland when he could have found one here. I know Dr. Eames would have hired him. So why did he go?"

Jenna shrugged. "I don't know. He just told us that he had found a job in Edinburgh. I didn't ask why. Maybe it was the only one he could get."

"That's not true! Dr. Eames would have hired him!" I said more loudly than I intended.

Jenna's eyes widened at my reaction.

I sighed heavily. "Sorry," I apologized, feeling bad about taking my anger and frustration out on her. "I know it's not your fault."

She stared at me for a moment before asking, "So, what's going on with you and Simon?"

I paused to swallow past the lump forming in my

throat. "I don't know. I haven't heard from him in months."

She looked at me with an expression somewhere between surprise and sympathy. "Oh."

What else could she say? I mean, I was talking about her brother. "It's just that I was really looking forward to being with him this summer, and now he's in Edinburgh and he didn't even tell me." My voice cracked and I turned away from her to give Posy's girth another tug.

I had promised myself that I was done crying over Simon Fitzgerald. I swallowed past the hard knot in my throat and walked around to Posy's other side so that I could finish adjusting my stirrups, blinking back the tears that threatened to fall as I did so. I could feel Jenna's eyes on me.

"Lily, I don't know why he didn't tell you. It just sort of happened. One day he came home and told us he had a job in Edinburgh, then he was gone. Perhaps it was a really good job for him," she said gently.

"Okay, so why didn't he tell me?" I asked.

"Maybe he's been so busy he hasn't had the chance."

I rolled my eyes at her. "Come on, Jenna. How long does it take to send a text?" I turned and fiddled with the stirrup leather. "He should have told me," I added. "If he was going to dump me, the least he could have done was tell me instead of slithering off to Scotland without saying a word."

Jenna gave me a sympathetic look, opened her mouth as if to say something, then closed it again without speaking.

"I'm sorry," I told her, realizing that I had put her in an awkward position. "I know he's your brother. I shouldn't have said that. Does he ... I mean, is he ... Did he say anything about me to you?"

Jenna gave me an apologetic shake of her head.

I hesitated before asking the next question. I wasn't sure I wanted to know, but I couldn't seem to keep myself from asking. "Is he ... does he have ... I mean, has he met someone else?" I finally managed to ask.

"No." She shook her head emphatically. "Don't be daft. It's not like that. He's just taken a job that's all." She settled her riding helmet on top of her curly red hair and fastened the chin strap. "So, where do you want to ride today?" she asked in an overly cheery voice as she changed the subject. "Shelton Wood?"

I looked at her over Posy's withers. "Fine."

"Brilliant. A lovely little ride through the woods is just what you need." She cast a reassuring smile my way. "I'm sure Simon will ring you as soon as he finds out you've come back to Brynmoor." She threw her leg over Dancer's back and settled into the saddle.

I would have liked to think she was right, but I knew better. It wasn't the new job that kept Simon from calling me. Simon had shut me out months ago.

I placed my left foot in the stirrup and swung my right leg over Posy's back. "Let's go." For some reason, knowing that Simon hadn't dumped me for someone else made things better. Not great, but definitely better. I tapped Posy's sides with my heels and followed Jenna down the gravel drive to the bridle path.

A lazy sun hung in the afternoon sky and the air was cool and fresh. Jenna was right. A ride in the woods was exactly what I needed. Although, I doubted that it would keep me from thinking about Simon. Just being back at Brynmoor reminded me of him. After all, he had been the first person I met when I first arrived last summer.

I had flown to England for the first time. My mom had met me at Heathrow airport and we drove directly to Brynmoor Manor. Simon helped us unload our luggage from the car. He had nodded politely to me before carrying my suitcases into the manor house. I remember thinking that he wasn't bad-looking, if you liked tall, muscular, broad-shouldered redheads.

My mother, worried that I wouldn't have anything to

do while she planned their wedding, decided that I should learn to ride horses. She was marrying into the British aristocracy and I guess she felt one of us should be able to "pip pip and cheerio" with the horsey set. So, she had asked Simon to teach me.

I have to admit, I wasn't a very enthusiastic student when I first started. I had never even petted a horse before coming to Brynmoor, much less ridden one. Simon, however, was a kind and patient teacher, and eventually I began enjoying myself. Simon and I ended up spending a lot of time together. One thing led to another. At least it had until sometime after my visit last December.

The memory of Simon sitting on the paddock fence, the afternoon sun turning his copper hair into spun gold as he encouraged me to try my first jump, flashed before my eyes. I gave my head a resolute shake. I was *not* going to think about him. "What trail do you want to take?" I asked Jenna.

"You choose."

"Do you want to ride past the stable ruins?"

Jenna's eyebrows knit together. "I don't know," she said. "That place still gives me the willies."

"She's not there anymore," I said.

"I know but ..." Her voice trailed off and she shrugged apologetically.

"No problem. If you want, we can go someplace else," I offered.

"You don't mind?"

"No."

Jenna's face brightened. "I know. Why don't we ride down to the meadow?" she suggested.

"Okay. I'm good with that."

She flashed me a grin that showed off the Fitzgibbon dimples and nudged Dancer with her heels. "Last one to the woods is a rotten egg!" she called over her shoulder as she flew down the bridle path.

For a city girl like me, who grew up in brown, dry Southern California, riding in Sheldon Wood was a magical experience. We rode along the trail as sunlight streamed through the leafy canopy overhead, dappling the ground with the patterns of light and shadow. Small delicate flowers and strange-shaped mushrooms peeked at us from behind shrubs and logs. The lush rich colors that saturated the wood were like something out of a fairytale, and every time I rode here, I felt like I was in a scene from a Disney movie. If seven tiny men appeared on the trail one day, carrying pickaxes and singing "Heigh-Ho," it wouldn't have surprised me at all.

We walked the horses single file along the trail, Jenna in the lead. She chattered nonstop, full of excitement about starting university next fall. She was going to study to be a teacher. I listened, happy for her but contributing very little to the conversation. I had been admitted to a few decent colleges in California, but I wasn't excited about any of them. At this point in my life, I wasn't sure that going to college in the States was the right choice for me, so Jenna did most of the talking.

We rode for about thirty minutes before Jenna said she had to turn back. She needed to pick up her little brother, Charlie, who was playing at a friend's house. I didn't have any pressing engagements, so I decided to take a detour to the site of the old stable before returning to Brynmoor.

Posy and I took a leisurely walk along the trail enjoying the tranquility of the wood. When we reached the charred remains of the original stable building, I pulled on Posy's reins and stopped. A thick tangle of blackberry vines had grown over the ruins in the years since the fire. We had dug them up last summer and the scarred earth was still visible beneath the newly sprouted vines. I sat still and closed my eyes and let the hushed quiet of the afternoon cast its spell on me.

This was once the site of Brynmoor Manor's original

stable. It had burned to the ground in 1851. The "new" stable had been built closer to the manor house. In a strange twist of history repeating itself, that building had also burned to the ground last summer.

Jenna didn't like to come here. I could understand why it made her uncomfortable; a young girl had died in the fire. Perhaps because I associated the wood with fairytales, I didn't feel the same way. To me, this was the place where she had lay sleeping until she was rescued by her true love. I looked at the tangle of blackberry vines, thinking about the scene in the Disney movie where the prince fights his way through the thorns to save Sleeping Beauty.

Posy, spying a patch of nearby grass, pulled the reins out of my hands to steal a quick nibble, jolting me out of my daydream.

"Hey," I scolded her with a firm tug on the reins. "No more of that." I nudged her with my heels and we headed home.

We rode through the lych gate and returned to Brynmoor, leisurely crossing the estate grounds. I spied Mr. Fitzgibbon talking to one of the day gardeners. The jaunty wave he gave me as I passed made me think of Simon. Again.

I sighed heavily. I kept promising myself that I wasn't going to think about him anymore, but it wasn't easy. Especially since I kept tripping over Fitzgibbons everywhere I went. The entire Fitzgibbon family lived in a cottage on Sir Richard's estate. His mother ran the day-to-day operations of the manor house, his father maintained the grounds and gardens. Between them, his sister, Jenna, his little brother, Charlie, I didn't go a day without running into a dimpled, red-headed someone who reminded me of Simon.

"Enough of that," I said aloud. I reached down and gave Posy's neck a pat. "Who needs him when I have you, Posy? Right, girl?"

Dismounting in front of the stables, I removed her

bridle, slipping the halter over her head. I had just finished tying her to the post when I heard someone call out to me.

"Hullo."

I turned. The young gardener I'd seen talking to Mr. Fitzgibbon entered the stable. He was about my height five foot eight, pale with brown hair and a pleasant smile. Given his lack of a tan, I figured he was new to the job.

"The manure is in the bins behind the building," I told him, as I loosened Posy's girth.

"Manure?" he repeated, his forehead furrowed in confusion.

"Yeah. If you wait a second, I can show you where it is after I take off her saddle," I offered.

He looked amused. "That would be grand. Except, I don't need any manure."

Still thinking he was a gardener, I asked, "Oh. You've got enough then?"

"Most people think I've more than my share of, uhm, manure," he said, cocking his head a little to the side and grinning at me.

"I bet they do," I said, unable to resist his smile.

His grin grew wider. "Actually, I'm looking for Jenna. Is she about?"

"Jenna?"

"Aye. My uncle said you might know where she is."

"Your uncle?" Now it was my turn to be confused.

"Right. I'm Jenna's cousin."

I felt myself blushing. "You're not one of the gardeners?"

His grin grew wider. "No. I'm Jenna's cousin. Mr. Fitzgibbon is my uncle."

I looked at him in surprise. "But you don't have red hair," I blurted.

He burst out laughing.

My face felt like it was on fire. "Sorry. That was stupid."

"No, it wasn't stupid. Red hair is a Fitzgibbon family

trait, but then I'm not a true Fitzgibbon. I'm a Hickman." He raked his fingers through his thick brown hair, making it stand on end. "As you see, I take after my dad's side." He thrust a hand toward me. "My name is Ben. Ben Hickman."

Feeling awkward, I shook hands with him. "I'm Lily. Lily Deene."

"Nice to meet you, Lily Deene." He glanced around the stables. "So, is Jenna's about?"

I shook my head. "I don't think so. We were out riding, but she came back earlier. She had to go pick up Charlie. She might be back at the cottage by now."

"Right. I'll check at the cottage then."

He turned to go, but I was curious about his accent and, I have to admit, more than a little curious to find out if he knew anything about Simon. "Mr. Fitzgibbon is your uncle? You're Scottish?" I asked.

"Aye. You've noticed I've a wee bit of an accent, I see," he said with a laugh, exaggerating his accent for my benefit.

"You do sound a little like Mr. Fitzgibbon."

"My mum is a Fitzgibbon, and, yes, she has red hair. Jenna's dad is my mum's brother," he said by way of explanation. The corners of his mouth twitched. "What about you? I notice that you've a wee bit of an accent, too."

"I'm American. My mom is married to Sir Richard. I mean, Lord Yarlbury," I corrected. While technically Richard was a knight, his title of Earl of Yarlbury was how most people knew him.

"Ah." He nodded as if suddenly placing me. "You're the stepdaughter. The one Simon saved from the fire."

"Yeah, that's me." Wanting to change the subject, I quickly asked, "So, how long are you staying at Brynmoor?"

"Only the night. I'm on my way home from university and Jenna's dad called and asked if I could give her a lift to

Balairie. It's a bit north of Edinburgh, but no more than a few hours."

"Edinburgh, Scotland?" I asked stupidly.

"That's the one."

"You live in Edinburgh?"

He nodded. "Born and bred there."

"In Scotland?"

"Aye."

"And Jenna is going to Scotland with you?"

He nodded again.

"To Scotland? With you?"

"Aye." Ben was beginning to look at me as if I was slightly demented.

"Why?" I took a breath. "I mean, why is Jenna going to Scotland with you?"

Ben shrugged. "An old friend of my parents has moved to the village of Balairie with his daughter. He's bought a place and is turning it into a bed-and-breakfast. The village is a bit isolated, so he asked Mum if Jenna would come up and visit for the summer and keep his daughter company. Jenna didn't tell you?"

"No," I told him dryly. "Apparently red hair is not the only Fitzgibbon trait the family shares."

Ben gave me a quizzical look. He paused a moment, but when I didn't add anything else, he said, "I'll be off then. If you see Jenna, please let her know that I'm looking for her."

"Oh, I will. Definitely," I told him. Ben wasn't the only one who wanted to talk to Jenna.

The first thing I did when I got back to manor house was to look up Balairie. It took me a little while to find it because I couldn't figure out the spelling. When I finally did find it, I realized that Ben wasn't exaggerating when he said it was isolated.

It turned out the Balairie was a village in the Scottish

Highlands, population of 280 people. Located north of a town called Lairg that boasted a population of a whopping 900 people, its claim to fame was some old stone ruins and its "wild windswept beauty."

The village didn't even have its own post office, which made me feel a little better. If I was going to be stuck helping my mom pick out christening gowns for the new baby this summer, then it was only fair that Jenna was going to be stuck in some minuscule village in the middle of nowhere. It didn't quite take the sting out of being ditched by yet another member of the Fitzgibbon family, but it helped.

Jenna came to see me just before tea. I was sitting in the Blue drawing room nursing my wounded pride.

I turned to look at her without even trying to hide my annoyance. "Why didn't you tell me?" I asked.

"I … I wanted to, but we were talking about Simon and you seemed so …" she stopped, her expression troubled. "I didn't want to make things worse."

"So what?" I asked sarcastically. "Were you going to leave without telling me, too?"

She bit her lower lip and shook her head. "No. I was going to tell you, but … I didn't think Ben was going to come so soon. Please don't be cross with me, Lily. I'm sorry I didn't tell you."

I sighed. "It's okay. I'm not mad, I'm just …" It was my turn to be tongue-tied. I was just what? Hurt? Unhappy? Abandoned? "It's just that I was planning on spending the summer with you and Simon. Now you're both going to be gone."

Jenna sat next to me on the window seat. "I'm sorry."

I turned and gazed at the portrait of Christian Hulse, the famous ghost of Brynmoor. He stared back at me from his gilt frame, looking rakishly handsome in his red hunting jacket and riding boots, his dark glossy curls spilling out from under his black hat. With his confident smile and dazzling blue eyes, he could make any modern girl's heart skip a beat. I should know. Last summer he had haunted my dreams. It had made for an exciting summer, but like Simon and Jenna, he too had abandoned me.

"I just wanted this summer to be like last summer."

Jenna looked at me, eyebrows lifted. "I don't think you're going to find another ghost at Brynmoor."

"I know." I sighed and turned back to study Christian's portrait. "I just wish we could spend one more summer together before everything changes. You'll be going to university and I'll be ..." I paused, not really sure what to say. "And I'll be somewhere," I finished lamely.

"Me, too. I mean, I wish we could spend the summer together, too."

We contemplated the painting in silence for a few minutes.

"Why not?" Jenna asked suddenly, her face lighting up. "Why can't we spend the summer together?"

"Uhm, because you're going to be in Scotland and I'm going to be here."

Jenna's face creased into a smile. "Right. But, what if you came to Scotland?"

"Me? Go to Scotland? What are you talking about?"

"You can go to Scotland the same way I am. If Katie needs company, two friends are better than one. Right?" Her grin grew wider. "You could come with me! We could both go!"

I shook my head. "I don't know. I mean, my mom's having a baby in less than two months."

"You could come back, if you wanted to. Maybe you could come for a month. Come back after the baby is born. Ask your mom. I bet she'd think it was a great idea!"

"Your friend might not want two people staying with her."

"It would be fine. I'm sure of it. I can ask my dad and see what he says. Why don't you ask your mum," Jenna enthused. "If you're mum says it's okay, then we'll ask my dad to call Katie's dad."

I felt a smile spread across my face. Why not, I thought. Scotland sounded like it could be an adventure. Although, if I had known how much of an adventure it was going to be, I'm not sure I would have been so eager to go.

ANNIE GRACE ROBERTS

CHAPTER 3

12 November 1901

Dearest Elizabeth:

I have given some thought to the question you posed to me at our last visit. I believe I have found a solution to your situation. Colonel George Morris, an acquaintance of Warren's, has recently returned to Edinburgh. He has made it quite clear that he is looking for a wife and asked Warren if he would provide him with introductions to the families of several eligible young women of our acquaintance. I will say that none of the young women in question surpass Mairi in terms of either beauty or breeding. According to Warren, Colonel Morris is a man of resolute character, well respected by his peers, without any marked deficiency in intellect or temper. Though quite a bit older, I believe he will make a satisfactory match for Mairi being a man of firm disposition and clear faculty. If you wish, I shall arrange a dinner party and facilitate their introduction.

Affectionately Your Friend,
Agnes McDermott

***

I didn't think Jenna and I were going to get everything organized in time. It delayed our departure by a day, but in the end, we did it.

I squeezed into the back seat of Ben's car, next to his laundry and my travel bag.

"You all right back there?" he asked, looking into the rearview mirror.

Jenna craned her neck around to look at me from the front passenger seat.

I gave Ben a thumbs up. "Comfy cozy," I chirped.

"Then we're off." He started the engine.

Mrs. Fitzgibbon and my mother stood in front of the manor house and waved to us as we pulled out of the circular drive.

Jenna stuck her hand out the window, waving back at them. "Ta!" she yelled before leaning back in her seat. "Whew. We've escaped. The way my mum was carrying on, I thought she was never going to let us leave. You would think I was eight and not eighteen," she groused. She glanced at me over her shoulder. "I wish she would be more like your mum."

"No, you don't."

"Yes, I do. Your mum didn't even bat an eye about your traveling to Scotland."

I shrugged. "I flew here from California by myself. I guess she figures if I can do that, I can make it to Scotland safely."

"Not my mum. You should have seen her. She was making me crazy with all her fussing, and poor Ben ..." She glanced over at him. "I don't know how you stood it." She raised her voice mimicking her mother: "Now, Ben, you be sure to drive safe and slow. You've precious cargo in that car of yours."

Ben shrugged good-naturedly. "It's not like I haven't heard the same from my mum." He grinned and began to whistle.

Recognizing the song, Jenna started laughing then launched into song. "You take the high road and I'll take the low road and I'll be in Scotland afore ye," she sang loudly.

I didn't know the words, but Ben chimed in and they finished the verse something about meeting a true love at the bonnie bonnie banks of Loch Lomond.

I was on my way to Scotland!

We stopped for lunch at a curry house, but aside from that and another stop for gas, we drove straight to Edinburgh. The plan was to spend the night at Ben's house, then drive up north to Balairie the next day.

After eight hours driving, I was more than ready to get out of the car when we arrived at Ben's house. Ben found a parking spot on the street and I pried myself out of the back seat, stiff from hours of sitting like a pretzel. He walked around the back of the car and popped open the trunk.

"Look at all this stuff. Jenna, give me a hand, will you?" Ben said, grunting as he lifted a large, overstuffed duffle from the trunk.

"I'll take this one," Jenna said. She pulled out a small blue suitcase from the trunk. "Come with me, Lily. I'll introduce you to my aunt Nancy."

I grabbed my travel bag from the back seat and followed her across the street.

"Hey! Aren't you two going to give me hand?" Ben called.

Jenna smiled over her shoulder. "Cheers, Ben. Thanks for the lift," she said as she turned toward a row of neat townhomes lining the street, leaving poor Ben to wrestle the rest of his things out of the trunk by himself.

The Hickmans lived in a neat two-story townhouse attached to its neighbors on either side. The stone exterior was gray and brown, the front door a deep green. I could see the Fitzgibbon influence in the bright red and pink geraniums flowering in the window boxes and the potted herbs that lined the front steps.

We mounted the steps just as the front door flew open. A woman with a cap of curly red hair stood in the doorway, a wide, welcoming smile on her face. She looked like a shorter, softer version of Mr. Fitzgibbon.

She hugged Jenna. "Come inside and we'll get to the introductions. Nick, come downstairs," she called out. "Your brother and Jenna are here." She ushered us into the house.

I stepped inside and my breath caught in my throat as I caught sight of a familiar face.

The welcoming smile on Simon's face froze when he saw me. He held my gaze for a moment. "Lily," he said, his voice tight and unnatural.

He looked the same: tall, built, and gorgeous. Damn him! Why did he have to look so good? My traitorous heart somersaulted in my chest. "Hi," I creaked.

"Hey! Will one of you give me a hand?" Ben called loudly from across the street.

Simon moved past me toward the open door. "Looks like Ben could use some help," he said to Mrs. Hickman. Then he was gone.

I stood in the hallway, feeling as if I had been run over by a truck. I swayed, slightly dizzy as I tried to remember how to breathe.

You look like you could use a cup of tea, my dear," Mrs. Hickman said, peering at my pale face with concern. "Why don't you leave your things by the door. The lads will take care of them. You two come with me."

She herded us into the kitchen. "You just sit down and I'll put the kettle on."

Jenna and I sat at the table. Jenna glanced worriedly at me but said nothing.

"A spot of trouble with your stomach, is it?" Mrs. Hickman asked, looking me over. "Not to worry. I have just the thing. I have the same trouble myself when I'm in the car too long." She filled a copper kettle with water and placed it on the stove. "You just sit here quietly and rest a bit. I'll have the lads put your things upstairs for you. Jenna, keep an eye on the kettle. I'll be back in a tic."

I was feeling queasy, though it had nothing to do with the car ride.

"Are you all right?" Jenna asked.

"I'm fine."

"I'm so sorry, Lily. I didn't know he was going to be here. Really, I didn't. My mum must have called him."

"It's fine," I told her.

"I really am sorry, Lily."

"It's okay. It's no big deal," I said, though my words didn't sound convincing, even to myself.

Dinner was painful. We crowded around the Hickman's dining room table: Ben's younger brother, Nick; Mr. and Mrs. Hickman; Ben; Jenna; Simon, and me. Jenna kept shooting me troubled looks over her meatloaf, while everyone else joked and chatted. I smiled wanly at most of the jokes and managed to answer a few of the questions that came my way, before mumbling something about not feeling well and excusing myself.

"You poor, wee thing," Mrs. Hickman clucked. "You go right on up and lie down. I'll send up some more tea for you."

Grateful to escape, I climbed the stairs to Nick's room. The poor kid had been forced to share a room with Ben for the night so that Jenna and I had a place to sleep.

I sat on the bed and stared unseeingly at the posters of various soccer teams adorning the walls. This wasn't how I had imagined seeing Simon again. I had planned on being cool and collected, not to mention dressed in something besides jeans and an old sweatshirt. I consoled myself with the fact that at least I hadn't embarrassed myself by crying in front of him.

The bedroom window was open and I heard people talking outside. I walked over to close the window, but then I recognized the voices.

"Well, how was I supposed to know you were going to be here," Jenna hissed.

"Right! You just happened to invite Lily to come with you. I'm supposed to believe that?"

Jenna's voice rose. "Mum never said anything about you being at Aunt Nancy's!"

"Come off it, Jenna. I'm working in Edinburgh. Twenty minutes from their house."

"Don't blame me, Simon!"

I could hear Simon exhale loudly in exasperation. "How long?"

"How long what?"

"How long is she staying?" he asked, working to keep his temper under control.

"She's not staying. She's coming with me to the McAfees."

"The two of you are going to Balairie? Whose brilliant idea was that?" Anger sharpened his voice.

"Mine." I didn't have to see Jenna to know that her chin was thrust at a defiant angle.

"That's just brilliant!" Simon's voice rose. "You know I've been helping out at the McAfees," he said. "How am I going to manage that if she's there?"

"You're helping the McAfees?" Jenna sounded surprised.

"Yes."

"With what?"

Simon sighed heavily. "This and that."

"Do they have animals?"

"No. But Da asked me to pop by, and one thing's lead to another," he said. "Now I'm a bit stuck."

"Well, you'll just have to get unstuck."

"It will be better if Lily goes back to Brynmoor. You

need to talk to her. Tell her to go back."

"If you want her to go back to Brynmoor, you tell her."

"I don't want to see her."

"Too bad. I'm not going to do your dirty work for you, Simon. If you want her to leave, you talk to her."

"You don't understand." The anger had leached out of his voice. Now Simon sounded tired and resigned.

"You're right. I don't."

"Look. Just ask her to go back to Brynmoor. It's better that way."

"Sorry, Simon. Lily's coming with me to Balairie, and if you don't like it, too bad! Just because you're a bloody git doesn't mean I have to be one!"

I heard the back door slam as someone, Jenna most likely, returned to the house. I quietly moved away from the window as hot tears ran down my cheeks. I couldn't stop them. I had no idea what I had done to make Simon dislike me so much.

That night I cried myself to sleep. But when I woke up in the morning, I decided for the millionth time that I was done crying. This time I meant it. I promised myself that I wasn't going to shed one more tear over Simon Fitzgibbon. He wasn't worth it.

"You look much better," Mrs. Hickman commented to me when she saw me. "I'm just about to start breakfast. You can keep me company if you like," she said, pushing open the kitchen door. "We eat breakfast in the kitchen, so much easier to get everyone out the door in the morning."

I followed her into the kitchen.

"Why don't you have a seat at the table? Coffee or tea?" she asked.

"Coffee, please," I told her, pulling out a chair and sitting down. "Thank you for the chamomile tea yesterday. It really helped."

She smiled and nodded as she prepared my coffee. "I'll

send some tea with you to Balairie. The ride isn't as long, but it is in hill country and you may need something to settle your stomach once you arrive."

She poured coffee into a mug and handed it to me.

I took a sip. "My mom is drinking a lot of chamomile right now. She can't have any caffeine because of the baby."

Mrs. Hickman nodded. "Yes, it's good practice to avoid caffeine when you're expecting, and chamomile soothes the stomach," she said, removing a package of sausage from the refrigerator. "The tea you had last night has some chamomile in it, though I add a bit of lavender and rose hips. It's my own special blend."

Jenna pushed open the kitchen door and slid into the seat next to me at the table. "Aunt Nancy's a great one for making tinctures and potions and the like. She's our family witch."

"Now, Jenna," Mrs. Hickman tutted with a laugh. "Don't you go spreading rumors. It's bad enough all the silly lassies who come here looking for love potions." She looked over at me. "I'm an herbalist," she explained. "I've a little shop 'round the corner. Now, how do you girls want your eggs?" she asked, holding an egg over the frying pan.

"Scrambled," we both said in unison.

The kitchen door swung open again and twelve-year-old Nick stumbled sleepily into the kitchen. "Mum, what's for breakfast?" he asked, yawning.

I stifled a smile. His hair was sticking up on one side of his head and he was wearing what I guessed passed for pajamas: soccer shorts and a very wrinkled T-shirt.

"Oh, you!" his mother admonished. "Look at you! And we've company this morning."

Nick pulled out a chair and sat next to Jenna. "Jenna's not company."

"Aye? Well, what about her friend?"

He shrugged, unconcerned. "Are you making breakfast

then?" he asked, eyeing the sizzling pan on the stove.

Mrs. Hickman rolled her eyes at him. "We've eggs, sausages, toast, and tomato juice for the *guests*," she said, stressing the last word."

"What about me?"

"You can march upstairs and make yourself presentable," she ordered, waving her spatula in the direction of the kitchen door. "When you're properly dressed, you may join us."

Nick glowered unhappily but did as he was told.

She had finished cooking by the time Nick returned. He sat down and promptly inhaled four sausages and a mountain of scrambled eggs within thirty seconds, leaving us to enjoy a leisurely breakfast with Mrs. Hickman. I skipped the sausages and tomato juice, but I ate the eggs and toast, washing them down with coffee.

I was sipping a second cup of coffee when Simon and Ben came into the kitchen.

"Mum, we finished loading those plants for you."

"Good lads. You boys ready for breakfast?"

"You have to ask?" Ben said with a grin, sliding into the chair next to mine.

Simon hesitated. I glanced up at him with what I hoped was a neutral expression on my face. His gaze rested on me for a moment before turning to look at Mrs. Hickman. "Smells great, Aunt Nancy," he said before pulling out a chair next to Jenna and sitting down.

I turned toward Ben. "What time do you want to leave?" I asked.

"I don't know." He looked over at Simon. "What do you say, maybe an hour?"

"Works for me," Simon said with a nod.

"What do you mean that works for you?" Jenna asked Simon.

"I'm going up to Balairie with you," Simon answered.

I almost choked on my coffee.

"Are you all right?" Ben asked solicitously.

"Fine," I spluttered.

Jenna shot a glance in my direction. "Why?" she asked Simon, narrow-eyed. "Why are you coming to Balairie?"

"I need to talk to John McAfee."

Jenna favored Simon with a long look. "If you need to talk to him so badly, why don't you just ring him?"

Simon shook his head. "I can't. They don't have service."

Jenna's eyebrows shot up to her hairline. "Are you joking?" she asked.

He shook his head. "No. Anchoret House is in a blind spot. No phones."

"No service, at all?" she asked, holding up her cell phone.

"No. The house is in a valley. You have to drive up to the top of the hill to get any service, and even then it doesn't always work."

"Bugger that," Jenna mumbled under her breath.

"What did you say, dear?" Mrs. Hickman asked, turning to face us, spatula in hand.

Jenna's face turned the same color as her red hair. "Uhm. I said, Mum didn't tell me that."

"Well, I expect she didn't know," Mrs. Hickman said, turning back around to finish scrambling the rest of the eggs for Simon and Ben.

"Nice save," Ben whispered to Jenna, laughing.

She made a face at him.

I pushed back my chair and stood. It was funny and normally I would have joined in the laughter, but seeing Simon again had robbed me of my sense of humor. "If we're leaving in an hour, I guess I'd better get packed." I turned and gave Simon a frosty smile. "I wouldn't want you to leave without me."

I thanked Mrs. Hickman for letting me stay over before going upstairs to pack. It didn't take me very long. I stuffed my few things in my bag and lugged it down the stairs. I reached the first-floor landing just as Simon pushed open the kitchen door. We both froze.

Simon recovered first. "I'll take that to the car for you," he said, reaching for my bag.

I hugged my bag close to my body. "I don't need your help," I said archly.

He gave me an unhappy look. "Lily, I'm just …"

Before he could finish what he was saying, Mrs. Hickman pushed open the kitchen door. "Oh, there you are. Just the person I was looking for," she said to me. "I forgot to give you your tea. Come into the kitchen. It won't take a moment." She looked at Simon. "Simon, take Lily's things to the car for her. That's a good lad."

Unable to keep my bag without creating a scene, I reluctantly handed it to Simon and followed Mrs. Hickman into the kitchen.

"Have a seat, my dear," Mrs. Hickman said as she pulled various jars of dried herbs from the cabinets. "It won't take a moment to finish this up."

I sat down. "Thank you. I really appreciate it."

"Think nothing of it. I'm happy to help."

I watched her scoop dried herbs from various glass jars and mix them together as she made my tea.

The truth is, I've never suffered from motion sickness. I'm actually the kind of person who can go on a roller coaster three or four times in a row and never get sick, but it was easier to have Mrs. Hickman think that I had motion sickness than explain what I was really suffering from. Besides, I didn't think there was a herbal remedy that could cure a broken heart.

She scooped the mixture into a small plastic bag. "There, that should do it. Do you have a tea strainer?"

I shook my head.

"No? Well, I have a spare you can take with you." She opened a drawer and brought out what looked like a spoon with a small strainer attached to it. "Where shall we put this? Hmm." She opened a drawer and pulled out a small paper bag. "This way you can keep everything together," she said to me as she dropped the strainer and the herbs into it. Rolling the top of the bag closed, she set it on the table in front of me. "There now. You're all settled."

I started to rise, but she placed a hand on my shoulder. "My brother told me a bit about what happened last year at Brynmoor."

"Oh?" I said, sitting back down in my chair.

"Aye. He told me how you found that poor wee lass. The one that was burned in the fire so long ago. After he told me, I thought to myself that young girl has the sight."

"The sight?"

She fixed her sharp, bright eyes on me. "*An Da Shealladh*. The Second Sight."

"Uhm …" I mumbled. "I'm not sure what you mean."

She pulled out a chair and sat down. "The Second Sight, luve." She looked at me expectantly.

I smiled apologetically at her, beginning to feel a little bit like Alice after she fell down the rabbit hole.

"I knew it the moment I set eyes on you. You have the sight."

I continued to smile blankly at her, having no idea what she was talking about.

"The dead, they speak to you," she said firmly.

"Oh," I answered, not sure how to respond.

She nodded briskly. "That's how you knew where to find the poor dead lassie. Isn't it?"

"Kind of," I said, feeling uncomfortable. This wasn't something I talked about with most people.

She looked pleased.

"Uhm. Well, I mean, I don't know if I actually have any second sight. It was only the one, uhm, ghost. And I didn't actually speak to anyone. The ghost just kind of showed up in my dreams."

"But that makes perfect sense, doesn't it?"

"It does?"

"Of course it does, luve. When you're sleeping, your subconscious mind is free to listen without your conscious mind telling it all sorts of stuff and nonsense and interfering with the reception."

"You mean like getting rid of static so you can hear the music better on the radio."

She smiled and nodded. "Exactly."

I pondered that for a moment. It did make sense in a weird kind of way.

"You do have the sight, luve." She gave me a sympathetic look. "I don't have it myself, though I've heard it is both a blessing and curse. I imagine it can be a bit troublesome and frightening to dream of the dead."

"It was kind of strange, but it only happened with the one, uhm, spirit. It's not like I experience it all the time."

"Aye. Well, if it happened once, there is always the possibility it could happen again. You'll need to take care at Anchoret House."

"Anchoret House?" I asked.

"John McAfee's house."

"Oh. I didn't know that was the name of his house." I paused. "Why do I need to be careful at his house?" I asked.

"Well, Anchoret House is a house of tragedy. Then there's Balairie, of course. It's an old village built on an even older village."

I looked at her blankly.

"Restless spirits, luve. There is many a poor lost soul wandering the moors. It may cause some trouble for you."

"Pour lost souls?" I asked, as a strange feeling of foreboding rippled along my backbone.

"The dead, luve. They do wander." She fixed me with a serious look. "You'll need to protect yourself."

"Protect myself?" I repeated, noticing that I was beginning to sound a bit like a parrot.

"From the dead, lass. You'll need to protect yourself from the dead."

The kitchen door swung open. Ben stuck his head in and laughed loudly. "Oh, no. Mum, you aren't scaring poor Lily with your stories, are you?" He looked at me. "She's a good one for stories about bogles and fairies and such."

Mrs. Hickman ignored her son and smiling benignly at me patted my hand. "Never you mind Ben Hickman. We're just having a wee chat."

"Well, if you two are done with your wee chat, we're ready to go."

I stood eager to escape the kitchen, but Mrs. Hickman placed her hand over mine once more. "You go on, Ben. Lily will be along in a tic."

Ben rolled his eyes and mouthed the word, "sorry," to me before letting the door swing closed.

Mrs. Hickman released my hand and stood up, her manner brisk and business-like. "Drink the tea before you go to bed and put this under your pillow. She handed me a small sachet tied with a black ribbon. "St. John's wort and fennel. It has protective properties and will help keep the dreams away and the spirits in their proper places."

A shiver ran up my spine. Last summer I had been haunted by strange dreams, but after the burial, the dreams had stopped. I had convinced myself it was a singular event, something that could only happen once in your life, like getting struck by lightning. Now Mrs. Hickman was telling me that it could happen again. "I'm not sure I understand," I said feebly.

"But of course you do, my dear. These things will help keep the spirits in their place. You take care in Balairie and remember to stay away from the moors at night."

"Uhm. Okay. Thanks," I mumbled and hurried out of the kitchen to the car.

I climbed in the backseat next to Jenna. Simon sat in front next to Ben.

"Sorry," I apologized.

Ben twisted around in his seat to look at me. "Not your

fault." He grinned. "My mum was telling her Scottish ghost stories," he explained to Simon and Jenna. "Once my mum gets going, there's no stopping her."

He turned back around and started the car. "Did she tell you the one about the kelpie?" he asked, eyeing me in the rearview mirror.

"No."

"I'm surprised. It's one of her favorites. The first time she told it to me was just after she'd caught me swimming in Blackford Pond with my mates. I was nine. It gave me nightmares for a month," he said with a crooked grin.

"You're as bad as your mother," Jenna complained.

"What? I wasn't going to tell it."

Jenna rolled her eyes at him. "Right."

"Wait a minute. What's a kelpie?" I asked.

"It's a waterhorse," Jenna explained.

"Okay, so what's a waterhorse?"

"A waterhorse is a spirit that lives in the lochs and ponds in Scotland," Ben answered. "According to my mum, it looks like a beautiful black horse and rises out of the depths of the lochs and gives people rides on its back."

"That doesn't sound bad enough to scare a nine-year-old boy."

"Well, it wouldn't, except for the fact that kelpies like to drown and eat children. So, do you want to hear the story?" he asked with a lift of his eyebrows.

"As if we could stop you." Jenna laughed.

"Well, if you insist," he said, catching my eye in the rearview mirror with a smirk.

Jenna smacked him on the back of his head.

"Hey! I'm driving!"

Jenna rolled her eyes.

Ben glanced back at me in the rearview mirror. "This is called the story of the kelpie and the ten children," he began. "Once, long ago, a group of children were playing by a loch when a beautiful black kelpie rose out of the water. The kelpie offered to give them a ride out into the middle of the loch. Nine of the children climbed on the kelpie's back, but the tenth boy was afraid. Instead of climbing on its back, he just petted its neck.

"The kelpie, who loved nothing better than drowning and eating children, dove under the water. The children who had climbed onto its back tried to jump off, but they were stuck fast. So, as the kelpie dove deeper and deeper into the water, one by one they drowned.

"Now, the tenth boy, when he realized what the kelpie was up to, also tried to get free. Because he had been petting the kelpie's neck, only his hand was stuck fast. The kelpie dove deeper and deeper into the black waters of the loch, dragging the poor wee lad down to the bottom. The boy, knowing that he would surely drown if he couldn't free himself, took a knife out of his pocket and began chopping his fingers off, one by one." Ben enacted the story by tucking his fingers into the palm of his hand, waving his stunted hand in the air. "When the last of his fingers slowly sank in the black waters to the bottom of the loch, he pulled himself free of the kelpie and swam through his own blood to the shore."

Ben finished the story with a grin. "That story had me sleeping with the light on for more than a month."

"It probably kept you from swimming in Blackford Pond, too," Jenna commented wryly. "Which is why I expect your mum told it to you."

"Right you are. I never did go swimming in Blackford Pond again." Ben glanced over at Simon. "Lots of lochs up near Balairie, right, mate?"

Simon nodded.

Ben gave Jenna and me a sly look. "Hope you two don't run into any kelpies when you're out and about," he joked.

I didn't laugh.

CHAPTER 4

7 July 1902

My dear Blaire,

 I was overcome with joy when the colonel brought your letter to me, dear sister. You cannot imagine the dull and dreary existence I lead at present surrounded as I am by nothing but empty moorlands and besieged by bleak, tiresome weather. It has rained steadily for a fortnight. There is little enough here with which I can amuse myself: As you know I am not one for books or embroidery. I have had no human companionship save the colonel during the last two months. The isolation and boredom are sometimes more than I can tolerate. At times, I find myself pacing rooms like a caged animal snapping and snarling at the staff in irritation. Yesterday, I spied a gypsy caravan traveling along the moors from the window of my room. In desperation, I wrapped myself in a cloak and braved the inclement weather to walk out and meet them. I can see you furrowing your brow with worry as you read this. Yes, I will admit that I did speak with them. I even paid one of the toothless old women a penny to read my fortune. She told me the usual drivel saying that I would find love and death in this place, etc. As fortunes go it was not terribly original, though I must admit the way she looked at me when she spoke raised gooseflesh on the back of my arms. Please speak again to Mother about arranging a visit to Anchoret House. If you were to come, I would no longer have to consort with gypsies for companionship. I pine for Edinburgh and miss you all terribly. Yes, you are quite correct in asserting that the roads in the Highlands are rather precarious, but please do not let the roads or mother discourage you from visiting.

Your loving and lonely sister,
Mairi

***

I was not prepared for the desolate loneliness of the Scottish Highlands. After we left Edinburgh, we drove for miles along the A9 without seeing a single building. The land rose and fell abruptly with jagged rock formations thrusting themselves upward as if breaking through a tattered blanket of grass and heather. Pools of dark, still water appeared in the valleys and low-lying areas. I found the landscape of the highlands beautiful, unsettling, and a little frightening. It made perfect sense to me that the people living among these vast, untamed lands would create stories of beautiful waterhorses who ate children.

We drove through the highlands for a long time, passing a couple of towns and small villages along the way, until we reached the village of Balairie. The village center turned out to be a small collection of six white frame houses with gray slate roofs and a signpost. Simon directed Ben to a dirt track just north of the last house. The track was marked by a cairn of small stones piled on the side of the road.

"This is the way to Anchoret House?" Ben asked dubiously.

Simon nodded.

"John McAfee's going to need a better sign than this if he wants paying guests to find him," Ben commented with a small shake of his head.

We followed the single track for about forty minutes. No one spoke. We didn't want to distract Ben from driving. The car bounced and dipped as he navigated over ruts and swerved to avoid rocks.

As we left the village behind, the brooding isolation of the landscape seemed to weigh on me. I looked out the window and couldn't help but think of Mrs. Hickman's lost souls wandering about the stark, barren land that stretched before us.

At one point, the road climbed steeply. Ben stepped on the brake and stopped the car as we crested the hill.

"There it is," Simon said, pointing. "In the corrie over there."

It took me a second to pick out the house in the valley below us. The two-story stone house had been built in the shadow of two rocky hills. With its mottled brown and gray facade it seemed to merge into surrounding landscape.

"I see why they call it Anchoret House," Ben commented.

"What do you mean?" I asked. I had assumed that Anchoret was the name of the family who had built the house."

"*Anchoret* is the Scottish word for hermit. You'd have to be a hermit to want to build a house out here," he said, gesturing toward the surrounding moor with one arm.

I heartily agreed with him. Anchoret House looked neither warm nor welcoming as it squatted in brooding silence on the vast, vacant moor. There wasn't another house or building to be seen anywhere.

I shivered as I looked out over the moorlands below. The empty landscape went on for miles and miles. Here and there, small creeks and pools of water caught the sunlight, their surfaces shimmering like droplets of molten glass against the gray-brown color of terrain.

"Is that a loch?" I asked, pointing to the largest of shining pools.

"Yes. Loch Shuftey," Simon answered.

"Didn't I tell you? Kelpies," Ben said with a wicked grin.

Jenna rolled her eyes. "I'm more worried about your driving than kelpies," she said.

"Ow! Have you no faith in me?"

Jenna shrugged. "Just get us down this hill without smashing the car."

Ben carefully maneuvered the car down the single track to the base of the valley floor. Simon acted as his navigator pointing out gullies and rocks as we descended.

"Not a drive I'd chance in the dark," Ben said through gritted teeth as we swerved around a large rock.

"No," Simon agreed. "Or in bad weather."

I glanced out the passenger side window as Ben wrenched the wheel to avoid a large rock. The car veered so close to the edge of the track that less than two feet of space existed between the car and steep embankment. I closed my eyes and put my faith in Ben and Simon.

It was slow progress, but we did manage to make it to the valley floor in one piece.

"Well, that was fun," Ben chirped as he hit the valley floor. "Almost as good as going to M and D's."

Jenna snorted.

"M and D's?" I asked.

"It's an amusement park in Edinburgh," she explained, giving Ben a sour look.

Ben parked in front of the house next to a battered jeep.

We had barely come to a stop when the front door of the house flew open and a girl came running out to greet us. She was pretty, in a little girl kind of way: petite, probably not more than five feet tall, with fair skin, dark hair, and large grey eyes.

"Simon!" she called out, her face breaking into a wide, welcoming smile.

By the time I had climbed out of the back seat, she was

clinging to Simon's arm and gazing up at him like an adoring puppy. *So, this was Katie McAfee*, I thought. Interesting. She seemed younger than fifteen. It wasn't just her small size that made me think that, though it added to the impression.

"Oh, Simon," she pouted prettily. "I thought you were coming up yesterday. I waited by the window all day for you."

It was enough to turn my stomach. Simon, I noticed, at least had the decency to appear a little embarrassed. He gently extricated himself from her grip.

"Katie, this is my cousin Ben, and Jenna's friend, Lily," Simon told her.

Hmm. I thought. It appeared that I was now Jenna's friend, not his. If I had any doubt of where I stood with Simon before, I certainly didn't any longer.

Of course, it didn't matter to Katie whose friend I was. She only had eyes for Simon. Jenna, Ben, and I could have been day-old porridge for all the attention she gave us. Jenna glanced over at me worriedly. I pretended not to notice.

"It's nice to meet you, Katie," I said cheerfully, forcing her to acknowledge me. "Simon's told me so much about you," I lied. Simon's head snapped in my direction.

Katie gazed up at Simon. "You told them about me?" she asked breathlessly.

Simon looked at me, his eyes narrowing in warning. "I told Lily about those delicious scones you made for me the last time I was here," he answered without taking his eyes off me.

"Oh, yes. I'm sure Katie is quite the little cook," I agreed, smiling coolly at Simon.

"What a good idea. We'll have to make scones while we're here," Jenna interjected quickly. Her gaze darting between Simon and me. "Lily is American. I don't think she's ever made scones before."

Katie clapped her hands together. "Brilliant!" she said.

"We can make some today and have them at tea."

I gave Simon a sour look. "Won't that be lovely," I said.

Katie didn't seem to notice my sarcasm.

Ben popped the trunk open. "Should we take the luggage into the house?" he asked Katie.

"We can leave the luggage in the boot for now," Simon replied for her. He looked down at Katie, who looked up at him, her eyes shining like polished stones.

"Is your dad about?" he asked her.

"I think he's in the workshop with Fraser."

"Right. Why don't you show the others to the workshop? I need to have a word with Lily."

Katie's gaze shifted uncertainly between Simon and me. "We can wait, if you like."

"You go on. This won't take long," Simon said with a reassuring smile.

Jenna looked at me, eyebrows raised in a silent question.

I nodded.

Simon waited until the others were out of hearing distance before speaking. "We need to talk."

"You had plenty of time to talk to me. Months, in fact. Apparently, you didn't have anything to say to me then. Now, I don't have anything to say to you," I snapped. I started to turn away.

He grabbed my arm. "You are free to be as cross with me as you like, but leave Katie be," he said carefully.

I yanked my arm free. "What do you think I'm going to do? Chase your adoring little Katie away?"

He had an odd look on his face. "You don't need to be jealous of her," he said quietly.

I felt a hot spark of anger zip along my backbone. "Jealous? You think I'm jealous? What do I care if she follows you around yipping at your heels like an adoring little puppy dog? Hah! Don't make me laugh! I'm not the least bit jealous!" I took a breath, part of me realizing how childish I sounded.

The muscle in Simon's jaw twitched.

I glared at him, daring him to say something.

He inhaled deeply and let out a long, slow breath. "Katie is a lonely, little girl who is going through a rough patch. Her parents are getting a divorce and she's not had an easy time of it. She could use some kindness."

My throat tightened with emotion. I couldn't tell if it was from anger or because I was working so hard not to cry. I swallowed hard. "Don't worry," I managed. "I won't hurt your precious little Katie."

Simon gave his head a little shake. "Please don't. She doesn't deserve that. Not from you." He turned abruptly and walked briskly toward the others.

My face flamed hot with shame, embarrassment, and fury. I was jealous and angry and hurt, all at the same time. Although, I think I was angrier with myself than I was with Simon. I had allowed myself to lose the veneer of cool indifference I had worked so hard to achieve. How could I have been so stupid? Why did I open my big, fat mouth? Worst of all, he was right. How dare he be right! There was no reason for me to treat Katie badly when Simon was the person I was angry with.

I breathed in deeply. Okay, time to start over. I took a moment to collect myself, straightened my shoulders, and followed Simon to the workshop.

The workshop was in a converted stable.

Mr. McAfee greeted me with the same welcoming smile as his daughter and a firm handshake. He was a compact man, short and square.

"Welcome to Anchoret House," he said heartily.

"Thank you."

He clapped Simon on the back. "Did you manage the track all right?

"It was a bit rough in parts, but we managed all right," Simon said with a tilt of his head in Ben's direction.

"Glad to hear it. We had some rain last week. I was

worried it might have washed out the track."

"It's still in pretty good shape," Simon said. "Though you'll need to do something about it soon."

"You're right about that. All in good time, eh, Fraser? The Carriage House first."

Fraser, looking like a Scottish version of a garden gnome, glanced up. A long strip of wood lay on the workbench. It looked like someone was in the process of painting it.

Fraser pushed his cap to the back of his head and scratched his wiry gray hair. "Got tae finish w' the house afore we go fixin' thon track," he agreed.

"Right you are," Mr. McAfee said. "Inside before outside, that's my motto." He smiled expansively. "Jenna, Ben, Lily, allow me to introduce Mr. Lachlan Fraser. Fraser is helping me transform Anchoret House into a world-class B and B. With a bit of help from Simon, of course." He nodded in Simon's direction.

We introduced ourselves. Fraser acknowledged each of us with an upward flick of his eyebrows, his sour expression never changing.

"His lovely bride, Mrs. Fraser, makes all of our delicious meals," Mr. McAfee added when we finished.

"Are you from the Balairie then," Ben asked Fraser.

"Aye," he said, turning his attention back to the piece of wood he was working on.

"Fraser is a true Highlander," Mr. McAfee explained. "He was born and raised in the village. Isn't that right, Fraser?"

"Aye," Fraser answered without looking up.

"We're hoping to finish up the Carriage House sometime this summer and be open for business by the late fall. So …" Mr. McAfee looked at Ben and Simon. "You lads staying the night?" he asked.

"If you have a room, we can use it, otherwise we'll head back this afternoon," Simon said.

"I don't want to chance the track in the dark," Ben

added.

"No, you don't," agreed Mr. McAfee. "You'll stay the night then. I'm glad to see you, Simon. We've been waiting for you to finish the chandelier. What do you say, Fraser? Perhaps we can talk the lads into giving us a hand."

"I wouldnae say no to a bit o' help from two brawny lads," Fraser agreed, eyeing Simon and Ben.

"You know me, I'm happy to help," Simon said.

"Count me in," Ben agreed. "I'm always willing to work for my supper."

Mr. McAfee smiled expansively. "Good. Then why don't I show you your rooms. Then we'll see if Mrs. Fraser has lunch ready and put you boys to work after we eat. Can't expect you to work on an empty stomach, now, can we?"

We followed Mr. McAfee back to Anchoret House.

As unappealing as the house was from the outside, I liked it even less from the inside. It was cold and gloomy. I couldn't help but compare it to Brynmoor Manor. The entry hall at Brynmoor Manor was filled with color and light, gilded portraits hung on apricot-colored walls and vases of freshly cut flowers decorated the end tables. In comparison, Anchoret's entryway had a dark, sinister feeling. The small, narrow windows provided little natural light. The ghost-like silhouettes of furniture draped in white cloths, coupled with the dark wood paneling and heavy drapery only added to the gloomy feeling of the place.

"It's a little dark in here right now. As you can see, we've taken down the chandelier. Mr. McAfee gestured toward a hole in the ceiling with exposed wires dangling from a beam. "Once we get her up and running again that will cheer this place up." He walked over to the staircase. "We've just finished bringing the plumbing and electricity up to date, so there'll be plenty of hot water for you lot.

Your rooms are right up the stairs. Mind yourself on the first step. It's loose."

We trailed up the stairs after him, careful to avoid the first step.

"The rooms are still in need of a bit of repair, but you'll be comfortable enough. Jenna, you'll be next to Katie in one of the remodeled rooms," he said. Lily, you're a bit farther along the hall. We've not worked on your room yet, but truth is, it won't need much work at all, and Katie's made a proper job of fixing it up for you," he said, casting a quick smile in his daughter's direction. "I'm certain you'll find it nice and comfortable."

"You, lads, will be in the room down the hall," Mr. McAfee continued. "It's a bit more primitive, but we males don't need all the frippery the lassies do. Right, lads?"

"Right," Simon and Ben chorused.

Jenna looked at me, one eyebrow lifted. I rolled my eyes as we reached the second-story landing.

The upstairs hallway was lined with faded rose-colored wallpaper. Its busy Victorian pattern was enough to make you cross-eyed if you stared at it long enough.

"Of course, the wallpaper will have to go," Mr. McAfee added. "We're going to paint the walls something bright. Cheer the place up a bit."

He stopped in front of a doorway. "Here you go," he said, pushing open the door. "Lily, this will be your room."

There was no doubt that this room had once belonged to a woman. The yellow wallpaper was festooned with faded pink roses. A cream-colored, four-poster bed sat at one end of the room, a mirrored vanity trimmed with gold paint sat in the other. I set my bag on the bed and followed the others down the hall.

"All right, that's the last of the bedrooms," Mr. McAfee announced after we'd finished looking at the room Simon and Ben would share. "We can go down the servant's staircase. I'll give you a quick tour of the ground floor before lunch."

We followed behind him like obedient ducklings, descending the narrow servants' stairway at the far end of the hall.

"The kitchen is to our right, but we'll save that for another time. We don't want to disturb Mrs. Fraser when she's hard at work preparing our lunch," he told us with a wink. "We'll start over here." He turned left and pushed open a door. "This is the colonel's library."

The library was a long rectangular room. Similar in layout to the library at Brynmoor Manor, the room was furnished with bookcases and overstuffed armchairs. But unlike the library at Brynmoor, which was bright and cheery, this room felt closed and claustrophobic. I didn't like it all.

"The colonel's library?" asked Jenna.

"Colonel Morris. This was his house." Mr. McAfee gestured toward a portrait hanging over the fireplace at the far end of the room. "The colonel wasn't the original owner, but the man who originally built the house never occupied it. Lost all his money. Diamond mines in Africa, I think. The colonel bought it in 1899. He spent several years and a great deal of money remaking it to suit him. For example, this was originally meant to be the formal dining room or perhaps a ballroom, but the colonel wasn't one for parties, so he converted it into a library."

I studied the man in the painting. He wore a military uniform and looked just like the kind of man who would build a dark, gloomy house like this. His thin, humorless mouth stretched taut under a thick gray mustache. His eyes were cold. I couldn't imagine this man smiling, much less dancing or entertaining guests.

"Colonel Morris was a member of the Royal Scots Dragoon Guards. If you look closely, you'll see that he carved their motto into the fireplace mantel."

I could just make out the words. They were written in a circle around something that looked like a stalk with a spiky ball attached.

"Is that a thistle?" I asked.

"Yes," Mr. McAfee beamed. "That is a thistle, the national flower of Scotland."

"Oh," I said, wondering privately why Scotland would choose a thorny weed for its national flower.

The thought must have shown on my face because Mr. McAfee continued. "As an American you might think that the thistle is a strange choice, but it has been the national emblem of Scotland since the thirteenth century, when it saved Scotland from the Vikings." He paused looking expectantly at me.

"Please, Dad, she doesn't want to hear about it," Katie said, making a face at her father.

"Just because you've heard the history before doesn't mean that our American guest won't be interested." He admonished her before turning back to look at me with an eager expression on his face. "Are you familiar with the history of our national emblem?"

Now I knew whom Katie had inherited her eager puppy-dog look from. "No, I'm not. How did the thistle save Scotland from the Vikings?" I asked dutifully.

Mr. McAfee's smile broadened, and he straightened up, puffing out his chest. "As you may be aware, in their day the Vikings were the scourge of Europe. They invaded and plundered at will all of the lands in the northern areas, including Scotland."

I murmured something appropriately encouraging.

"Well, one dark and silent night the Vikings arrived on the shores of Scotland while the Scots lay peacefully sleeping under a starlit sky, completely unaware of the danger they were in." He paused dramatically. "The Vikings pulled their boats ashore, planning to mount a surprise attack, removing their shoes so they could march quietly to the village."

Mr. McAfee's face creased into a wide grin again. I noticed that his Scottish accent seemed to grow stronger as the story unfolded.

"Unfortunately for the Vikings, they didn't know that the fields surrounding the village were filled with thistles. As they crept closer to the village, the tough spikes of the thistles pierced their bare feet, causing the Viking men to cry out in agony. Their shouting and yelling awoke the sleeping Scots, who fought them fiercely with every weapon they could lay their hands on. The Norsemen faced with such furious resistance fled back to their boats in defeat."

"Don't you mean they fled back to their boats on de feet," Ben said lifting one foot in the air.

"What? Ho. Very clever!" Mr. McAfee let out a belly laugh. "Yes. You're right, lad. They fled on de feet in defeat. I'll have to remember that one."

Ben glanced at Jenna and me, pleased with himself.

Jenna shook her head, but I couldn't hide my smile.

Mr. McAfee turned to gaze back at the engraving of the thistle. "The lowly thistle may not be as elegant as a rose, but it is the perfect emblem of Scotland because it is both fierce and beautiful."

"And difficult to uproot," Simon added, a smile flickering across his face.

Mr. McAfee looked at Simon, his eyes gleaming with good humor. "Aye, lad. That is true. I suspect you've heard this story a time or two from your dad, have ye?"

Simon nodded. "A time or two."

Mr. McAfee said, "Your da is a true Scot and a good man."

"Not to mention a gardener," Simon added.

"Right. Da always adds the uprooting part to the story when he tells it," Jenna chimed in.

Everyone laughed.

"So, what does the *Nemo me impune lacessit* mean," I asked, struggling to read the unfamiliar Latin words carved into the mantel beneath the colonel's portrait.

"That is the motto for Colonel Morris's regiment: 'No one harms me without punishment.'"

"Ouch! Not exactly an inspiring and uplifting motto," Ben commented.

I glanced up again at the hard, cruel face of Colonel Morris. He looked like a man who would carve those words into his fireplace. In fact, he looked like a man who would take those words to heart.

Mr. McAfee cleared his throat. "Hmm. Now, where were we? Ah, yes. The colonel made a fortune in the West Indies and bought Anchoret House when he returned. He spent several years and a great deal of money remodeling it for his bride." He turned toward the opposite wall of the library. "We've hung her portrait on the opposite wall."

We turned to look.

The girl in the portrait looked like she could have been his daughter, not his wife. She wore a long pale pink dress and sat demurely with her hands in her lap. Her hair was pinned on top of her head in a sophisticated hairstyle more appropriate for an older, more mature woman. The elegant hair and gown did not disguise her youth or the sadness of her smile. I knew without asking that she was the owner of the bedroom with the yellow wallpaper.

"She's so young," I said.

"Right you are," Mr. McAfee agreed. "Just eighteen when she married the colonel. He brought her here from Edinburgh. Poor wee lassie. She died not long after her marriage. They say the colonel was so distraught that he put her portrait on the wall and sat there night after night mourning her for the next twenty years."

"Is that why they call this Anchoret House?" Ben asked.

"Aye." Mr. McAfee nodded. "He never left the house after her death. He just sat here." He walked over to an armchair that was positioned to face the portrait. "Night after night, he would sit in this chair, drink his whisky, and mourn his poor dead wife."

A draft of cold air whispered across my skin. I felt the hairs on the back of my neck and arms suddenly stand on end. This must have been the tragedy that Ben's mother had meant when she had warned me about Anchoret House.

As if drawn by a magnet, I drew closer to her portrait. "What was her name?" I asked, staring up at the painting.

"Mairi."

"How did she die?"

He gestured with his arm. "She was lost out on the moor, most likely drowned. Some of the villagers found her scarf tangled in the heather above Loch Shuftey."

Ben's story about the kelpie popped into my head and I felt a sudden eerie prickling sensation like bony fingers scraping up my spine.

"How terrible," Jenna commented.

I stood still and studied the two portraits, my gaze shifting from one end of the room to the other. Colonel Morris's painting hung over a stone fireplace. Mairi's painting hung over a wall with similar stonework but without the fireplace. Something seemed off about the wall. I looked again at Colonel Morris's end of the room when I suddenly realized what was bothering me. "There were two fireplaces," I said aloud. "But this one has been covered up."

Mr. McAfee grinned. "You have a good eye, lass. Right you are. When the house was originally built there were two fireplaces, one at each end of the room. I guess the good colonel changed his mind or maybe he just didn't want the expense and trouble of keeping two fireplaces lighting the one room. At some point, he closed up the second one, just keeping the one to warm himself. I suppose, he wouldn't have need for two, would he? Living alone as he did after his wife died." He pursed his lips, studying the wall under Mairi's painting. "I'm trying to decide whether we should knock through that wall to make a doorway to the small sitting room next door and expand this room. I'd like to make this a game room for the guests, keeping the books of course, but perhaps adding a billiards table and a small bar. I don't really want to go to the expense of knocking down walls, but it would be nice for the guests to have someplace to have a drink at the end of the day and relax after tramping across the moor," Mr. McAfee continued. "It's something that Fraser and I are thinking about at any rate."

I studied the stonework below Mairi's portrait while he spoke. It was strange, but even I could see that the workmanship was not of the same quality as the rest of the walls in the room. The stones were rougher and not as uniform in shape and color. I reached out to touch one of the stones.

As soon as my hand touched the cold, rough surface, I felt a sudden surge, like the shock from an electrical current charge through my body. It rushed through me, leaving me feeling as raw and exposed as if I had lost a layer of skin. My heart slammed into my chest and the room around me suddenly vanished. I saw nothing but darkness, so black and impenetrable it was like a solid wall. Pain! Sorrow! Rage! Emotions jolted through me, shuddering up my spine and exploding inside my head. I think I grabbed my head with both my hands, but I'm not sure. The only thing I was aware of was the pain as the dark pressed against me, stealing my breath away.

Strangled choked sounds creaked out of my throat. I couldn't talk. I couldn't move. I was like one of the children in Ben's story about the kelpie unable to free myself. Some part of my brain knew I was being dragged down deeper and deeper into the icy black water, but I could do nothing about it. All I knew was pain. Deep, raw pain. I forgot where I was. I forgot who I was. I had no sense of anything except that I was drowning in pain.

It wasn't until Simon gently pried my hand away from the stones that the library swam into view again.

Half-moaning, half-sobbing I collapsed against him, burying my face in his chest. He gathered me into his arms and carried me out of the library while the others stood staring at us in various states of shock and confusion.

ANNIE GRACE ROBERTS

CHAPTER 5

3 November 1902

Liza,

You are right to complain about Mairi's ingratitude. She does you wrong in thinking that you do not love her as you ought. It is your responsibility as her mother to ensure that she fulfills her wifely duties. You must not give in to Mairi's pleadings. She is a grown woman and must make her home with her husband and not her mother. As we know, marriage is a lonely business, but women must defer to their husbands. If her husband does not wish to allow her to travel to Edinburgh for the holidays, as is his right, then she must not undertake the journey. My deliberate opinion is that Mairi will never find any satisfaction in marriage if she is allowed to run home to Edinburgh at the slightest hint of unhappiness. As a wife, she must learn to prize the daily presence of her husband and give up her selfish interests or learn, as we all do eventually, to turn his opinion by the use of womanly arts.

Yours in sisterly affection,
Jane

***

Lunch, as you might have expected, was awkward. Jenna tried to cover for me. She chatted about people with sensitivity to jetlag, but no one believed her. Not even me. So, we sat at the table eating our tomato sandwiches and everyone tried to behave as if I hadn't had a major breakdown for no apparent reason. Mr. McAfee chattered away with breezy good cheer and everyone else played along, sneaking sidelong glances at me when they thought I wouldn't notice.

We finished lunch and Mr. McAfee, casting a concerned look in my direction, suggested that Katie show the garden to Jenna and me so that we could "relax" after our long drive. I knew he was suggesting it for my benefit. After all, everyone knows it's important to keep emotionally, unstable people calm and happy. The fact of the matter was that I didn't really mind. The thought of sitting outside in a garden sounded like a good idea. The episode in the library had affected me more profoundly than I would have liked. I told everyone that I was fine, but I couldn't quite shake the lingering, oppressive feeling I had experienced in the library, nor the slight throbbing pressure behind my eyes that was threatening to turn into a headache.

Katie walked us over to the small walled garden attached to the side of Anchoret House and gave us a tour. Remembering my conversation with Simon, I worked hard to be an enthusiastic guest.

"Simon brought these for me," Katie said, pointing to several tomato seedlings. "He's so kind. He always brings me something when he comes here," she said, her eyes flicking to me before quickly looking away again.

I murmured something appropriate and smiled encouragingly.

I knew that poor little star-struck Katie was trying to figure out my relationship with Simon. More than once, I had caught her staring at us at lunch, her eyes darting between the two of us as she tried to work it out. The scene in the library must have been confusing for her. It certainly was for me.

I had heard nothing from Simon for months. When I finally did see him again, he barely acknowledged my existence, except to give me a lecture on being nice to a Katie, a girl who obviously has a crush on him. Then, the moment I fall apart, he scoops me into his arms and tenderly ministers to me. Yes, I said tenderly. He was very kind, very gentle, and very tender. He folded me in his arms and carried me out of the library as if I was as fragile as a piece of spun glass. He cradled me against his chest, rocking me gently while I listened to the deep, slow rhythm of his heartbeat. For a moment, it was like old times.

I blinked to chase the image away. Simon had always been good about helping anyone or anything in distress, I reminded myself. He took care of injured animals, being steady and strong in a crisis was part of his job. I was in pain and he reacted. He would have done the same thing for anyone in the same situation. However much I hoped differently, Simon's reaction to my distress was nothing more than that. He had made it abundantly clear that he no longer cared for me. I had no idea what had gone so wrong between us, but pretending that nothing had changed was a waste of time. I needed to move on. He obviously had. So would I.

"We can sit here," Katie said, pointing to a small wooden bench surrounded by rose bushes. "It's nice and sunny in this spot."

We sat down. The wall around the garden blocked the wind, but the temperature was still cool. This far north, the summer month of June did not necessarily mean summer temperatures. At least not the summer temperatures that I was used to in LA. I tilted my face toward the sun and closed my eyes, enjoying the warmth on my skin. I inhaled deeply and let the subtle fragrance of the roses and fresh herbs waft over me. Katie and Jenna were chatting about something, but I kept my eyes closed and their conversation flew past me.

As I sat in the garden, I found myself thinking about Mairi Morris. I wondered if she had been the one who started this garden. I imagined her walking among the various plants wearing a large brimmed sunhat and carrying a small basket with pruning shears. After working in the garden, she probably would have sat on this very bench breathing in the scent of freshly cut flowers just as I was doing now. I imagined that the peace and tranquility of the garden would have provided Mairi with a welcome escape from the gloom of Anchoret House as well as from her marriage to the grim and humorless Colonel Morris.

Poor Mairi. She must have been terribly lonely. Even if Colonel Morris had hosted parties and dinners, Anchoret House was so isolated that Mairi would have had few opportunities to socialize with other people on her own. I couldn't imagine choosing to live out here.

With a sudden pang of conscience, Simon's description of Katie popped into my head. Like Mairi, she must be feeling very lonely, too. Divorce was never easy. I was too young to remember my parents' divorce, but I'd seen enough of my friends go through it to know how hard it was on the kids when the adults in their lives screwed up. No wonder Katie looked at Simon with stars in her eyes.

I felt a nudge in my side. My eyes popped open and I turned to face Jenna. "What?"

"I said," Jenna repeated. "Do you want to walk out on the moor?"

"No. Not right now." I rubbed my temples. The dull throbbing behind my eyes was still there and still threatening to become something worse. "I'm pretty tired. I think I'll go back to the house and unpack."

Jenna's eyebrows drew together as she looked worriedly at me. "Are you all right?" she asked.

"I'm fine. I just have a little headache."

"I brought some paracetamol with me," Jenna said. "I'll get them for you." She turned to look at Katie. "We can go for a walk later, after Lily's headache is better."

"You two can go for a walk. I'll be fine," I told her.

"No, we'll wait until you're feeling better," Jenna said firmly. I knew she was still thinking about the library incident.

Katie nodded. "We can wait. This time of the year we don't have to worry about it getting dark. We've plenty of time for a walk later, if you like."

"Right, then. Let's go back to the house and I'll get you that paracetamol," Jenna said, standing.

We walked back to the house and I linked arms with Jenna. Leaning toward her, I whispered, "You don't have to worry about me. I'm okay. Really."

She gave my arm a little squeeze as we climbed the steps. Katie pushed open the front door.

"Hold up, lassies," Mr. McAfee called out to us as we entered the entry hall. "We're just about done."

We stopped and gawked.

Ben stood balancing on top of a ladder in the center of the hall while Fraser steadied it. Simon, biceps bulging, pulled on a rope, slowly lifting the heavy crystal chandelier off the floor with the use of a primitive pulley system they had strung over the rafters. Mr. McAfee stood to the side directing the project.

I noticed that Katie couldn't tear her eyes away from the sight of Simon as he strained at the pulley cable, but my eyes kept straying to the top of the ladder where Ben balanced precariously on the topmost rung.

"Steady now," Mr. McAfee called, though I wasn't sure if he was directing his command to Simon, Fraser, or Ben.

We stood gawping as the huge chandelier majestically ascended.

"Just a bit more," Ben called down to Simon as he reached for the top of the chandelier. He grabbed the cable. "Got it. Now hold her steady and I'll get the wiring fixed up."

We watched while Ben quickly and competently twisted and capped the electrical wires linking the chandelier to the ceiling.

"Wow. Where'd he learn to do that?" I whispered to Jenna.

"His dad owns a construction business. Ben and Nick work for him during the summers."

"Right, then. That's done." Ben called down. "Flip the switch and let's make sure she works before I bolt her to the ceiling."

Mr. McAfee walked over to the light switch and turned it on. The crystal chandelier blazed to life.

"Brilliant!" Ben crowed, looking down at us with a cocky grin.

I caught his eye and applauded.

Still grinning, with a sweeping gesture, he bowed, or at least bowed as much as he could while standing on top of a ladder.

"Mind yerself, laddie," Fraser admonished, tightening his grip on the ladder.

"What is he doing? He's going to fall," I said, my heart skipping with anxiety.

"He won't fall," Jenna said, her eyes focused upward. "He was in gymnastics when he was young. Though I expect my aunt Nancy would have a thing or two to say to him if she saw this."

Mr. McAfee flipped the light switch to off. "Let's bolt her in then," he called up to Ben.

"Right. Simon, give her another yank and I'll finish up," Ben called down.

It was like watching a high wire act in the circus. I kept my eyes fixed on Ben, admiring his confidence and cat-like grace as he tugged the chandelier into place and secured the bolts to the ceiling. At one point he dangled in space, one arm thrown casually around an exposed beam, one foot barely resting on the ladder.

"All right then," he called down after the last bolt was in place. "Who wants to do the honors?"

"I will," Katie said eagerly. Her father stepped aside and allowed her to turn on the light.

We looked up and admired the glittering crystals of the chandelier as Ben climbed down the ladder.

"Well, what do you think?" Mr. McAfee asked Fraser.

Fraser looked up at the chandelier, squinting. "She'll do," he said.

Mr. McAfee clapped Ben on the back. "That's high praise indeed coming from Fraser. Well done, lad."

"Thank you," Ben said, looking pleased.

Mr. McAfee tilted his head to look up at the chandelier again. "That was quite an acrobatic act of yours. You looked as comfortable as a monkey up there."

"He's discovered your secret then, Ben," Simon said with a sly grin.

"You've a secret?" Mr. McAfee asked, turning to look at Ben.

"Aye," Ben replied, his expression solemn. Without warning, he bent his knees and began scratching himself and hooting.

Caught by surprise, I laughed aloud.

Ben smacked his lips together loudly, twirled in a circle, and hooted once more before giving me a conspiratorial wink.

I felt a happy little flutter in my stomach and grinned back at him. Though he was not your stereotypical "hot guy," there was something endearing about him. "Careful, Ben, or we'll have to check you for lice," I joked.

Ben's smile widened as he looked at me, but before he could reply, Simon stepped between us. His eyes flicked toward me before he clamped a hand on Ben's shoulder. "Well done, mate," he said. "Now, you can help me haul the ladder back to the workshop."

The men cleaned up the tools. Katie, Jenna, and I went up to our rooms. Jenna dropped off the bottle of paracetamol, the British equivalent of Tylenol, for me. I swallowed two pills and unpacked my bag, which took me all of five minutes.

The cream-colored bureau drawers were empty, so I stuffed my clothes in them and threw my toiletry bag on top. That was pretty much the extent of my unpacking. When I finished, I went over to the bed, sat down on top of the soft-down comforter, and looked around my room. I was absolutely certain that this had been Mairi's room.

Poor Mairi, I thought. She had tried to create a soft, feminine oasis for herself among the dark, depressing decor of Anchoret House. Her choice of furnishings—the dainty cream-colored furniture, the soft yellow wallpaper with its pale pink roses, the plush Persian rugs—had been an attempt to design a place of beauty and joy in a house that lacked both. Unfortunately, it hadn't worked. I had a strong sense that the terrible sadness and grief I had felt in the library had come from her. She had not been happy at Anchoret House. How could she be? A young girl, isolated from friends and family and trapped in the highlands with no one to keep her company but a grim and humorless husband. This beautiful room had been nothing more than a gilded cage for Mairi.

I leaned back against the pillows and closed my eyes. The pounding behind my eyes seemed to be growing stronger. I slowed my breath and tried to relax as I waited for Jenna's paracetamol to work.

I must have dozed because I woke up to the sound of someone knocking on my door.

Dragging myself back to consciousness, I called out a groggy, "Who is it," as I sat up.

"Me." Jenna's voice called from the other side of the door.

"Jenna?"

"Who else?"

"Come in."

Jenna opened the door, peering worriedly at me. "What

took you so long?" she asked.

"Sorry. I fell asleep," I said with a yawn.

"Asleep?"

I shrugged and gave her a sheepish grin. "My head was still bothering me, so I laid down and closed my eyes. I guess I fell asleep."

She stepped inside and closed the door behind her. She studied me for a moment. "Is your headache gone?"

"Just about."

Jenna walked over to the bed. "Well, that's good. Budge up," she ordered before hopping up onto the bed and sitting next to me. "So, tell me what happened to you in the library?"

"I don't know."

"What do you mean you don't know? Is it another ghost?"

"I'm not sure."

She gave me a look. "You're not sure?"

"I can't explain it. I don't know what it was."

Jenna's eyes drilled into me like lasers. "Try," she ordered.

I closed my eyes and rubbed my temples. "I touched the wall and then the room kind of disappeared and all I could see was darkness. Then I felt sad. This awful, overwhelming, deep, dark sadness and pain. I don't know why."

"You were shaking and crying and looked like you were about to pass out. That's a little more than feeling sad," she said.

"You're right. It was more than sad, but I don't know how to explain it. I'm not sure what it was. I didn't see anything or hear anything. I just felt this ... this terrible, awful black nothingness. It was like all these emotions had seeped into the walls and I was touching them. Everything was black, but I could feel wave after wave of intense, raw anger, grief, and pain surging through me. I've never felt anything like it in my life. It hurt. Physically hurt." I tapped my heart. "I mean, it was like my heart was breaking. Really breaking. I couldn't breathe it hurt so bad." Tears pricked the back of my eyes at the memory. "Something really horrible happened to her."

Jenna's eyebrows shot up to her hairline. "Her? You mean Mairi?"

I nodded. "I think so."

"There is a ghost! I knew it!" Jenna crowed.

"Maybe," I hedged. "Like I said, I didn't see anything."

"But you sensed something," Jenna insisted.

"Yes, but I'm not sure if it was Mairi or …" I broke off. "I don't know what or who it was."

"It has to be her!" Jenna said. "You said you felt like you couldn't breathe, right? Like you were drowning."

I nodded.

"One"—she held up a finger—"you felt this under her portrait." She held up a second finger. "Two. Mairi drowned." She held up a third finger. "Three. You are a ghost magnet. So, the conclusion is, you've found the ghost of Mairi!" She grinned at me triumphantly. "And you thought this summer was going to be boring. Now we just have to figure out why she's still here!"

I didn't return her smile. I wasn't sure I wanted to find out what had happened to Mairi because I knew that whatever it was, was bad, really bad.

CHAPTER 6

2 December 1902

Dear Father,

I am sorry to hear that Mother is unwell. I too am suffering a terrible catarrh, which has kept me in a most sorry state for the last three days. Even now I am sitting by the fire with a huge uncomfortable comforter and gargling at intervals with a vile concoction made by the cook who insists that it will cure me. The colonel has taken pity on me in my sorry state and brought me a most wonderful early Christmas present, though I am not yet well enough to enjoy her. I am laughing as I write this because I know I have piqued your curiosity. I will put you out of your suspense and tell you that I am the proud new owner of a lively Highland pony. I have named her Biscuit, as she looks like one, being rather round and small. I hope to be well enough to begin riding her soon. I am sure we will be great friends. Please give my love to Mother, Alec, Blaire, and Isobel.

Your Affectionate Daughter,
Mairi

***

I woke up in the library with absolutely no recollection of how I got there. I was in my bare feet, wearing my pajamas. It was dark and freezing cold. I stood rooted to the spot with terror and confusion, adrenaline sparking through me. What was I doing here? My eyes darted wildly around the room as my heart rate spiked with fear.

I thought I sensed something, just behind me. Fighting the urge to flee, I slowly turned around as my heart thudded against my chest and my eyes strained against the gloom. Mairi's portrait glimmered faintly in the darkness. I could almost feel her spiritual imprint in this room. It clung to the walls and saturated the air as if it was an actual physical entity.

"Mairi?" I whispered.

I waited, heart hammering in my chest, and listened. I heard nothing except silence and the sound of my own shallow, panicked panting. Had she brought me here? If so, why? I stared at her portrait, trying to calm my unsteady nerves. I supposed I could have touched the stone wall. Perhaps that was what she wanted me to do, but I wasn't willing to experience that again. I waited for several minutes, shivering in my pajamas in the cold and dark, before turning away from her.

Chiding myself for my overactive imagination, I quietly made my way back upstairs to my room. I turned on the lights and sat on the bed sorting through the possible logical explanations of my freaky nighttime excursion. Jet lag? Maybe. Sometimes, with all the traveling I did, I did end up getting so tired that I was barely functioning. When that happened my memories of events tended to become pretty fuzzy. Maybe my sleepy brain thought it was time to get up and I just didn't remember getting out of bed and walking down the stairs. I had heard of people doing that sort of thing. Maybe I was subconsciously thinking about Mairi and somehow ended up in the library, kind of like sleepwalking. Just because I'd never done anything like that before didn't mean it wasn't possible.

Of course, I wasn't ready to totally discount a supernatural explanation for my late-night trip there. After all, I had definitely sensed some kind of presence in that room earlier in the day. Was it possible that Mairi had somehow called to me? Maybe. Perhaps she had reached out to me in my dreams. In the past I had always remembered those kinds of dreams, this time I didn't remember anything. If Mairi had been trying to communicate with me, why hadn't I seen or felt anything? Why couldn't I remember anything?

Sighing, I hopped off the bed and walked over to the bureau, grabbing the herbal sachet that Mrs. Hickman had given me. She had said it would help to keep the "spirits in their place," maybe it would keep me in my place too. I figured it couldn't hurt to try. I slipped it under my pillow before turning off the lights.

I was sitting in the garden at Anchoret House. Except now the wall around the garden was yellow and covered with pale pink roses. Why was Mairi's wallpaper in the garden? As I stared at the wall in confusion, a monkey suddenly appeared on top of the wall. It started hooting and laughing. I watched as it performed a perfect backflip off the wall, landing right in front of me. Except when the monkey stood up, he wasn't a monkey at all. He was Ben Hickman. He tilted his head at me and winked. The next thing I knew I was in Ben's arms. We were kissing. We were still kissing when I heard a sudden explosive thunderclap.

I jolted awake. My first disoriented thought was about Ben. I opened my eyes and realized that I was still in my bed. I was relieved, if somewhat bemused by my strange dream, to find that I hadn't wandered off again after I'd gone back to sleep. I sat up yawning sleepily and reached under my pillow to feel for the sachet that Mrs. Hickman had given me. I wasn't sure I really believed that a bag of herbs could keep the spirits away, but I decided that it wouldn't hurt to leave it there for the duration of my visit. Smiling to myself at the strange workings of my subconscious mind, I wondered idly if she had given me one of her love potions by mistake.

Bang! A loud clanging noise startled me.

That must have been what woke me, I thought. I waited, listening. The noise sounded again. Bang! Bang!

Curious, I climbed out of bed, opened the door to the hall, and stuck my head out. The banging had stopped. I stepped into the hallway and cocked my head, listening.

Bang! Bang! Bang!

The noise seemed to be coming from downstairs. I walked over the stairwell and leaned over the banister.

Fraser and Mr. McAfee stood on the ground floor looking glumly at a thick newel post attached to the bottom of the stairwell banister.

"We'll need tae take out thon stone," Fraser said glumly.

"But, we can't do that without damaging the floor."

"Nae, I wouldnae think so."

I looked at the newel post. It was a thick piece of carved wood. The handrail rested on the top of it, but the bottom was encased in a heavy stone base.

"Let's give her one more go," Mr. McAfee suggested.

Fraser swung the rubber mallet he was holding against the newel post.

Bang!

The post shivered. Mr. McAfee, red-faced with strain, tried to pull the post loose of its stone base.

"Och, thae's no budging her," Fraser said, shaking his head. "She's stuck fast."

Katie and Jenna's door opened behind me. They poked their heads out, looking sleepy-eyed and cranky.

"What is that noise?' Katie asked grumpily.

"Uhm, I think your dad and Fraser are trying to do something to the handrail and the post is stuck."

"This early? Are you joking?" Katie stomped out of her room looking as adorable as a rumpled kitten and peered over the railing at her father below.

"Daaaaad," she wailed. "What are you doing?"

He looked up at us and beamed. "Ah, I see everyone's awake. Good. Mrs. Fraser's left breakfast in the dining room for you lot."

Katie glared at her father, who cheerfully ignored her. Glowering, she stomped past me back to her room, shutting the door firmly behind her.

Jenna grinned at me. "See you downstairs."

"So, how is your headache this morning?" Jenna asked as she spooned oatmeal into her bowl.

"Better. Thanks."

Katie slid into a seat across from me. "No thanks to my dad and Fraser," she said crossly. "I can't believe they were making all that noise so early."

"Noise? What noise?" Ben asked as he entered the room.

"You didn't hear all that banging this morning?" Katie asked.

Simon followed Ben into the room.

"No. I didn't hear a thing except Simon's snoring," Ben said.

"I wasn't the one snoring," Simon retorted. He jerked his thumb toward Ben. "I've treated pugs and bulldogs that are quieter than Ben."

I laughed.

Simon glanced at me, his mouth curving upward.

I looked away. It still hurt too much to be near him.

"I don't know what you're talking about, Simon," Ben said, feigning offense. He walked over to the seat next to me, winked, and let out a loud snort.

For some reason, the image from my dream of the two of us kissing him suddenly popped into my head. Embarrassed, I quickly looked down, hoping no one would notice my red face. I ate a few bites of my oatmeal, waiting for my color to return to normal. When I looked up again, I caught Simon staring at me with an odd expression on his face. Ben was at the sideboard filling his breakfast plate.

I ignored Simon and focused my attention on Ben, trying to figure out what had made my subconscious mind consider him a love interest. He was cute, in a nerdy kind of way, with short and wiry thick brown hair and an infectious laugh. He would be fun to go out with, I decided. Though he wasn't the type of guy I usually fell for. I tended toward the tall and athletic guys like ... I stopped myself mid-thought.

Looking down at my bowl, I very slowly and deliberately ate another spoonful of oatmeal to keep myself from glancing at Simon.

Ben put his plate down next to mine. "So, what's on for today?" Ben asked.

I swallowed and looked up at him, shrugging. "I don't know," I replied, working to keep my tone light.

Jenna glanced at Katie. "What are we doing today?"

"Well, my dad keeps asking me to take an inventory of all the things stored in the attic." She wrinkled her nose. "I haven't done it because I don't like to be up there by myself. Maybe the three of us can do that today."

"That's a great idea," Jenna enthused with a knowing look in my direction. "I love searching through old things. You never know what you're going to find. Right, Lily?"

"Yeah. Sounds like fun," I agreed. I turned to Ben. "So, when are you guys leaving?"

"What? Are you trying to get rid of us already?" he joked.

I could feel Simon's eyes on me. I shrugged and kept my gaze focused on Ben. "Just wondering. That's all."

"You're stuck with us until after lunch. Katie's dad needs a couple of "big brawny lads" to help him this morning," he said, flexing his biceps and grinning.

I smiled back at him. Ben's good humor was almost impossible to resist.

Jenna rolled her eyes. "Don't encourage him, Lily," she warned. "If you do, we'll have to listen to him all morning."

"You're just jealous."

"Jealous? Of what?"

I listened to the two of them going back and forth, enjoying their banter. It must be nice to have siblings and cousins. As an only child, I always felt that I'd missed out on something wonderful. In my little family, there were no siblings or cousins. Just me. Although most of my friends at school insisted that the fact that I didn't have siblings made me the lucky one, I wasn't so sure.

I guess everyone always wants what they don't have. I had always wanted a sister or a brother. Now, at the ripe old age of eighteen, I was finally going to become a big sister. Or at least, I would become one, once my mom had the baby. I wondered idly about the kind of relationship my little brother and I would have as I listened to Jenna and Ben bicker good-naturedly.

After we finished breakfast, Katie led Jenna and me to the attic. The attic ceiling was low and slanted. Katie was small enough to stand upright, but I had to hunch over to avoid the overhead beams as I climbed up the ladder.

I could see why she hadn't wanted to work here by herself. The only light came from a very small dormer window located at the far end of the room. Strange shapes lurked in the darkened corners, reminding me of the monsters that had populated my childhood nightmares. It was definitely a spooky place.

There's a light switch somewhere," Katie said as she

patted the wall searching for the switch. "My dad had the electrician put it in when they were working on the rest of the house." She found the switch and pressed it. Overhead two bare light bulbs cast harsh white light, turning the "monsters" into a jumble of dust-covered items: old furniture, boxes, trunks, crates, stacks of old papers. With the light on it wasn't quite as spooky, though it still wasn't the cheeriest place to spend an afternoon by yourself.

"It looks like Colonel Morris never threw anything away," I said, picking up a battered brass umbrella stand. "Why would anyone keep all this stuff?"

"No one to pick up the rubbish," Jenna explained. "If you live out here, you have to haul it into town yourself. Colonel Morris probably decided it was easier to store it than to bring it into town."

"We bury it," Katie said. "Well, as much as we can. We have a compost outback by the workshop and another pit for some of the other stuff."

The three of us surveyed the mass of accumulated bric-a-brac.

"So, where should we start?" Jenna asked.

I let my gaze sweep across the room. "I think we should divide it up. It'll go faster if each of us focuses on one area."

"Good idea. I'll start on this side," Jenna said, gesturing to an old bed frame, a bureau, and stack of boxes to her left.

"Don't forget to open the drawers. You never know what might be stuffed inside them," I reminded her with a grin. "Maybe we'll get lucky and find some buried treasure."

Jenna's eyes gleamed. "Wouldn't that be grand? You know those stories where somebody cleans out their attic and finds a priceless painting. Maybe we'll find something like that rolled up in a corner somewhere."

"A priceless painting would be nice," I agreed. "But I'm looking for gold and diamonds."

"Right," Jenna agreed, laughing. "Good luck with that."

"You never know," I told her. "I read about someone who bought a second-hand couch, and when they tried to reupholster it, they found out it was filled with thousands of dollars."

"You're having me on."

"No. It's true. Really."

Jenna looked at me, her eyebrows arched in disbelief. "Well then, I'd best get to it. If I'm to find those gold coins before you do," she joked.

"Where should I start?" Katie asked.

"Uhm. How about that back corner," I suggested, pointing to where two exotic-looking carved chairs were stacked on top of each other. "You work in that direction and if Jenna works opposite direction, when you two meet, you'll have finished that whole side of the room. I can start on this side and work my way toward the back of the room."

"All right, then," Jenna said. "Let's get started. First one to find a priceless painting or gold coins wins!"

I walked over to my corner and began sorting through a pile of cardboard boxes. They were filled with books, not paintings. I noted the title and author of each book on my inventory list, before repacking and closing the boxes.

We worked for a couple of hours, opening boxes and drawers, making notations of what we found and sharing the most exciting finds out loud. Katie had the most interesting area by far.

"Look at this!" Katie called excitedly. "A real tiger-skin rug!"

I leaned back and craned my neck to see as she unrolled it. "Well, that's definitely unexpected," I said.

Jenna walked over to admire the rug. "You know, Katie," she said, shooting a look my way, "maybe your dad could use this in one of the guest bedrooms."

"In one of the guest rooms?" Katie looked uncertainly at the tiger skin. "I don't know about that."

"I know you're joking, Jenna, but that's actually not a bad idea," I said, walking over to take a closer look at the rug. "There are a lot of hotels and bed-and-breakfast places that have theme rooms in California."

"Theme rooms?" Katie asked.

I nodded. "Yeah. They decorate the rooms in a theme, like the Jungle Room or the Moroccan Room, something like that.

"I bet," Jenna said. "I can just see it. Green painted walls, lots of tropical plants, an indoor waterfall, and this lovely bloke on the floor in front of the fireplace. Wouldn't that be grand?"

Katie shuddered. "I would never stay in a room with this on the floor. Look at his teeth. I couldn't stand going to sleep with him snarling at me like that. It would give me nightmares."

The three of us stared down at the tiger rug. Katie was right. He did look as if he was ready to gobble up a tasty human or two.

"I bet Mairi made Colonel Morris put it up here. I know that's what I would have done if I was married to him," Katie said.

"Do you think all these things belonged to him?" Jenna asked, picking up a brass paperweight sitting on top of a closed cardboard box. It was carved to look like a Hindu goddess.

"Well, maybe not everything, but the tiger-skin rug seems like the sort of thing he would have. Don't you think?"

"Yes," I agreed, thinking of the thin cruel mouth on his portrait. "He probably shot the poor tiger himself."

Katie eyed the Hindu goddess. "I guess some of these things could have belonged to someone else. I think a nephew lived here after Colonel Morris died. And then a cousin lived here for a while, too."

"No. I think you're right. I bet all this India stuff belonged to the colonel." Jenna bent down and rummaged through another box. "You are not going to believe this," she said as she lifted a stuffed cobra out of a cardboard box. It lay coiled and ready to strike in the palm of her hand.

"Ugh." Katie grimaced. "Why would anyone want to buy something like that?"

"For the same reason you would buy a snarling tiger skin," I said. "Or this." I pulled a long, curved dagger out of the box. "Souvenirs. I bet Colonel Morris liked to hunt. He probably brought these things back with him from India. Unless the nephew or cousin was in the army and went to India, too." I looked at Katie inquiringly.

She shook her head. "I don't know about the cousin, but the nephew was some sort of scientist. I think he studied bugs."

"Ah," I said. "That explains all the bug books and glass test tubes I found."

"So, all these bits and bobs must have belonged to Colonel Morris," Jenna commented, bending over to examine the rest of the contents of the box with the cobra. She pulled out a drawing of a knife-wielding, multi-armed woman with big breasts and held it up so we could see it. "Look at this," she said, a wicked grin on her face as she held up the voluptuous statue. "Oh, Colonel, you naughty, naughty lad."

We burst out laughing at her imitation of someone's maiden aunt.

Jenna stared at the statue and shook her head in mock sorrow. "Ah, Colonel. You're no better than the rest of them."

"The rest of who?" Katie asked.

"The rest of the male world. Like my mum says, boys will be boys. No matter the age, they never really grow up."

I winced. "I can't stand that saying. It's an excuse for bad behavior."

Jenna's mouth twitched. "I suppose that's because as

far as boys go, there's not enough good behavior to talk about." She looked over at Katie. "I think I should help you with this lot. It's far more interesting than the stuff I've got."

"Hey, what about me?" I asked.

"Sorry." Jenna grinned. "You're stuck with the bug books."

I made a face at her.

She just laughed. "Come on, Katie. Let's see what else naughty Colonel Morris brought home from India."

While Katie and Jenna finished inventorying Colonel Morris's Hindu goddesses and dead animals, I went back to my box of books on Scottish flora and fauna.

I closed the last box and I sat back on my heels, shifting my position to ease my stiff back and roll my shoulders and neck. As I did so, I caught a glimpse of something out of the corner of my eye. I turned to look.

A cream-colored wooden chest sat wedged in the corner of the room nearest the door. It was about three feet high and five feet long and decorated with gold trim. I hadn't noticed it earlier because it had been behind us when we entered the attic.

As soon as I saw it, my heart jumped. It looked identical to the furniture in Mairi's bedroom. I walked over to it and stroked the top of the smooth wood. Goosebumps prickled on the back of my neck. This chest had belonged to Mairi. I was sure of it.

I knelt down in front of it and carefully lifted the lid. The inside was lined with floral paper. I brushed my fingers against the pattern of delicate leaves and flowers.

With my heart bumping against my rib cage in anticipation, I looked inside.

The chest had been packed with care. White paper, now brittle and yellow with age, lovingly protected its contents. I took out the first item and carefully unwrapped it. Yards of delicate netting trailed from a crown of dried white roses, Mairi's wedding veil.

I lifted it out of the paper. I could see Mairi in my mind's eye as she waltzed down the church aisle, the delicate veil floating behind her, white roses gleaming against her dark upswept hair. She was a beautiful bride. The image was so vivid, that for a brief moment I felt as if it was a memory of a real event.

Smiling at my overactive imagination, I carefully rewrapped the veil and laid it on the floor next to me. The next item I unpacked was her wedding dress. It lay folded, nestled underneath the veil in more paper. The once white satin had taken on a yellowish cast, but other than that it had aged well. I lifted the dress out of the chest and gently lay it on the floor next to her veil.

At the bottom of the trunk I found a black lacquered box, a set of ivory-handled brushes and combs, a matching hand-held mirror, and a book.

I lifted the lacquered box out of the trunk. There was a brass plaque fitted on the top of the lid inscribed with the date 24 March 1902. Was that the date of Mairi's wedding? I opened it.

A small oblong case of red leather lay inside the box. I snapped the case open. A single strand of pearls gleamed on a pillow of faded blue satin.

The room around me seemed to fade, and once again I imagined Mairi. She was dressed in white, the crown of small white roses resting regally on her head, the pearls draped elegantly around her neck. She was standing inside a church. This was the day Mairi had dreamed about ever since she was a little girl. The church was festooned with flowers and ribbons. Friends and family crowded together in the pews, craning their necks to watch as Mairi, nervous and excited, waiting for the ceremony to begin. The vision felt so real that I could actually feel my heart skittering in my chest with nervous excitement, as if I was actually there.

I gingerly lifted the pearl necklace out of its case. I held it up to the light, examining it. The necklace was flawless.

Each perfect sphere glowed softly in the light, but they gave off no warmth.

How long did it take? I wondered, before Mairi discovered that she wasn't going to live happily ever after.

I gently lay the pearls back on their blue satin pillow. Noticing for the first time that the words "Hamilton and Inches, Edinburgh" were stamped on the underside of the lid. Closing the case, I set it aside.

Reaching once again into the chest, I picked up the book. It was small, bound in green leather. Embossed in faded gold letters on the front cover was the title *Burn's Poems*.

I opened the book and was surprised to find myself gazing at a faded, sepia-toned photograph of a boy and a horse.

The photograph had been stuck between the pages of the book. The boy was in his late teens or maybe early twenties. It was hard to tell. He stood next to a cream-colored pony, holding the reins and grinning at the camera with an easy confident air. He had dark, wavy hair and his eyes were filled with laughter.

I flipped the picture over, hoping to find a name or some information that might tell me who he was. There was nothing written on the back.

I glanced at the open book. The poem on the page in front of me was called "Highland Mary." It was about a girl called Highland Mary who met the poet "under the gray-green birk" and "hawthorne's blossom." It was a love poem but a sad one. In the third stanza, Highland Mary dies:

Wi' mony a vow and locked embrace
Our parting was fu' tender;
And, pledging aft to meet again,
We tore oursels asunder;
But, O, fell Death's untimely frost,
That nipt my flower sae early!

Now green's the sod, and cauld's the clay,
That wraps my Highland Mary!

I reread the poem. The similarity between the name of the girl in the poem and Mairi was too much to be just a coincidence. Someone had deliberately marked this poem by placing the photograph in the book at precisely this page. But who?

Because it was in Mairi's trunk, it made sense that she would be the one who had placed it there. Mairi, like the girl in the poem, had died. Had she placed the photograph here before her death, or had someone else noted the similarity of their names and marked this poem with the photograph before placing the book in the trunk?

I flipped open the cover, hoping to find an inscription. It was blank. The book could have belonged to anyone. But if someone else placed the photo there, why was it in Mairi's trunk? Who would have put it in the trunk with her wedding dress? The colonel? The boy in the photograph? But why would he do that? Maybe someone wanted to say good-bye to Mairi. That made sense if the poem was deliberately marked. Maybe the book was supposed to be buried with her, but if that was the case, then why was it in the trunk? How did it get there?

No. I shook my head. I was making things too complicated. I had found the poems in Mairi's trunk, so it made sense that the book belonged to her. Since it was hers, then it also made sense that she was the one who put the photograph in it. The poem was probably just a coincidence. Most likely, she had just tucked the picture of the boy between random pages for safekeeping.

I sat back and held up the photo, studying the boy with the laughing eyes. She must have loved him. Why else would she keep this picture? More importantly, who was he?

"Who are you?" I asked aloud.

"What?" Jenna asked.

I looked up, startled. I hadn't realized that I had spoken aloud. "Sorry. Just talking to myself."

"Having a good conversation, are you?" she joked. She wrinkled her nose and wiped a hand across her forehead. "All this dust is getting to me, too. Hey, what are you doing over there?" she asked, noticing I had moved. "I thought you were going to finish that other corner?"

"I got a little distracted when I saw this," I told her, gesturing toward the trunk. "It's Mairi's trunk. I found her wedding dress."

"A wedding dress? Oooh, I want to see," Katie squealed.

Jenna and Katie hurried over and inspected the things I had taken out of the trunk.

"Look at those pearls," Katie said breathlessly. "Wait till my dad sees them. Do you think they're real?"

"They look real to me," I said.

"I can't believe it. You actually found something," Jenna said, ogling the pearl necklace.

"Well, it's not a chest of gold coins, but a pearl necklace isn't too shabby," I agreed.

Katie snapped the lid closed on the jewelry box and picked it up. "I want to show these to my dad. Do you want to come?"

"You go ahead," I told her. "I'll put the rest of the things back in the trunk."

"Jenna?"

"I'll be down in a minute. I'll finish repacking the stuff we inventoried."

Katie's eyes lit up with excitement. "Right, then I'll see you downstairs."

Jenna and I watched as Katie hurried out of the attic with the jewelry box.

"So, what else did you find?" Jenna asked.

I picked up the photograph and handed it to her. "I found this stuck in between the pages of that book," I said, pointing to the book of poetry laying on the floor next to her.

Jenna took the picture and studied it.

"Who is he?"

"I don't know."

Just as I had done earlier, she flipped the photo over. "There's nothing written on the back."

"No. There's nothing written in the book either."

She turned the photograph back around. "I wonder who he is?"

"I don't know, but she loved him," I said simply. I knew that she loved this boy. I couldn't tell you how I knew it, but I was one hundred percent sure that Mairi loved this boy.

Jenna looked at me, her expression thoughtful. She accepted my statement that Mairi loved him without questioning it, as I knew she would. "Could he have been her brother?" she asked.

I shook my head. "I don't think so. It doesn't feel like that."

"Feel?"

I nodded.

"So your ghost antennas are, uhm, working?"

"I think so. I'm not seeing ghosts or dreaming like I was last summer, but I can sense Mairi's feelings."

"Like in the library?"

"I think so. Maybe. I'm still not sure."

Jenna looked at the photograph again. Her eyebrows drew together as she studied him. "You know who he reminds me of?" She held the picture so I could see it.

I shook my head. "Who?"

"Ben."

I took the photo from her hand and looked closely at the boy. She was right. He didn't look exactly like Ben, but there was something about him that was familiar. I wasn't sure if it was the dark hair or the laughter in his eyes, but Jenna was right, he did remind me of Ben.

"You're right. He does."

"Why don't we bring the photo and show it to Mr. McAfee? He might know who he is."

"Good idea," I agreed. "Help me put these things back and I'll bring the book and the photo, so we can show both of them to him."

We repacked the trunk, gathered up our inventory notes, and left the attic in search of Mr. McAfee.

We found Mr. McAfee in the dining room. The jewelry box lay on the table with its lid open. Mr. McAfee, Ben, Katie, and Simon stood next to the table, studying the gleaming strand of pearls.

They turned to look at Jenna and me when we entered.

"Lily found them in a trunk. They belonged to Mairi," Katie said as they turned to look at me. "Right?"

"Yes. They were with her wedding dress and a veil."

"Well done, Lily," Ben said.

"Thanks," I replied, feeling absurdly pleased by his compliment.

"Aye. Well done," Mr. McAfee agreed. He picked up the strand of pearls, holding them with both hands so that they caught the light. "Isn't Mairi wearing some sort of pearl necklace in her portrait? I wonder if this is the same one. Perhaps we should have a look?"

We trooped over to the library. I followed the others reluctantly, a heavy feeling of dread settling in the bottom of my stomach as I approached the library. I felt uneasy about entering the room. It was the same feeling I had last night, like when you catch just the barest glimpse of something out of the corner of your eye, but when you turn to look it's disappeared. Something was there, but not there. I hung back in the doorway while everyone else crowded around Mairi's portrait.

"It is the same necklace!" Katie said, pointing to the painting. "Look!"

I couldn't see very well from where I was standing, but

then I didn't need to. I knew the pearls belonged to Mairi.

Jenna nodded. "It does look like it is the same one," she agreed.

"Do you think he gave them to her?" Katie asked, turning around to look at Colonel Morris's portrait on the opposite wall.

Everyone followed her gaze, including me.

Colonel Morris's empty eyes surveyed the room with icy disdain. I felt a sudden chill and shivered involuntarily as a strong sensation of anger and revulsion rushed through my body, making me feel suddenly nauseous. Wrapping my arms around myself, I took a step back into the hallway. I did not want a repeat of what happened yesterday.

I leaned against the wall in the hallway, breathing deeply until my stomach settled. With my eyes closed, I listened through the open door as the others discussed Mairi.

"It's possible. The date on the box might have been their wedding day, though it might just as well be her birthday or an anniversary," Mr. McAfee said. "Perhaps you lassies can do a bit of research and find out for us."

Katie or Jenna, I wasn't sure which, said something, but I couldn't quite hear it from where I stood. I moved closer to the doorway.

"Aye. Well, I suspect Colonel Morris had her things stored in the attic after she died," Mr. McAfee replied. "It must have been a terrible blow losing her so young."

"I don't know how he could have stayed here after she died," Jenna said. "Day after day, living in this empty house with only his memories to keep him company."

"He couldn't leave her," Katie said. "He loved her too much. He had to stay here. That's why he spent every night in this room staring at her portrait. He loved her too much to leave her."

I leaned against the wall and closed my eyes. Katie was wrong about Colonel Morris. I didn't know why he had continued to stay in this house, but I knew it wasn't because he had been pining for his dead wife. Colonel Morris hadn't married Mairi because he loved her. He had married her because she was young and beautiful.

I thought about the things we had found in the attic that were part of the colonel's collection from India, the tiger skin, the various statues and paintings. Colonel Morris was a man who liked to own things, beautiful exotic things. He had brought those things back to Scotland as a way of displaying his power and wealth. For the colonel, Mairi had been just another acquisition. He had married her and, just as he had with the tiger he'd killed, he brought her to Anchoret House to be displayed for his own amusement. Poor Mairi. The pearls she had worn for her portrait might as well have been chains. She wasn't Colonel Morris's wife. She was his possession.

"Why don't we see what Mrs. Fraser has made us for lunch?" I heard Mr. McAfee suggest. "We need to get you lads fed and watered before you leave."

I tucked the book with the photograph under my arm as he stepped out into the hall. Now was not the right time to ask about the boy with the laughing eyes.

CHAPTER 7

February 9, 1903

Dear Father,

In answer to your inquiry, yes I am quite an accomplished equestrienne now. Biscuit has such a kindly nature. I could not ask for a better equine companion. She is gentle and patient, yet sturdy enough to manage the difficult terrain of the moor. She is my boon companion and the two of us roam freely among the lochs and lichen taking photographs with the camera you so kindly sent. Thank you for such a thoughtful gift! As you are well aware, unlike Blaire, I have never had the patience or skill necessary for drawing or painting. I am enclosing some photographs of Anchoret House for you to share with Mother and one of Biscuit for Isobel. Please give my love to Mother, Alec, Blaire, and little Isobel.

Your Devoted Daughter,
Mairi

***

During lunch, I felt a familiar pressure building behind my eyes. I pressed my fingers to my temples to try to relieve the pain. When I looked up, I caught Simon staring at me with concern. I dropped my hands.

Are you all right?" he asked.

I'm fine," I snapped.

"Jenna said you had a headache yesterday."

"I said, I'm fine," I repeated, turning my attention back to my soup. The last thing I wanted to do was have a conversation with Simon.

Simon leaned toward me. "Lily …"

I stood abruptly.

All eyes turned to look at me.

"If you don't mind, I think I'll skip lunch," I announced. "I'm not feeling very well."

"Another headache?" Jenna asked, her eyebrows knitting together worriedly.

I nodded.

"You still have the pills I gave you, right?"

I nodded again.

"Maybe you should go upstairs and take a couple."

"That's a good idea. Please excuse me," I said to Mr. McAfee.

"Of course, lass. If you need anything just let us know."

"I will. Thanks."

I could feel Simon's eyes following me as I fled the room, but I refused to look at him.

Once upstairs, I took a couple more paracetamol, swallowing them down with a glass of water from the bathroom faucet. Then I lay down on the bed, closed my eyes, and waited for the drugs to work.

After about thirty minutes, the pounding in my temples had settled into a dull ache. Hoping that the fresh air would help chase away the last of my lingering headache, I decided to take a walk outside.

I made it down the stairs and out the front door

without seeing anyone. I assumed Simon and Ben left for Edinburgh after lunch and that was fine with me. I didn't want to spend any more time in Simon's company. It was just too hard to be around him right now.

Outside, the day had turned cold and windy. A line of gray clouds edged the horizon, although the sky directly overhead was clear. Curling my hands inside the sleeves of my wool sweater for warmth, I stood on the front porch and looked out over the vast moor that bordered Anchoret House. The abrupt rise and fall of the surrounding landscape gave me the strangest feeling, almost like standing on a ship in the middle of a turbulent sea. Something about its wild beauty called to me, and without making a conscious decision to go, I suddenly found myself walking out on the vast, wild moor.

The quiet of the moor was like nothing I had ever experienced before. It was like stepping into a living, breathing world all on its own. I walked without any destination in mind, placing one foot in front of the other, accompanied only by the whisper and moan of the wind as it swept across the gray-green heather. I walked for a long while enjoying the wild, windswept beauty of the surrounding landscape.

I had probably walked two miles or so when I stumbled across the ruins of a curious stone structure. At first, I thought it was a natural stone outcropping, but as I got close to it, I could see that it was man-made.

Someone had stacked rough-hewn rocks on top of each other to form a small cone-shaped house. On one side of the structure, the stones formed a wall about five feet high. The other side of the wall had either collapsed or been knocked down so that it was much shorter. Rocks that had once been part of the wall lay strewn on the ground nearby.

I circled the structure studying it curiously. It was old. Very old. Most of the rocks were covered with lichen and in some places tufts of grass sprouted between the stacked stones. It looked like some sort of shelter. I wondered if it had been built to house travelers or shepherds passing through the area. It seemed far too small for someone to have lived in it for any length of time.

I walked all the way around the funny little house, then stepped through the doorway and stood in the center of the circle. As soon as I did my skin began to hum as if an electrical current was surging through my body.

I should have been afraid, but I wasn't. Happiness. Joy. Love. I could feel the soft golden glow of those emotions swirling about me like invisible snowflakes. I turned around with my arms outstretched, threw my head back, and opened my mouth as if I might be able to catch them or taste them on my tongue.

I stayed in the circle for a long time, drinking in the atmosphere of the stones, allowing it to scour the last traces of pain from my head. I had no idea what the stone circle represented, but I did know that it was a place of happiness.

I felt as if I was walking on sunbeams when I began my hike back to Anchoret House. Unfortunately, the weather didn't cooperate with my sunny mood. The clouds I had seen earlier caught up with me about halfway home, drenching me with cold, fat raindrops.

I dashed across the moor and into the house, shivering and laughing like a lunatic.

"G-g-g-got c-c-caught in the r-r-r-rain. N-n-need to change b-b-before d-d-d-dinner," I said through chattering teeth as I squelched up the stairwell.

Once in my room, I stripped off my wet clothes, changed, and hurried down to dinner.

"S-s-sorry, I'm l-l-late," I apologized as I slid, still shivering, into my seat.

"Here, lass. Take my seat," Mr. McAfee offered, pushing back his chair and standing. "You'll be warmer by the fire."

I smiled at him gratefully. "Th-th-thank you," I

stuttered.

We switched places. I leaned back allowing the heat from the fireplace to warm me.

"You have to keep an eye on the weather here," he said as he handed a plate to me. "It can turn very quickly. I don't expect you're used to that coming from California."

"N-n-n-no," I agreed as Mr. McAfee placed a serving of Mrs. Fraser's pasta in front of me. I rubbed my cold hands together under the table before reaching for my fork.

"What were you doing out on the moor?" Jenna asked, giving me a curious look.

I finished swallowing my noodles. "Walking."

"Walking? In this weather?"

I shrugged. "I wasn't planning on staying out so long, but I started walking and I guess I lost track of time."

"Ah, the allure of the moor." Mr. McAfee leaned back in his chair. "My heart's in the Highlands, my heart is not here; My heart's in the Highlands a-chasing the deer; a-chasing the wild-deer, and following the roe, my heart's in the Highlands wherever I go," he sang.

"Oh, Dad," Katie said with a roll of her eyes. "Please." She turned to look at Jenna and me. "Once he gets started, there's no stopping him."

"Och, Katie, my luve. Have you no appreciation for the greatest of our Scottish poets?" He sighed theatrically. "'Well, then I will say farewell. Farewell to the Highlands, farewell to the North, the birthplace of Valour, the country of Worth,'" Mr. McAfee quoted with a gleam in this eye.

"Dad!"

I hid a smile behind my hand.

"So, Lily," Mr. McAfee said, ignoring his daughter's outburst. "How did you find your tramp among our moors? Aside from getting a wee bit wet?"

"It wasn't raining when I started. The weather was actually very nice."

"Ah. How did you find the midges then? They can be

quite fierce during this time of year when the weather is clear."

"Midges?" I said, visualizing the Scottish version of a leprechaun. "I'm not sure. What is a midge?"

"Midges are the bane or savior of the Highlands. Depending upon who you ask," he replied with a loud laugh.

I gave him a blank look.

Katie wrinkled her nose. "Midges are horrible insects. They swarm all over you and bite you and make you itch. I can't stand them!"

"Oh. Well, I didn't notice any of those today."

"You were lucky then," Katie said.

"I expect the wind and rain kept them away," Mr. McAfee commented. "If you decide to walk the moor in fair weather, you'll want to ask Katie to get you some repellent before you go. So, did you enjoy your tramp through our bonny Highland moor?"

"I did," I said. "Do people live out on the moor?" I asked him, thinking about the small stone house I had found.

"No, not often. Once in a while you'll find a lonely little crofter's cottage, but for the most part people up here cluster together in villages. Anchoret House being the exception, of course."

"Oh. I found some ruins. I thought they might be a little house, but I wasn't sure because it was so small."

"Were the ruins built with stacked stones in the shape of a circle?"

I nodded.

"Well then, what you found was most likely a *broch,* or as they call them up here in the Highlands, an *airie.* There are a fair number of them scattered across the Highlands."

"The village is named for them. Balairie," Katie added.

"So, are they old houses?" I asked.

Mr. McAfee leaned back in his chair. "No one knows for certain what they were used for or who built them, though the experts say that they are more than a thousand years old. It's one of our Highland mysteries."

"Some people think they're graves. I don't like them," Katie said with a shiver. "I think they're haunted."

Jenna caught my eye and lifted an eyebrow in my direction. "Haunted?" she mouthed silently.

I gave my head a little shake. It wasn't that I didn't think the broch was haunted. It was. The feelings of happiness and joy I had sensed were so palpably strong there could be no other explanation. I just wasn't ready to share it with anyone, not even Jenna.

After dinner, we played some cards. It was either that or Monopoly. The options were pretty limited, given that we were staying someplace without internet or cell phone coverage. I stuck out a few games of Crazy Eight, but it wasn't too long before the paracetamol I had taken earlier started to wear off. I told Jenna and Katie that I was tired and went upstairs to my room. I took two more of Jenna's pills, this time washing them down with some of Mrs. Hickman's tea. It wasn't until I had crawled into bed that I realized I'd forgotten to ask about the photograph of the boy with laughing eyes. Exhausted, I fell asleep almost as soon as my head touched the pillow.

I had no memory of my dream when I woke up the next morning, but the name Robbie popped into my head. I picked up the photograph I'd been looking at before I'd fallen to sleep.

"Robbie?" I said the name aloud, trying it out as I studied his image. Maybe. Or then again, maybe not. I resolved to ask Katie and Mr. McAfee about him today.

Katie and Jenna were still sleeping, but I found Mr. McAfee in the stable eyeing the newel post he and Fraser had finally managed to extricate with Simon's help from the floor. He turned to greet me as I entered. "You're an early riser, I see," Mr. McAfee said with obvious approval. "Are Katie and Jenna awake?"

I shook my head. "I don't think so."

"No. I suspect Katie's still in bed. She's not likely to be up and about this early in the morning. Are you hungry, then? Mrs. Fraser usually doesn't put out the breakfast until a bit later, but I can ask her to set the things out earlier if you like."

"No. I'm fine. I can wait. I just came to find you because I wanted to ask you about something I found in the attic."

Mr. McAfee grinned. "Not another pearl necklace, is it?"

"No, Sorry. Though I did find it with Mairi's things." I handed him the book.

Mr. McAfee studied the book. "Burns. Well, that is a find." He opened the book and examined the title page. "Mairi Morris had fine taste."

"Inside the book I found this." I gave him the photograph. "I was hoping you might know who he is."

Mr. McAfee's eyebrows drew together as he studied the photo. He shook his head. "Sorry, lass. I've no idea. You found it in the book, did you?" he asked, handing the photo back to me.

"Yes." I glanced down at the photograph. "Do you know if Mairi had a brother?"

"Hmmm. I can't say. I don't know much about poor wee Mairi. I've done quite a bit of research on the colonel, but not much on his bride, I'm afraid. Though, you might find something about her in the colonel's papers."

"The colonel's papers?"

"Aye." He scratched his chin thoughtfully. "I keep meaning to sort through them. Unfortunately, I've not had the time. If you're interested in doing some sleuthing, I can show you the boxes. You're welcome to go through them."

"I'd love to!" I said enthusiastically.

"Well, then. Let's head back to the house and we'll get you started. The boxes are in the library."

I must have looked as uneasy as I felt at the thought of going to the library, because Mr. McAfee quickly offered to transfer the boxes to the music room. "I'll just get them and you can set yourself up in there. A bit more peace and quiet for you," he added thoughtfully.

I followed him back to the house.

"Here we are," he said, opening the door to the music room.

I stepped inside, expecting to see a piano or harp. I was surprised. Instead of a piano, an enormous roll-top desk sat in the center of the room.

"Why is this called the music room?" I asked, eyeing the desk.

"Ah, you've noticed the lack of musical instruments. Have you?" Mr. McAfee chuckled. He pointed to the crown molding near the ceiling. "I suspect the original owners had plans for a proper music room, but I don't believe this room has ever been used as such."

I looked up. A different musical instrument decorated the molding at each corner: violin, harp, trumpet, and flute.

"The colonel converted this room into his study after he bought the house. I was thinking perhaps I might convert it into a quiet sitting room once Anchoret House is accepting guests, but then there is the wee problem of the desk."

"The desk?" I asked, eyeing the mahogany desk. "What's wrong with it?"

"Nothing." He chuckled again. "Except that it's twice as wide as the door."

I looked from the wide desk to the door and saw that he was right. "You're right. Wow. How did the colonel get it in here?" I asked.

"I suspect he didn't."

I looked at him blankly.

"Have you ever seen one of those bottles with the ships in them?" he asked.

"Yes."

"I think that's how he managed it."

"Ship in a bottle?" I said, my gaze shifting between the door and the desk. It took me a moment. "Oh, I get it! He didn't bring the desk through the door at all. He built it inside the room."

"That would be my guess," Mr. McAfee said with a grin. "I'll go fetch those boxes for you now while you settle on a place to sort through them."

There were four boxes in all.

"It looks like you're in for quite a job," Mr. McAfee said, looking them over. "I can't promise there's anything in them that will help you identify your young man, but with a bit of luck, you might find something."

"That's okay. I really like doing things like this."

Mr. McAfee nodded. "Simon mentioned that you and Jenna uncovered some interesting history at Brynmoor Manor. Rooting through the past can be quite fun." He grinned. "Though one has to be careful as there is always the risk of finding a few hidden family skeletons," he added with a wink.

"Uhm. Right," I said, wondering if he knew about the skeleton we had found last summer.

He dusted off his hands. "Well, then I best let you get to it. Let me know if you need anything else."

"I will. Thanks."

I waited for him to leave before opening the first box.

The box was filled with Colonel Morris's military papers. I rifled through them. All of the papers appeared to be dated before the colonel's marriage to Mairi. Since I wasn't interested in Colonel Morris, I pushed the first box to the side and moved onto the second box.

This box held twenty years' worth of Anchoret House ledgers. One book for each year, the first one dated 1899. Columns of carefully calculated expenses filled the brittle pages of each leather-bound book. Payments for house repairs, food, clothing, and servants were all painstakingly noted in the colonel's very precise handwriting.

I studied a random page from the ledger for 1899: 6 shillings for tea, 3 shillings for sugar, 2 shillings for butter, and 2 pounds, six shillings to Mrs. A. Beattie, Cook. I closed the ledger and replaced it in the box.

I located the ledger from 1902. Opening it, I flipped through the pages until I found the page marked 24 March 1902. The same date engraved on Mairi's jewelry box. In the debit column, the colonel had written entries for two railway tickets, one carriage rental, and, most importantly, a payment to a Revd. James L. Craven, St. Cuthbert's Parish Church, for services rendered.

A slow smile spread across my face. So, I thought, pleased with myself, now I knew for certain that Mairi had been married on March 24th. I read the entry again. The colonel's firm handwriting marched across the page: *Services rendered.* I shook my head. Poor Mairi. She had married a man who treated their wedding with as much passion as his monthly purchase of butter. He had paid for a bride and brought her, as he would with any new acquisition, to Anchoret House.

I worked my way backward through the ledger to see if I could find any mention of the pearl necklace, thinking that Mr. McAfee might be interested in its history.

It took me a while, but I eventually found it: 17 January 1902. Colonel Morris made a payment to Hamilton and Inches, 90A Princes St. Edinburgh, for one gold band, one pearl necklace, and one pearl brooch. The total expense was fifty-five pounds. More than twice what the cook earned in an entire year.

I marked the page with a scrap of paper and closed the book, setting it aside to show Mr. McAfee later.

By the time I opened the third box, my head was beginning to ache again. I pressed my fingers to my temples. Just one more box, I told myself then I would take a break and get breakfast.

I opened the box. I was completely thrilled by what I found inside. Photographs! The box was filled with photographs.

The first photos I found were of Colonel Morris. There were several framed black and white images of him from his time in the Army. I pulled out a picture of him as a very young man. It must have been taken early in his Army career because his mustache was dark and luxurious. He stared at the camera with a self-satisfied gaze, his mouth twisted into an arrogant smile. I felt a surprisingly intense loathing for the man in the photo.

There were several more of the colonel posing in uniform and one of him sitting atop a large bay horse. I quickly set those aside, barely glancing at them.

I also found one framed photograph of Colonel Morris as an old man. I almost didn't recognize him. He was sitting in a chair, a small rug or blanket covering his lap. A younger man stood slightly behind him, resting a hand on his shoulder. In this photo, the colonel looked frail and surprisingly small. He no longer had a mustache, and without it, his pinched face resembled that of a withered apple.

I set that photograph next to the first one I'd found and studied them. For some reason, it gave me a sense of satisfaction to know that the arrogant young Colonel Morris in the first picture had ended up becoming the feeble old man in the second one.

The last framed photo in the box was a picture of Mairi. Like the portrait hanging in the library, Mairi wore her hair swept up on top of her head, exposing an elegant swan-like neck. She had posed sitting in a chair, her head turned slightly as if she was looking at someone standing to the left of the photographer. She smiled tentatively, almost self-consciously. I studied the photo for a long time before putting it aside.

The throbbing in my head was getting worse, but I was determined to finish going through this box. I rubbed my temples and promised myself that I would take a break after I finished looking. I lifted the last item out of the box. It was a photo album.

As soon as I saw the name written on the inside cover, my heart started beating excitedly. I had no doubt about the photographer's identity. This was Mairi's album.

She was a talented photographer. She did more than document place and time. She took time to compose her photographs, infusing them with a range of emotions. She had snapped a few photos of Anchoret House and the garden, but the majority of the images in the album were ones she had taken of the surrounding moor.

Her black-and-white photographs managed to capture the bleak and haunting beauty of the moor in a way I wouldn't have thought possible. In one photo, a storm-tossed sky, clouds roiling overhead, blotted out the sun as the wind whipped the heather below. In another, a lone tree stood like a sentinel guarding a rocky hill. A third photo depicted a small stream, water glistening on lichen-covered rocks as it meandered across a field. She had also taken a stunning series of images by aiming her camera at the surface of a loch and photographing the reflections of the sky and surrounding landscape in its dark, still waters. Her photos captured both the aching loneliness and haunting beauty of the highlands.

As I flipped through the pages, I felt like I was looking through a window into her world. Her days were filled with loneliness and isolation, but there were also moments of joy. I laughed aloud at her photo of a rather annoyed ram, his grumpy expression making it clear that he was displeased at having his picture taken.

Then I saw a photo that made my heart skip a beat. It was a photograph of the stony ruins of a broch. The same one I had stumbled upon yesterday.

Mairi had taken the photograph on a bright and sunny afternoon, most likely in the spring. A sprinkling of soft white snow-dusted ground, but many of the stones gleamed darkly in the bright sunlight, wet with newly melted snow. In the foreground, a small hearty wildflower had pushed its way up through the half-frozen earth in search of sunlight. It was an arresting image. Mairi had taken more than a photograph of the stone broch. It was an image of life and beauty thriving among ruins. More than any of the others, this photograph was a representation of Mairi's life at Anchoret House.

I thought of the feelings of happiness and joy I had felt when I was at the broch. Had the broch been Mairi's refuge from Anchoret House? Was that what I had sensed? I stared at the photograph, the throbbing in my temples intensifying. I pressed the flat of my hand against my forehead and turned the page.

For a second, the breath caught in my throat as I stared into a pair of startlingly familiar eyes. He was leaning casually against the broch's stone wall, his cap tilted at a jaunty angle, the corners of his mouth curving upward, as if he were about to tell me a secret.

Robbie!

The name jackhammered through my skull, blinding me with pain. I felt like my head had been struck by lightning. White blinding pain seared through my skull. The pounding in my head grew so violent that I felt physically sick. So much so, that I was afraid I was going to throw up. Moaning, I pressed my hands to the side of my head, lay down on the floor, and curled into a fetal position, praying that the pain would go away.

"The doctor thinks it's a migraine," Jenna told me as I lay in bed.

"K," I croaked. The effort of saying that one word sent

another bolt of pain rocketing through my skull. I discovered that as long as I didn't move, didn't speak, didn't open my eyes, the pain was tolerable. The moment I tried to do anything other than lie perfectly still triggered intense waves of pain. Unbearable pain.

"She said that we should keep the room dark and quiet and let you rest. If it doesn't get better by tomorrow, or if the pain gets worse, then we should take you to the hospital."

Jenna paused. I didn't move or respond.

"She said you should take these if you can keep them down."

I cracked one eye open and saw that she was holding some pills and a glass of water.

"Do you think you can take these? I can help you sit up if you like."

"K," I croaked again. I lifted my head—no easy task, as the movement felt like someone was beating my brains out with a sledgehammer. I managed to choke down the pills and some of the water before falling back onto the pillows exhausted, pain knifing through my head.

"Well," Jenna added uncertainly. "Uhm, I'll just go. I brought a bowl, in case you get sick again. I'll leave it on the bed next to you."

I didn't move or say anything. I couldn't. I was concentrating on keeping the pills and water from coming back up.

"Uhm. So, I guess I'll go now." She paused, waiting for me to say something. When I didn't respond, she continued. "I'll come back and check on you in a bit. Just to make sure you don't need anything."

I heard her softly closing the door behind her as she left.

I don't know if it was exhaustion or the pills, but somehow I managed to sleep. When I woke up I realized the pain in my head had subsided, leaving nothing more than a dull throbbing ache behind my eyes. I cautiously raised myself into a sitting position. The room was very dark, but I had no idea what time it was.

I sat in the dark, not yet willing to risk getting out of bed. Eventually, I heard footsteps outside my door. The door to my room opened and Jenna peaked inside.

"You're feeling better," she said.

"Yes," I replied weakly.

"Oh, I'm so glad. Do you want me to switch on the lights?"

"No. I'm not ready for that yet, but you can leave the door open." The hallway light softened the darkness of my room, but it wasn't so bright that it hurt my eyes or worsened my headache.

Jenna entered the room and stood uncertainly by my bed. "Uhm, Mrs. Fraser made you some soup. Do you want me to bring it up for you?"

"Not yet. Maybe in a little while." I exhaled slowly and tried to sit up a little taller.

"Let me help you," Jenna offered. She gently tucked the pillows behind my back and head. "How's that?"

"Good. Thanks."

"Does your head still hurt?"

"A little."

The doctor said you can have two more of those pills if you need them."

"I don't think I need them right now." I moved my head slowly, experimentally. The pain wasn't too bad. "What time is it?" I asked.

"Eleven o'clock."

"At night?"

"Uh-huh."

"I can't believe I slept that long."

"I think it was the pills. The doctor said that they would help you sleep. I guess they did." In the dim light, I could just make out the ghost of a smile on Jenna's face. She reached over and gave my arm a little squeeze. "I'm so glad you're feeling better."

"Me, too." I smiled weakly at her.

"When I first saw you curled up on the floor like that, I thought you were dead."

I leaned back against the pillows and closed my eyes. "I felt like I was dying."

"So, what happened? Was it like what happened to you in the library?"

"No. I was just looking at some old pictures. I had a headache, but it wasn't that bad. I thought my head hurt because I hadn't eaten breakfast. I should have stopped, but I got distracted by the photos. I guess I'll have to wait until tomorrow to look at the rest of the papers in the boxes."

Jenna shook her head and held up her hand. "The doctor said that you aren't supposed to read, watch the tele, listen to loud music, or play video games for the next twenty-four hours," she repeated, ticking off each item on her fingers.

"Hmm," I murmured noting that the doctor's orders hadn't included looking at photographs.

"So, do you think it was a migraine?"

"I don't know. I've never had one before. If it was a migraine, I have to tell you, I hope I never have another one again."

"I think you should take the pills." She held up the bottle. "Just to make sure."

"Okay," I agreed.

"I'll bring you some water."

I reached over and squeezed her hand. "Thanks, Jenna."

The next morning when I woke up, my headache was gone. I rolled my head experimentally from side to side. No pain. I was almost giddy with relief. I felt like I had been reborn. I swallowed two paracetamol pills as a precautionary measure and made my way downstairs to breakfast.

The dining room was empty. That was fine by me. I wanted to get to the back to look at the photographs and I didn't want to have to answer any questions. I ate quickly then hurried to the music room.

When I arrived, I was surprised to find Jenna sitting on the floor surrounded by photographs. She looked up when I entered the room.

"I knew you would come here as soon as you woke up," she said.

I grinned. "The doctor didn't say I couldn't look at pictures."

Jenna rolled her eyes. "Right."

"I'll stop if my head or eyes start to bother me."

"Promise?" Jenna said, lifting a skeptical eyebrow in my direction.

I held up my hand. "Trust me. I don't want a repeat of yesterday."

She sighed but moved over to make room for me.

I settled myself on the floor next to her. "So, what have you found?"

"Well, I saw the picture of our mystery man at the broch. You left the album open to that page. I looked through the rest of the album and found one more photo of him."

She opened the album and handed it to me.

The photograph showed a large bay horse standing in his stall. It might have been the same one in the framed photo of Colonel Morris. The horse stared curiously at the camera, ears pricked forward, nostrils flaring as he leaned over the door to his stall, eager to get a closer look at either the camera or the photographer.

"There." Jenna pointed. "Off to the side. I think that's him."

Robbie stood to the right of the stall, a bucket in his hand. He was looking at the horse, not the camera so his face wasn't visible, but I was certain she was right.

"I think you're right," I said, studying the image.

Jenna placed the photo from the book next to this one. "Same clothes. Same hair. Same build. It's him."

I nodded in agreement, as I shifted my gaze from one photograph to the other. "Too bad that doesn't tell us who he is."

"But it does," Jenna said. "Or at least I think it gives us a pretty good clue."

"What do you mean?"

"Look at him in this photo." She pointed to the photo with the horse. "What is he doing?"

"He's carrying a bucket."

"And ..." she prodded. "Why is he carrying a bucket?"

A light bulb went off in my head. "Because he is feeding the horses," I said excitedly. "He works for Colonel Morris!"

"Right. He probably took care of the colonel's horses, which means ..."

"That the colonel paid him. Which means that his name is listed in the ledgers! Which means we can figure out who he is!"

Jenna's face creased into a wide grin. "Exactly!"

"Jenna." I hugged her. "You're brilliant!"

"What? It's taken you this long to suss that out?"

I grabbed the ledger for 1902, the one where I had marked the page with the notation about Mairi's pearl necklace. "I'm sure we can find it in here," I told her. "Colonel Morris always paid his staff on the first of each month. So, all we have to do is check the list of paid servants."

I quickly thumbed through the pages, finding nothing until I turned to the first day of December. I ran my finger down the column of expenses looking for Robbie.

R. Cameron, Groom. 1 pound, 2 shillings.

A shiver of recognition rippled up my spine as I read his name. *R. Cameron. Robbie Cameron.* I had found him!

CHAPTER 8

14 February 1903

Dear Blaire,

I am disappointed that Mother is unable to travel with you to Anchoret House. I would so enjoy a sisterly visit for I have much to tell you. I suppose I must begin by confessing that I have found love again! The kind of love that makes your heart sing and the sun shine even on the worst of days. I know that you are wondering why is it that I am now confessing this so long after my wedding. My dear sister, I can only answer that one cannot always predict how and when one's heart will open itself to love. Unexpectedly love has shone its light on me and it is as if the world has been washed clean of all things base and ugly and made new again. For the first time in my life I understand the power of the words "for richer, for poorer, in sickness and in health, forever here and (please God) forever and ever in the world to come." I have found someone for whom I am ready to sacrifice everything on earth. I hope that one day you too shall find the partner of your heart and soul, for love is a great gift, perhaps the greatest gift one can bestow upon another and have bestowed upon us.

Yours in sisterly love,

Mairi

***

Over the next three days, I became obsessed with finding information about Robbie. I was feverish in my need to find him. It wasn't enough to see a photograph and find a name in a ledger. There was so much I needed to know: Who was he? Where was he from? How did he come to work at Anchoret House? Why did Mairi save his picture? Like my ever-present headache, his name was a constant echo thrumming through my skull, a song playing over and over in my head. I went on a manic hunting expedition. I woke up in the morning and began searching for clues to Robbie's identity, stopping only for meals and sleep. I examined every scrap of paper and every photograph. I read every ledger entry and tore through box after box in the attic in the hope that I would find something. After three exhaustive days, all I managed to discover was that Robbie had worked for Colonel Morris from December 1902 through November 1903. That was it.

I have to admit, I went a little crazy in my quest for information on Robbie. When I couldn't find any information about him in the colonel's papers or the attic, I brought the box of photographs up to my room and began inventing evidence. I studied the photos at night before I went to bed, desperately searching in the margins of the pictures for signs of Robbie. A harness slung casually over a fence meant that he led the colonel's horse to the paddock for him. An overturned bucket was where he had sat to clean the saddles. A wheelbarrow, a rake, hoof prints, each one was a possible connection to Robbie.

As I searched for Robbie, I found myself growing increasingly angry with Colonel Morris. In my mind's eye, I saw him tear up Mairi's photographs of Robbie and throw them into the fireplace, furiously stoking the flames as he watched them burn. I imagined him gathering Robbie's belongings and hiking across a gray and windy moor, then dumping them into the deep black waters of a loch. Robbie had lived here and worked here, and yet no trace of him remained. I was convinced that Colonel Morris had deliberately obliterated all signs of Robbie from Anchoret House, although I had no proof of it.

After three days of finding nothing, I started scouring the moors. As I walked, I would look at rocks or hills and wondered if Robbie had passed this same way. Inevitably, no matter which direction I started walking, I would find myself at the broch, brushing my hands against the stones, knowing that Robbie had done the same thing. Then I would climb inside the stone circle and wait as a mixture of giddy anticipation and anxiety fluttered beneath my breastbone.

I really wasn't sure what I was waiting for, though I knew I was waiting for something to do with Robbie Cameron. Was his spirit wandering the moors? Would he return to the broch? Part of me knew that I wasn't really thinking straight, but another part of me didn't care. It was almost like an addiction. I was waiting for Robbie. It didn't even matter that he was dead. I was convinced that he would come. So, I sat in the broch for hours, waiting for him to show up until the cold or the midges drove me back to Anchoret House.

Eventually, I removed the photo Mairi had taken of Robbie from the album. I placed it with the photograph I'd found in the attic on my bedside table and mooned over them as if I were a lovesick girl. In a way, I guess I was. I couldn't stop thinking about the boy with the laughing eyes. His was the last name on my lips when I went to sleep at night and the first thought in my head when I woke up. I thought of nothing else.

I barely spoke to Jenna or Katie. I became so intensely focused on my detective work that I noticed nothing else. At the time, it seemed perfectly normal. Sure, I was obsessing over a dead guy I'd never met, but then I'd done that last summer, too. So, it didn't seem so crazy. Maybe that's why it took Jenna so long to figure out what was going on.

"Lily, we're going to Wick," Jenna announced at breakfast. "And you're coming with us," she added.

I looked up from my bowl of oatmeal. "Wick?" I asked.

"It's just north of here. My dad needs to place an order with the Timber Merchant in Wick and he says we can go with him," Katie explained, her eyes lighting up at the prospect of getting away from Anchoret House.

"You guys go, I'm fine here."

"You are not staying here," Jenna said. "You're coming with us."

"There are some great shops in Wick," Katie added. "We can have lunch. The Bombay Café makes a really good curry, or if you don't like curry there are Italian restaurants, too. I know all the best places. We can even go to the cinema if you like."

"Uhm. I don't know." I glanced over at Jenna, who sat staring at me with her arms crossed in front of her.

"You are coming with us, Lily," she said in a firm voice. "You need to think about something besides dead people, and you need to check in with your mum."

"My mom? Why do I need to check in with my mom?"

Jenna gave me an exasperated look. Speaking slowly and clearly as if I wasn't too bright, she explained, "Because we'll have good mobile service in Wick and your very pregnant mother, who might be having a baby at any time, is probably worried about you because she hasn't heard from you in a week."

"Oh, right," I said, feeling slightly guilty. I hadn't even thought about my mom since I'd left Brynmoor. "Okay. I'll go," I agreed.

Katie clapped her hands together and smiled happily. "Brilliant!"

"Hmm," I murmured. I wasn't as enthused as Katie about the outing, but Jenna was right, I did need to call my mom.

Wick was a charming coastal town. Divided in two by the Wick River, the town hugged the shoreline of a sheltered bay with bright blue water that glinted invitingly in the sun. Sailboats dotted the horizon and several hearty people sunbathed on the shore, though no one was foolish enough to brave the frigid waters for a swim.

We approached the town from the south on the A99. As we neared the river, Mr. McAfee pointed to a building on our left.

"Guinness Book of Records," he said. "Wick's claim to fame is right over there."

Jenna and I exchanged confused looks.

Katie giggled. "It's the shortest street in the world."

Mr. McAfee nodded. "It's only two meters long. Little more than six feet," he explained converting the metric measurement for me, not that he needed to. I'd been in England long enough to grow comfortable with meters, liters, and kilos.

"Why would anyone want a two-meter-long street?" Jenna asked.

Mr. McAfee grinned. "It's part of the hotel."

I looked out my window. A long, narrow stone building stood along the road. From my angle, the building appeared to be three stories high, more than a dozen rooms in length and one room wide.

"See that door there." Mr. McAfee slowed the car so we could look at the front door of the hotel that was on the narrow end of the building. "When MacBride built that hotel in 1883, the city council told him he had to have his address posted above the front door. Well, as you can see the front door sits on that little bit of road where the two other streets meet. So, in order to be in compliance with the town council, Sinclair named that little bit of road himself." He pointed to the letters affixed to the front of the building. They spelled out 1 Ebenezer Place. "There you have it. Ebenezer Place, the shortest street in the world, according to *Guinness World Book of Records*."

I arched an eyebrow at Jenna.

Jenna read my mind. "So, does Wick get a lot of tourists then?" she asked. "To see the street, I mean."

Mr. McAfee laughed. "We get our fair share. Though most come for the scenery, not for Ebenezer Place, which is why," he added with is a touch of pride, "Anchoret House is going to give MacBride's hotel some competition. Once I get her up and running that is."

"Right," Jenna said.

I nodded in agreement, though I privately wondered how many tourists would choose isolated and gloomy Anchoret House over MacBride's hotel in downtown Wick.

We continued over the bridge and crossed the river to the north side of town. Mr. McAfee dropped us off on High Street before continuing on his way to the Timber Merchant.

High Street looked like a much more promising tourist attraction than Ebenezer Place. Benches and planters with flowers bordered the sidewalk while stately old Victorian buildings lined the street housing an assortment of small restaurants and shops.

"I want to go to the Confectionary Shop," Katie said, pointing to a store located on the ground floor of a pink and white building.

"Uhm, I should probably call my mom," I said, glancing at Jenna. "I'll hang out here and call her while you two shop."

Jenna nodded. "Good idea."

I sat on a bench and made the phone call. My mom

was thrilled to hear from me. She was happily ensconced at Brynmoor Manor still waiting for the 10th Earl of Yarlbury to make his appearance.

"Have you and Richard decided on a name yet?" I asked her.

"Not yet."

"You guys are cutting it a little close, aren't you? I mean, the baby is due pretty soon."

My mom laughed. "We have a few definite possibilities, we just haven't decided on anything yet."

"Such as …"

"Oh. Well, the list is a bit long, but don't worry. We'll have made a decision by the time he's born."

"Okay, but make it a good one. I don't want to be embarrassed by my little brother's name."

I could hear the smile in her voice. "Weren't you the one who suggested Percival?"

"I was just joking about Percival. Now I'm thinking that Alfred would be a much better name?" I said teasing her.

"Alfred? Do you really want a little brother named Alfie?"

"Okay. No Alfred. What about Felix?"

"Felix? Like the cat?"

"Eugene? We could call him Genie."

"Lily, you are impossible," my mother said laughing.

I chatted with my mom for a little longer and told her about Anchoret House and Mr. McAfee and Katie. I also told her about finding the broch. I didn't mention anything about Simon or tell her about my migraine headache. I didn't want to worry her, and I didn't want her to tell me to come home.

I finished my phone call with my mom, then I strolled over to the Confectionary Shop. Jenna was standing outside the shop talking to someone on her phone. She didn't see me at first. When she finally caught sight of me, her eyes widened.

"I'll ring you later. Yes. I've got to go," she said, ending her call abruptly. She turned to face me. "So, how is your mum?" she asked brightly.

"Fine. No baby yet, which is a good thing, since she and Sir Richard still haven't picked a name for him." I shook my head. "Poor little No Name. So, who were you talking to? Your mom?" I asked.

"Mmm," Jenna mumbled, her eyes sliding away from mine. "Oh, look! Katie's waving at us. Let's go inside."

The three of us spent the rest of the day shopping, mostly window shopping, but sometimes that's even better than actually buying things. Our sum total of purchases included two magazines (Jenna), a scarf (me), a bag of assorted candies (Katie), and lunch (all three of us). I surprised myself by having a pretty good time. I didn't even realize that my headache was gone until it came back, which it did as soon as we crested the hill above Anchoret House.

Mr. McAfee parked the car and I hurried up to my room to take a couple more paracetamol pills, mentally kicking myself for not buying more of them at the pharmacy in Wick.

I dumped my bag on the bed and grabbed for the bottle of pills. I wasn't about to take the chance on having another migraine headache.

Unfortunately, I was in such a hurry that I accidentally knocked the bottle off the top of the bureau. It fell onto the floor and rolled underneath.

Cursing under my breath, I got down on my knees to look for it. The bottle had rolled all the way to the back wall. I stuck my arm underneath the bureau and began feeling around for it. My arm was just long enough to reach it. As I slid my fingers along the back wall, I felt something strange. A metal ring of some sort was wedged under the baseboard. I gave it a tug, but it stayed put.

I pulled out the bottle and quickly downed two of the paracetamol pills. Curious about the metal ring, I crouched down and peered under the bureau. Without a flashlight, I couldn't really see much. I stuck my arm underneath and felt for the metal ring again. I tugged at it, but it was wedged tight and I wasn't able to move it.

I sat back on my heels thinking. It was probably nothing more exciting than a bent nail, but my curiosity was piqued. I eyed the bureau. It wasn't small, but I thought with a little effort I might be able to move it at least enough to get my arm behind it and pry the metal ring loose.

It took me a few shoves, but I eventually managed to shift the bureau far enough away from the wall to squeeze my upper body behind it. I hooked the metal ring with my fingers and wriggled back and forth until it came free from the baseboard. I pulled it out from behind the bureau, holding my hard-won prize up to the light.

I was wrong. It wasn't a ring, it was some kind of charm or pendant.

The pendant was made from two curved pieces of metal fused together to form a heart shape. The thick end of the metal pieces formed a square base at the bottom, their tapered shafts curving to form the heart. It looked like it was a pendant from a necklace or perhaps a charm from a bracelet.

I held it in the flat of my hand, running my finger over the smooth, polished metal. It was a quirky little piece, obviously made by hand. The heart was a little lopsided. I wasn't sure if it was because it had been designed that way or if it had bent it when I had pulled it out from under the baseboard.

There was something oddly familiar about the shape of the two metal pieces forming the pendant. I stared at it for a moment, and then it came to me. Horseshoe nails. I was looking at two horseshoe nails fused together and bent into the shape of a heart. My heart leapt with recognition.

Robbie had made this pendant!

I know I should have given the pendant to Mr. McAfee or Katie, but I didn't want to share it with anyone else. I felt like it was a gift, a special gift from Robbie to me. Logically, I understood that Robbie could not possibly have left the pendant for me and that he might not even have been the person who made it, but I wasn't thinking logically. In my heart, I felt that Robbie had made this for me. So, I kept it. I removed the ribbon from the sachet of herbs that Mrs. Hickman had given me, threaded it through the pendant, and hung it around my neck. That night at dinner, I wore Robbie's heart next to mine.

"Did you buy that in Wick?" Mr. McAfee asked, noticing the pendant as he handed me a plate.

Jenna's head swiveled in my direction. Her eyes narrowing thoughtfully as she looked at the small heart hanging around my neck.

I clasped it self-consciously. "No. I bought a scarf."

Katie giggled. "She bought a winter scarf in June! The woman in the shop tried to talk her out of it, but Lily said no. She said it still felt like winter to her because she's from California."

Grateful for the distraction, I tucked the pedant inside my shirt.

Mr. McAfee leaned back in his chair. "Ah, California. The land of golden sunshine. I suspect our summer is a bit like winter where you come from." He glanced over at me. "I've always wondered what it was like to live in the land of perpetual sunshine and famous celebrities."

"Do you know some celebrities?" Katie asked eagerly.

I laughed. People who have never visited California seem to think that we have celebrities on every corner. I've lived in LA all my life, and the closest I've ever come to meeting a "movie star" was at a friend's party when I was introduced to her uncle, a man who had been an in a movie no one had ever seen. "Not really," I said.

We talked about Los Angeles and Hollywood and then the conversation turned back to Anchoret House.

"Jenna and Katie tell me you've been going through the colonel's photographs with a fine-tooth comb. Have you found anything interesting?" Mr. McAfee asked me. I had shown Mr. McAfee the ledger entry for the purchase of the pearl necklace earlier.

"Not really. Although, I don't think that all of the photos belong to the colonel."

Mr. McAfee frowned. "Really?"

"Well, I mean, I guess, technically, they did belong to the colonel, but I don't think he took them. I think Mairi did. Maybe not all of them, but I think she took the photos in the album. The pictures in the frames were probably taken by other people, but I think I think the album belonged to her or at least it did when she was alive."

"Why do you think she took the photos?" Jenna asked.

"They just don't seem like something the colonel would do. Take pictures, I mean."

"Why not? Maybe it was his hobby."

I shook my head. "No. The photos in the album are artistic. You've looked at them. I can't see the colonel wandering the moors taking artsy photographs. Think about it. The guy converted the ballroom into a library and the music room into an office. He was not artistic. And the photos in the album are definitely artistic. Besides, her name is written inside the cover," I added.

"He could have given the album to her as a gift," Katie said.

I shook my head. "I can't see that. Like I said, the photos just aren't his style."

"Hmm." Mr. McAfee scratched his chin. "I suspect Lily's right. She did find that photograph in her trunk."

"Inside a book that was inside the trunk. Anyone could have put it there," Jenna countered. She looked at me. "We don't even know if it was Mairi's book. There was no name written in it. The book might have been put in her trunk by mistake."

"Okay. The book might not be hers, but that's not why I think she took the photos," I argued. "Why would he take pictures of his groom? There are two pictures of Robbie. The colonel wouldn't have taken those photos. He might take one of his favorite horse, but not the servant who took care of the horse. No way."

"So, you think Mairi took pictures of the servants?" Katie asked.

I looked at Katie. "Mairi didn't take pictures of the servants. She took pictures of one servant, Robbie Cameron."

"But why?"

"Because she was in love with him."

"But she was married to the colonel," Katie protested.

I shrugged. "I don't think the colonel was a very nice man. I think Mairi was lonely and found someone who made her happy." I glanced at Mr. McAfee, belatedly remembering that he was getting divorced from Katie's mother. Luckily, he didn't look too bothered by my comment. Katie, on the other hand, frowned unhappily at me.

"You're just guessing. You don't know any of this," Jenna protested.

I swung my gaze back to Jenna. "You're right. I don't know, but it makes sense." I turned to Mr. McAfee. "You told us that they never found Mairi's body. Right?"

He nodded.

"When did that happen?"

He scratched his chin thoughtfully. "Hmm. I'm sorry, lass. I don't know the date. Though I can tell you she hadn't been married for very long before she died. If she was married in March 1902, she must have died sometime in 1903, or perhaps early 1904."

"The last mention of Robbie in the colonel's ledgers is November 1903," I said, giving Jenna a triumphant look.

"They both disappeared around the same time."

"You don't know that. We don't know the exact date that Mairi died," Jenna said.

"Okay, so we don't the exact date, that doesn't mean it isn't possible. We don't know that they didn't both disappear at the same time."

Jenna snorted in disbelief. "Just because Robbie Cameron isn't in the ledger doesn't mean he disappeared. For all we know, he got a new job. Colonel Morris could have sold his horses. There are a million different reasons why he might have left Anchoret House that have nothing to do with him running away with Mairi."

"It doesn't mean they weren't together," I insisted stubbornly.

"Dad, where can we find the date that Mairi died?" Katie interjected suddenly.

Jenna and I both turned to look at Mr. McAfee.

"Well, I suppose there'll be a record of it somewhere, though I've no idea where. Church registries, perhaps. Old copies of the daily?" He leaned back in his chair and scratched his chin again. "Hmm. I'll have to think on it. Trying to find the past is a bit like playing detective, isn't it?" he said, smiling at us. "You girls will have to put your heads together and see what you can suss out."

CHAPTER 9

31 May 1903

Dearest Mother,

I have news to share with you! Even as I lift my pen to write this letter, I find I can scarcely believe it. First, I must tell you that I have not been feeling very well these last few weeks, suffering from what I thought was a stomach ailment. I had very little appetite, and when I did eat, I suffered terribly from nausea. The colonel was quite cross with me one evening when I abruptly excused myself from the table. It was either that or risk a much worse embarrassment. When my health showed no improvement after several weeks' time, he called the doctor to come to Anchoret House. Now I find that I am to have a baby! A beautiful baby for the new year, or so the doctor tells me. I am very happy, yet I cannot help but feel a trifle frightened as I know so little about babies and birthing. The doctor assures me that it is an entirely natural process and that I shall have no difficulty, but I do not find his words comforting, for he is a man and cannot know first-hand the travails of childbirth. I know you will find me foolish, but I do so yearn for womanly companionship and advice. I cannot help but feel that a woman would have better insight into the divine mysteries of childbirth than Dr.Hunter. Please write to me right away, as I am anxious to hear from you. My love to all.

Your daughter,
Mairi

***

Jenna came to my room after dinner to talk. She wanted to go to check the records at the churches in Wick and look for information on Robbie and Mairi. I thought it was a waste of time. "We did it last time and it worked," she insisted.

Last summer it had worked, but this time things were different. "Last time we had information to look up," I told her. "This time we don't. We don't know when he was born nor when he died. We don't even know what church he belonged to. We don't even know if he was from around here. The only information we have is the name of the church where Mairi was married, and that was in Edinburgh."

We argued. I told her I wasn't going to waste my time going through a lot of worthless church records, but she was welcome to do it if she wanted. She accused me of not wanting to find out the truth about Robbie and Mairi: "You don't want the facts because they might not fit with your romantic fantasy of what happened," she accused, just before marching out of my room.

I sat on my bed and clasped the heart pendant hanging around my neck. I felt bad about arguing with Jenna, but she was wrong. It wasn't a romantic fantasy; I knew Robbie would never have left Anchoret House without Mairi. I just didn't know how to prove it.

A sudden thought popped into my head and I found myself slowly smiling at my cleverness. Maybe I did know how to prove it. I reached under the pillow and pulled out Mrs. Hickman's herb sachet. The small silk bag smelled faintly of licorice. Maybe it was time to find out what had happened at Anchoret House. I was willing to take my chances with dreams and spirits, if it meant finding out the truth. I placed the sachet on the nightstand next to my bed and turned out the light.

I couldn't breathe! I clawed at my throat, my mouth opening and closing like a fish out of water as I choked and wheezed. The blood roared in my ears as my body frantically sought the oxygen it needed to stay alive. Air! I needed air! Panicking, I kicked off the bedsheets and crashed onto the floor, gasping desperately. Then suddenly, miraculously, my lungs inflated. I greedily gulped the air as I lay on the floor in the dark. Breathing, just breathing precious air as tears streamed down my face.

I had been wrong! Totally and completely wrong! Mairi hadn't run away with Robbie. Jenna was right. Mr. McAfee was right. I now knew, without a doubt, that Mairi had drowned.

What a terrifying, horrible way to die, I thought as I inhaled deeply, filling my lungs with the cold, night air. Poor, poor Mairi. I lay awake for a long time, grieving for her.

The next morning, I awoke red-eyed and exhausted. I sat up in bed trying to piece together what had happened. In the light of day, I was no longer certain that my experience last night was related to Mairi or her death. Maybe it had just been a bad nightmare.

I tried to remember the details before I'd woken up gasping for air. I couldn't recall anything. In the past, my interactions with dead people had occurred in my dreams. Not that I had a lot of experience in this area, but dreams seemed to be the way my connection with the supernatural world worked. Since I couldn't remember dreaming about Mairi or anyone else, it seemed unlikely last night was the result of an encounter with the spirit world. But if there wasn't some sort of supernatural explanation, I wasn't sure how to explain what had happened.

Logically, I supposed there was any number of explanations that didn't involve dead people. Asthma? Possibly, though I'd never had an asthma episode before. Allergies? Also possible, though I wasn't allergic to anything that I knew of. Panic attack? Possible, though unlikely, since I didn't remember dreaming about anything that would have made me panic. Of course, waking up unable to breathe had definitely caused me to panic. Maybe I had choked in my sleep, then panicked, and because I panicked, I forgot what I had been dreaming about. Maybe I had that disease where people stop breathing at night. I was so confused. Nothing made any sense.

I had just assumed that after I removed Mrs. Hickman's sachet that I would have a dream that would reveal what had happened to Mairi.

Maybe I had. If Mairi had drowned in the loch, that would explain what I had experienced last night. Perhaps Jenna was right, I was ignoring the truth because I didn't want to believe that Mairi had drowned. But if that was the case, I argued with myself, why didn't I remember the dream? I should have remembered something. At least, that's how it had worked last summer.

I sighed in frustration. This was getting me nowhere. I got out of bed, threw on a pair of jeans and sweater before stumbling down to breakfast. I must have looked as terrible as I felt because the first thing Jenna asked me was if I had another headache.

I nodded. It was easier than explaining what had happened.

"Maybe you should see a doctor," she suggested.

"Or maybe you need glasses," Katie said helpfully. "I heard that people who get a lot of headaches sometimes need glasses."

"I don't need glasses," I told her. I looked at Jenna. "And I don't need to see a doctor."

Jenna raised a skeptical eyebrow in my direction but didn't say anything.

I nibbled on a piece of toast and sipped some tea. I didn't have much of an appetite. My thoughts kept returning to the night before.

Jenna asked me again if I wanted to go to Wick with them. I shook my head and excused myself from the breakfast table before they finished eating.

After the McAfee's and Jenna left, I wandered over to the workshop. Fraser was inside, using a table saw to cut a large piece of wood. I paused in the doorway and watched him work. The original stable had been built to accommodate four horse stalls. Mr. McAfee and Fraser had removed two of the partitions separating them to create a large workspace, though the rest of the building retained its original structure.

It took a few minutes before Fraser noticed me. He turned off the saw and looked up.

"Aye?" he asked.

"Uhm, I was just wondering if I could have a look around. I mean, if it won't disturb you."

"And what is it ye'll be looking for, lass?"

"I'm not really sure. I was just curious, that's all. You know, about the buildings and the history of Anchoret House."

Fraser gave me a long look. "Please yerself. Though you'll not find much tae look at in here."

"Thanks," I smiled.

"Hmmpf." Fraser made a disapproving noise in the back of his throat and returned to his task.

I wandered around the stable, poking my nose into the remaining stalls, but Fraser was right. Other than a couple of hooks on the walls where the feed and water buckets once hung, there wasn't really anything to see.

I returned to the work area. "Uhm, excuse me," I

shouted to Fraser over the noise of the saw.

Fraser shut it off. "Aye?" he asked gruffly.

I graced him with my most charming smile. "I'm sorry to interrupt you again, but I was wondering if you knew where the groom might have slept?"

Fraser's eyes beneath his bushy gray eyebrows fixed me with a look of incredulity.

"I was just thinking about the groom that worked here. With the horses. Colonel Morris's servant. I-I thought you might know where he lived," I stammered. "I wasn't sure if the servants lived here, or maybe if they went back to the village when the colonel owned the house. I was thinking that maybe the servants who took care of the horses might have stayed here, and so maybe if they stayed, I thought you might know where they lived. But then maybe they lived in the house, though that doesn't seem to make sense, so I was just wondering if you knew," I blathered nervously.

Fraser watched me the way one might watch an exotic and slightly erratic wild animal. "Hmmpf," he said when I finally stopped jabbering.

I waited and looked at him with what I hoped was a charming smile on my face.

"I dinna, ken," he said finally.

"Oh," I said disappointed. "Well, thanks anyway. I'm sorry I interrupted your work."

As I turned to leave, Fraser cleared his throat. "I canna be certain, but there's a wee room behind the harness room," he said gruffly, gesturing with a jerk of his head. "I expect thae stable lads wouldae bidden-a-wee in thon room. Ye may want tae ha'e a look," he finished abruptly, powering up the saw and turning back to his work before I could thank him.

I walked over to the harness room, which was almost identical to the one we had at the stable at Brynmoor. The one we had before the fire, I corrected myself. It was long and narrow with rough plank walls. The walls were lined with pegs, hooks, and wooden saddle racks. During Colonel Morris's time carriage harnesses, bridles, and saddles would have been stored here. Now, it housed Mr. McAfee's tools.

I walked through the harness room and pushed open the door at the far end. It opened onto a cramped, windowless room, though I'm not sure that "room" was the appropriate term for it. About the size of a closet. The walls were made from rough rocks piled one on top of the other. The floor was dirt. At one time, it probably had a thatch roof, though someone, Mr. McAfee most likely, had recently installed a sheet of corrugated metal over the rafters. It had more in common with the stone ruins I'd found on the moor than a bedroom.

I stepped inside and ran my hands over the rough stone walls. Without insulation or a stove for heat, it would have been horribly cold in the winter. I couldn't imagine Robbie living in this terrible place. Sleeping with the animals would have been better than this. If I had had the choice between sleeping here or with the horses, I know what I would have chosen.

I touched the pendant hanging around my neck, my lips curving into a slow smile. *Why not?* I thought. If I would have slept in the stable instead of in this cold wretched room, I bet Robbie had made the same decision. After all, why would he choose to sleep here when he could sleep somewhere much warmer and more comfortable?

The stable hayloft had been built using the posts of the horse stalls as supports. It formed a partial second floor inside the stable building. Wood nailed onto one of the posts formed a crude ladder to the entrance. Testing each rung carefully, I climbed up to the loft.

Once I reached the top of the ladder, I inhaled deeply, breathing in the earthy-sweet scent of hay. Despite the fact that the hayloft had not been in use for many years, scattered bits of straw and hay still covered the floor. I touched the pendant again. This was where Robbie had slept. I knew it.

I walked the length of the hayloft and sat down on the rough planks. Drawing my knees up to my chin, I rested my head on my arms and closed my eyes, envisioning the loft filled with bales of hay. Robbie had walked this very same floor. He had touched these walls. At night, he had curled up on the hay and listened to the snorts and sighs of the sleeping horses below. The hay would have made a soft bed and helped keep him warm at night. Yes, this was where he had slept.

With a sigh, I leaned my back against the wall. As I did so, I caught sight of something. Its red color obvious against the worn wood planking. Curious, I leaned over to take a look at it.

My heart skipped a beat when I saw what it was. I recognized it immediately. It was a different shape, square instead of oblong, but it was a perfect match to the jewelry case that held the pearl necklace.

My heart racing with excitement, I picked it up and opened it. It was empty.

Disappointed, I stared at the empty case, thinking. There was no doubt that it matched the other jewelry case. The one that had been inside Mairi's trunk. The one that held the pearl necklace. It was the same color, and like the box that had held the pearl necklace, the names of Hamilton and Inches were inscribed inside the lid.

This jewelry case belonged to Mairi. That much was obvious. I snapped the lid closed and rubbed my finger over the smooth leather. So, what was it doing in the hayloft? Had Mairi come up here? That was possible, but why would she bring a jewelry case with her?

In his ledger, Colonel Morris noted paying Hamilton and Inches for a pearl necklace and a pearl brooch. I turned the case over in my hand. It was the right size and shape for it to be the case for the pearl brooch, but that didn't help me answer the question about how it ended up in the hayloft. And, I thought, it also didn't answer the question about where the brooch was.

I climbed down the ladder, relieved to find Fraser gone and the stable empty. I decided to walk back to Anchoret House. I would show the jewelry case to Mr. McAfee when he returned from Wick. I wasn't hopeful, but maybe he knew what happened to the pearl brooch.

I walked through the wide double doors of the stable and started back toward the house. I hadn't taken more than a few steps when I saw Simon. I stopped, unable to move, my heart in my throat.

He stood with his back to me, broad-shouldered, legs slightly apart, the afternoon sun tinting his copper hair gold. My traitorous heart skipped and bumped in my chest at the sight of him. For a brief moment, I forgot everything except how much I loved him. A quiet, strangled sob escaped from the back of my throat.

Surprised, he turned to look at me.

Blinking back my tears, I tossed my head defiantly. "What are you doing here?" I asked brusquely.

"I came to see you."

"You came to see me? Why? "I asked suspiciously.

"I was worried about you."

"Well," I said coldly, "as you can see, I'm fine." I turned abruptly and began walking toward the house.

He quickly caught up with me and stepped in front of me, forcing me to stop. "Lily, please. I want to talk to you."

I felt a flash of anger. It settled in my stomach like a smoldering hot coal. "Well, I don't want to talk to you," I said acidly.

He didn't move. "Lily," he said. "Something's not right. I can see that just by looking at you. You've lost weight. You've dark circles under your eyes. You're having headaches. You need to leave here."

"What? Now you're treating human patients, too?" I said sarcastically, glaring at him.

Simon held my gaze. "I'm worried about you."

"Oh, yes!" I told him, my voice rising. "The great and all-knowing Simon Fitzgibbon says something's not right. So, it must be so! Let me rush inside, pack my things and leave, right now!"

"Lily, please listen …" he began.

"No! You listen! There is nothing wrong with me except for the fact that I was once stupid enough to think I loved you! Now, please leave me alone!" Much to my utter humiliation, my eyes filled with tears. Shaking with emotion, I tried to push my way past him, but he grabbed my arm.

We stood close together, too close. I knew I should have pushed him away, but I couldn't make myself do it. I leaned into him and breathed in the musky citrus scent of his aftershave. God, how I'd missed him. At that moment, I would have given anything to have him wrap me in his arms, pull me close, and tell me that he still loved me.

"Lily," he said, his voice hoarse.

I looked up at him, hope and love blazing in my eyes.

He gazed down at me, a pained expression on his face, then abruptly released me. He took a step back. "You should go back to Brynmoor," he said gruffly.

The words were like a physical blow. I turned and fled, hot tears streaming down my cheeks.

I ran straight up the stairs to the safety and security of my room. Wiping the tears from my eyes, I swallowed two more of Jenna's pills and lay down on my bed, hoping that the pills would stop the hammering inside my head, though I knew they would do nothing to fix the pain in my heart.

I didn't go down to dinner that night. I told Jenna that I wasn't feeling well. It was cowardly, but I didn't care. I couldn't face Simon again.

Jenna brought a tray to my room after dinner. "I

brought you some lasagna. I thought you might be hungry."

I was sitting in my bed, Colonel Morris's 1904 ledger resting on my lap, the empty jewelry case lying on the table next to the photograph of Robbie.

The rich scent of garlic, tomato, and cheese made my stomach grumble and my mouth water. "Thanks," I said as I closed the ledger and placed it on the bedside table.

Jenna carried the tray over to me. "Are you feeling better?" she asked, handing me the tray.

"Yeah. I'm fine."

I moved over and made room for her on the bed. She climbed up next to me and watched me as I hungrily shoveled lasagna into my mouth.

"You even brought garlic bread," I said, happily sopping up sauce and cheese with it.

She watched me eat for a moment before saying anything. "You are feeling better."

I nodded—my mouth too full to answer.

"I'm glad. I've been worried about you."

"Why is everyone suddenly worried about me?" I rolled my eyes as I swallowed the last bite of lasagna.

"You haven't been yourself lately and you keep having these headaches."

"Lots of people have headaches," I said.

"Not you. Not like this."

"Look, Jenna, I'm fine. Really."

Jenna shook her head. "No. I don't think you are," she said. "I think there's something about this place that is making you sick."

"What are you talking about?"

"I don't know exactly, but you're not acting right. You've become obsessed with him." She gestured to the photograph of Robbie.

"I am not!" I said defensively. "Just because I want to find out who he was, doesn't mean I'm obsessing."

"Lily, I think maybe it would be good for you to go

back to Brynmoor," she suggested hesitantly.

I looked at her, struck by the sudden memory of the phone call she'd made in Wick. "You called him," I said. "You called Simon and asked him to come here."

The guilty expression on her face said it all.

"I can't believe it," I snapped. "You called Simon."

She lifted her chin defiantly, a gesture I knew well. "Who else was I supposed to call? You keep getting these headaches and you spend all your time wandering around the moor by yourself. Staying away for hours."

"I'm fine."

"No, you're not."

"Yes, I am."

"No. You are not fine. This is not like last summer. This is different. Something is not right. You've been acting strange. Sometimes it's like you're a different person. Then when you had the migraine and I ... I thought you were dead when I saw you lying on the floor." She looked at me with her eyes brimming with tears, her voice hurt and angry. "I didn't know what to do. I didn't want to worry your mum, not with the baby and all. So, I called Simon and I told him everything that's been going on and he said he would come out and see to things." Her chin bumped up another notch. "I would do it again, too," she said belligerently.

She stared at me, head high, eyes flashing, daring me to argue with her, but how could I? She had been worried. I would have been, too, if she'd been the one with the headaches.

"Okay," I said.

Her eyes widened in surprise at my sudden capitulation. "Okay? You'll go back to Brynmoor."

"No," I said. "I'm not going back to Brynmoor right now, but I understand why you did what you did. I probably would have done the same thing if I were you. I wouldn't have called Simon, but I would have called somebody," I said with a little smile. "Let's not argue, okay."

She gave me a half-smile in return. "I didn't know who else to call," she said softly.

I hugged her. "I know."

I folded my napkin and laid it on top of the tray. I picked up the jewelry case and handed it to her. "So, look what I found today while I was wandering around."

"It's a jewelry case just like the other one."

"Open it."

She opened the box then looked at me with a disappointed expression on her face. "It's empty," she said.

"Yes," I said, still grinning. "But it matches the case for the pearl necklace. See." I pointed to the Hamilton and Inches logo stamped inside the lid. "I reread the entry in Colonel Morris's ledger to make sure, and he bought a necklace and brooch. This has to the box for the brooch." Jenna snapped the lid closed. "You might be right. Where did you find it?"

"In the hayloft."

She wrinkled her forehead, puzzled. "Why would Mairi's jewelry case be in the hayloft?"

"Because she gave it to Robbie."

Jenna's eyebrows drew together. "Why would she do that?"

"He needed money and she gave it to him so that he could sell it," I said confidently.

"How do you know?"

"I just do."

"Did you dream it?"

"No. I haven't been having those kinds of dreams while I've been here."

"If you aren't having your dreams, then how do you know that's what happened?"

"I just do," I insisted, stubbornly. "I can feel things. I don't know. Maybe Mairi is somehow sharing her feelings with me. Kind of like what happened in the library but not as intense."

Jenna looked thoughtful. "Do you think that is why you are getting these headaches?"

"No."

Jenna didn't look convinced.

"Look," I argued, "I don't know exactly how I know, but I do know that Mairi gave the brooch to Robbie. Colonel Morris would never even have noticed it was gone."

Jenna turned the brooch case over in her hand. "You really found this in the hayloft? In the stable?"

I nodded. "Where Robbie Cameron worked and lived."

"I don't know," Jenna said, staring at the small red box thoughtfully. "Just because you found it in the hayloft doesn't mean that she gave it to Robbie or even that Robbie had anything to do with it."

"Of course it does. How else could it have gotten in the hayloft?"

"Mairi might have dropped it."

"In the hayloft? No way! She'd have no reason to go up there." I paused. "Unless she was meeting Robbie, but that only makes it more likely that she gave it to him. Don't you see? They were planning to run away together and they needed money, so she gave it to him to sell. It's the only thing that makes sense," I said, full of enthusiasm "That has to be what happened!"

"You don't know?"

"Not exactly. But it has to be how it happened."

"So, you don't really know for certain that she gave it to him?"

"Yes, I do."

"What if she didn't give it to him?" Jenna countered.

"She did," I insisted.

"But what if she didn't? What if he stole it? That makes better sense. It would explain why he wasn't working here anymore and why you found the empty jewelry case in the hayloft. Maybe Colonel Morris found out that he stole the brooch and fired him. Or maybe he stole it and ran away."

"No! That's not what happened!" I said indignantly. "You're wrong!"

"How do you know?"

"Because she gave it to him," I said, irritated by her stubborn refusal to see the truth.

"But, he could just as easily have stolen it."

I angrily snatched the jewelry box out of her hands. "Why are you against him? He's not a thief!"

"You don't know that," she argued.

"Yes, I do!" I was practically shouting. "I gave it to him!"

Jenna looked at me wide-eyed with surprise at my outburst. She slid off the bed and picked up the tray. "I'll just take this downstairs for you," she said carefully.

I didn't bother to respond.

I waited until she had closed the door behind her before dropping the jewelry case into my lap. She was wrong!

My head had begun to ache again and my hand instinctively sought Robbie's pendant as I leaned back and closed my eyes. I clutched it tightly. Jenna was wrong!

CHAPTER 10

30 June 1903

Dear Mother,

There was a terrible accident and I lost the baby. I was riding out on the moor when Biscuit lost her footing climbing the brae and I tumbled off her back. The colonel is most angry; he has sent my poor dear Biscuit away. Oh, Mother, I am suffering so unbearably. I spend my days weeping over my lost little baby. Please, may I come home to visit? I miss you and Father terribly and I want to see Blaire and hug little Isobel. I have asked the colonel to provide a carriage for me, but he is not willing to do so at this time. He says he is far too busy and does not wish me to travel alone in my delicate condition. If you would come to fetch me, I am sure he would allow me to travel to Edinburgh. I will eagerly await your next letter. Please write a reply as quickly as you can.

Your daughter,
Mairi

***

I woke up the next morning, Jenna's betrayal pricking at me like a piece of broken glass. I wasn't ready to face her or anyone else at Anchoret House, so I skipped breakfast and snuck out the front door while everyone was still sleeping.

The morning was sullen and dreary. A pale sun shone in the gray sky giving off a weak, watery light that offered little warmth. Cold and bleak, in spite of the June date on the calendar, the day suited my mood perfectly. I curled my hands inside the sleeves of my sweater and walked briskly and onto the moor.

It had rained the night before and the ground was saturated with water. I squelched in and out of gullies as the landscape rose and fell beneath my feet, walking as hard and fast as I was able. By the time I reached the broch, I was beginning to perspire and no longer felt the cold. I stepped inside the stones, breathing hard from my sprint across the moor. Like Mairi, this place had become my refuge.

As I had done many times before, I sat resting my back against the lichen-covered stones. A feeling of anticipation fluttered beneath my breastbone as I waited. I closed my eyes, enjoying the quiet solitude, and waited. Although, if someone had asked me, I couldn't have told them what exactly I was waiting for.

The ground outside was so spongy and soft from the rain the night before that I didn't hear the footsteps.

"Hullo?" A masculine voice called from the other side of the stones.

I felt a jolt of pure joy shoot through me. Leaping to my feet, I called out, "Here I am!"

He stepped through the stones and I launched myself into his arms, happiness exploding inside of me. He had come for me!

Unprepared for my assault, Ben wrapped his arms around me to keep us both from falling over as I kissed him repeatedly.

"Lily!" The name cracked sharp and angry like a rifle shot.

Startled, Ben and I jumped apart. Simon stood staring at the two of us, his expression grim. "What the hell are you doing?"

"Simon, it's not what you think," Ben said.

The muscle in Simon's jaw jumped. His gaze shifted from Ben to me. "I need to talk to Lily, he said quietly, though his voice was edged with steel. "Alone."

I clutched Ben's arm tightly. "Don't go," I pleaded. "Don't leave me!"

With an apologetic look, Ben gently extricated his arm from my grasp and turned away from me. "You'll be all right," he said kindly.

Simon moved aside to let him pass, his eyes never leaving my face.

I watched Ben leave and suddenly the world tilted beneath my feet. "Robbie! Don't leave me!" I cried as I fell to my knees and doubled over, my body racked with sobs.

"I hate you! I hate you! You've sent him away!" I yelled. "Robbie! Robbie!" I repeated his name over and over as I wept.

Simon let me cry. He said nothing. Nor did he try to touch me or comfort me in any way. He stood silently and waited until all the tears were gone.

"Lily?" He said gently. "Who am I?"

"What?" I looked up at him, my face tear-stained and blotchy.

"Who am I?"

"Simon, what is wrong with you?"

"Good. You recognize me."

I shook my head to clear it. "What are you talking about? Of course, I recognize you."

He tilted his head to one side and regarded me carefully. "You called Ben, Robbie."

"I ..." I paused. "I guess I was ... I mean I was

thinking about …" I struggled to my feet. I didn't take Simon's proffered hand. For some reason, I didn't understand; I didn't want to touch him. Had I called Ben by Robbie's name? Yes, I had. Why? What was going on with me? No, not me, Mairi. Mairi and Robbie. Robbie and me. Ben and Robbie. I held my head in my hands. My thoughts were jumbled together and I was having a hard time sorting through them. I felt hollowed out inside, empty. Confused.

"You're leaving this place now," Simon said. "With me. Today."

I didn't argue. I didn't have the strength to. There was nothing left. I didn't even have the strength to lift my head and look at him. Jenna and Simon were right, something was terribly wrong with me. I didn't recognize myself anymore.

We walked back to Anchoret House in silence, Simon holding my arm tightly as if he was afraid that I might suddenly float away.

When we returned to Anchoret House, Simon asked Jenna to help me pack. I meekly followed Jenna to my room and stood silently watching as she stuffed my clothes and things in my bag.

"Lily, this is for the best. You'll see. Once you're away from here, things will get better."

I didn't bother to respond. What could I say?

Jenna quickly finished packing my things and I followed her downstairs. Simon was waiting with Ben next to the car. Jenna handed my bag to Simon. He tossed it in the trunk and opened the door for me to get in.

Mr. McAfee and Katie watched silently as I slid into the passenger seat. I couldn't help but notice that Mr. McAfee looked relieved. Katie, on the other hand, looked stricken.

"Hope you feel better, lass," Mr. McAfee said.

I didn't respond.

Simon nodded to Ben, then slid into the seat next to me. I stared numbly out the window as he reached over and fastened my seatbelt.

I leaned back against the seat and closed my eyes as we drove away from Anchoret House.

CHAPTER 11

13 July 1903

Dear Mother,

I received your letter of the 29th. Your letter was so full of maternal advice that I can hardly think what to write in response. As you say, I am a wife now and must respect my husband's wishes. I had written to you hoping to find solace in the bosom of my family, but I see that you, as you have always done, elevate proper etiquette and public opinion over sentimental attachments. Do not trouble yourself on my account. I will manage as best as I am able. My love to Father.

Mairi

***

"Are you saying that you think that I was possessed?" I asked, my voice edging toward hysteria.

"Oh, dear." Mrs. Hickman shook her head, pursing her lips in disapproval. "That is such a dramatic word, isn't it?

It has such terrible connotations: demons, spinning heads, levitating. Perhaps it would be better to say that you are overly perceptive to the spirit realm." Her expression brightened. "Yes. You are a very perceptive young woman and I think perhaps that was causing the problem at Anchoret House. You are open to suggestions from the dead, and if you are not on your guard, they may be able to convince you to do or say things you normally wouldn't do."

Simon had driven me to Ben's house in Edinburgh, though I have no real memory of the trip. I must have looked pretty bad because the moment we showed up, Mrs. Hickman sent me to bed with one of her herbal remedies. I slept for twelve hours. Apparently, while I slept, Simon and Ben explained the situation to Ben's mom, which was why I was currently sitting in Mrs. Hickman's kitchen once again having a "wee chat" with her.

"But you think Mairi was inside my head? I mean, really inside my head?" I asked. Just the thought of it made the hairs on the back of my arms and neck rise. As soon as I said it, I realized that it was true. Mairi had been inside my head, hijacking my thoughts and feelings. It was beyond creepy, like something out of an alien invasion movie.

Mrs. Hickman nodded. "Well, yes. I suspect that is what happened," she said matter-of-factly.

I looked at her trying hard not to hyperventilate. "You mean, she was inside me? Inside my head. Feeling everything I felt? Doing everything I was doing?"

"Well, I don't know about that, luve. Perhaps. Aye. It is possible, isn't it? A bit of a two-way communication, I expect. The both of you could be sharing the same feelings."

I thought about what had happened at the broch. "So, if she liked someone I would like them, and if she didn't like someone, then I would feel the same way."

Mrs. Hickman nodded. "I expect so."

"Could she make me do things?"

"Hmm. Possibly. Though I suspect only if you wanted to do them." Her eyebrows drew together thoughtfully. "I think she found someone who was sympathetic to her, and, well, I suppose that spirits are much like the rest of us, aren't they?"

I looked at her blankly.

"Sometimes when you find someone who is willing to listen to you, it's a bit tempting, isn't it, to take advantage of their good nature?" She looked at me expectantly.

I leaned forward, pressing my forehead into my hands. I couldn't believe I was having this conversation. It wasn't that I hadn't had some experience with the supernatural world, I just wasn't ready to admit that I had been possessed by a ghost. Though if I had to choose, I guess being possessed was better than having a brain tumor. Maybe.

"Oh, dear. Have you got another headache?"

"No," I said, looking up. "I'm just having a hard time absorbing the fact that a dead person took over my brain. It's so different from what happened last summer. Last summer, I could see and feel things, but I was always in control of myself. Mairi has made me do things, things that I would never normally do. It's like she was controlling me."

"Oh, I wouldn't say that, my dear. I think she might have influenced you a bit, but you are a very strong-willed young woman. I suspect that is why you had so many headaches." She took a sip of tea. "You haven't had headaches since you left Anchoret House, have you?"

I shook my head. "No. I didn't have one when I went to Wick either."

She stood up and smiled. "Well then. That must be it," she said, turning toward the sink. "I think you'll find that you won't be troubled by headaches while you are here."

"Okay, so what am I supposed to do now?" I asked. "Go back to Brynmoor?"

She paused, teacup and saucer in her hand, and gave me a strange look. "Well, it's up to you, luve. If you feel that's best, Ben can drive you tomorrow. Of course, if you do that, Mairi's poor, wee spirit won't know any peace, will she?"

I went outside and sat in Mrs. Hickman's herb garden, thinking about what she had said. I had no idea what I should do.

While I don't claim to be an expert on paranormal existence, my own experiences have convinced me that the dead stay with us when they have something they need to do before they can leave: some important work that has been left undone, a wrong that needs to be righted, or a person who needs to be protected or avenged. Mairi's spirit was here because something or someone had tethered her to our world. If I returned to Brynmoor, Mairi's spirit would not find peace. She was suffering, I knew that. I had felt her pain and grief intimately. At Anchoret House, she had been reaching out to me for help in the only way she knew, by jumping inside my skull. The problem was, I wasn't sure what I should or even could do to help her. I shuddered, remembering the night I woke gasping for air in the dark. If I did choose to help her, what might it cost me?

In the end, I guess it came down to whether or not I could feel comfortable walking away from someone who was hurting, when it might be in my power to help them. Mairi was suffering. I didn't know why, but I did know that her unfinished business involved Robbie Cameron. She was searching for him. I decided that I would do my best to help her. The only problem was that I wasn't sure what I could do. How could I find Robbie for her? I had nothing to work with except a very common Scottish name and photograph.

The back door opened and I turned to look. Ben

greeted me with a cheery "hullo."

I hadn't seen him since Balairie, when I hadn't been myself, to put it mildly.

"Hi," I replied, feeling extremely awkward. I mean, what can you say to a guy you practically sexually assaulted? "Uhm, I'm sorry about what happened at the broch," I said, an embarrassed heat creeping up my neck.

Ben yawned. "That's all right," he said, feigning boredom. "I'm used to it. It happens to me all the time. I'm out walking, minding me own business, when suddenly a beautiful lassie jumps into my arms and plasters me with kisses."

My face flamed beet red. "Uhm, I-I wasn't really myself," I stammered.

His mouth twitched. "I know. My mum explained to Simon and me."

Relief washed through me.

"Though I have to say, for a dead woman, she kisses pretty well," he added with a theatrical sigh.

I made a little choking sound.

Ben laughed aloud at my horrified expression. "I'm having you on," he said. "Sorry. I couldn't resist. I have to admit I always thought people who were possessed did things like vomit blood."

I blanched.

"Much better the kissing than the vomiting, don't you agree?"

I smiled weakly. "Yes. I do."

"Though, if Mairi takes another fancy to me, you'll need to have a wee chat with her. Simon's made it quite clear that I am to keep my hands, and all other body parts, off you."

My stomach fluttered. "Simon said that?" I asked, trying to keep the hope out of my voice.

"Aye. He was quite cross with me. Offered to break my nose, should I need reminding," Ben said offhandedly, as he plopped down on the bench beside me.

Could it be that Simon was jealous? The thought kindled a warm glow in the pit of my stomach.

"You'll be going back to Brynmoor tomorrow?" Ben asked.

The corners of my mouth curved upward. "No, I don't think I will."

Ben nodded. "My mum said you'd more than likely be staying for a bit."

"She did?"

"Aye. She also said that I'm to help you."

"Thanks. I'd like that."

Ben stood. "Shall we let my mum know you'll be staying on then?"

I nodded.

We walked back to the house in companionable silence.

St. Cuthbert's Church was near Edinburgh Castle. Its domed roof, flanked by two imposing towers of colored stone, peeked out from behind a small forest of trees. Ben and I stood on the sidewalk in front of the church trying to decide what to do.

As soon as I made the decision to stay in Edinburgh, I knew that I had to do what I could to help Mairi while I was here. It was obvious that she wanted me to find Robbie. Unfortunately, it was just as obvious that I didn't have enough information to do that. I talked it over with Mrs. Hickman, who suggested I start with the information I did have: Mairi's wedding date and place.

"You might be able to work your way around to the lad if you start from the other end of the puzzle," she'd advised.

Since I had no other place to start, I decided to follow her advice.

"Where do you think the church office is?" I'd asked Ben.

He shrugged. "In the back I suppose."

"Maybe we should go inside and see if we can find someone to ask."

"Why not? It's as good a place to start as any."

I had called St. Cuthbert's earlier and was told very politely, but firmly, that the church was unable to assist with any historical inquiries. However, I wasn't willing to give up so easily. I talked Ben into driving me to the church in the hope that if I pled my case in person, I might get a different answer.

The door to the church was closed but not locked. Ben pushed it open and we stepped inside, leaving the noise and bustle of the street behind us.

It was a beautiful church, boasting a richly painted vaulted ceiling and ornate stained-glass windows. As I stood inside the church, I thought of Mairi. She had walked down this very aisle on the day of her wedding. Today the church was empty, but when Mairi was here, the wooden pews would have been filled with family and friends, the church decorated with flowers.

"I'm sorry. The church isn't open for visitors just now."

I turned to look.

A woman about my mother's age with short blonde hair smiled warmly at Ben and me. "Our visiting hours are posted in the front of the church," she said. "You are more than welcome to come back then."

"We're not tourists," Ben told her. "We are looking for the church office."

The woman smiled warmly at us. "Well then, perhaps I can be of some help. I'm Reverend Anne Gowans. Reverend Anne, if you like. What can I do for you?"

I hadn't noticed the white collar around her neck until she introduced herself.

"Uhm, we're hoping to speak to someone about the marriage registry," I said.

Reverend Anne looked Ben and me over. "Have you already spoken with our wedding coordinator?" she asked.

I glanced at Ben, puzzled.

He laughed. "We're not interested in getting married," he told Reverend Anne.

"You're not?" she said with a little frown.

"No."

"I guess I'm a bit confused then. What is it you need?" she asked, her gaze shifting between Ben and me.

"We're looking for information on a wedding that took place at St. Cuthbert's in 1902," Ben told her.

"Ah. I see. Unfortunately, I can't help you with that. We don't keep any records here. All of our registry records are stored at the General Register House."

"Oh," I said, my disappointment obvious.

Reverend Anne smiled consolingly at me. "It's not far. Just up the road a bit on Princes Street. I'm sure they'll be able to help you." She turned to Ben. "You're from Edinburgh?"

"Aye."

"Then you'll know the Register House."

He nodded. "It's hard to miss," he said dryly.

Ben was right. The Register House was hard to miss. Large, solid, and imposing, it took up an entire city block. It was so big that it dwarfed the outsized statue of the Duke of Wellington displayed in front of it.

I craned my neck back to look up at the building's domed roof. "Now what?" I asked him, somewhat intimidated.

"We go in and find Mairi's marriage record."

"You make it sound easy," I said doubtfully.

"With my help, we'll be in and out in tic," Ben said with a wink.

"I hope you're right."

It wasn't. Easy that is, but Ben was amazing. Dealing with bureaucracy has never been my strong suit, but Ben patiently filled out forms, asked questions, and eventually searched out a reel of microfilm for marriages registered with the government of Scotland between the months of January through July of 1902.

After receiving a quick lesson on how to use the scanner machine, we inserted the microfilm and began reviewing the files.

They were brutally difficult to read. The microfilm contained scans of the actual parish ledgers. The entries were handwritten, sometimes with faded ink and cursive writing that was almost impossible to decipher. Ben and I huddled together, hunched in front of the viewer for an hour as we searched for Mairi's marriage registration.

"Wait! St. Cuthbert's!" I said as we sped through another section. Ben hit the pause button and reversed.

"There." I pointed.

We quickly scanned the registration entry. "No. Wrong date," I said. "That says July. Go back a little more."

The scanner whirred as Ben fiddled with the knobs.

"There!"

He stopped the machine.

We slowly skimmed through the entries until we found March 24th. We eagerly leaned forward and read the entries.

"There it is!" Ben whispered, pointing to an entry near the bottom of the page.

On the *24th* Day of *March* 19 *02*
Colonel George Morris of the Royal Scots Dragoon Guards, bachelor
46, son of Graham Morris deceased.
Usual Residence: *Balairie, Scotland,*
and
Mairi Bain, spinster 18, daughter of Archibald Bain, architect.
Usual Residence: *25 Thistlewhite Road, Edinburgh*
Married After Banns according to the forms of
Parish Church of St. Cuthbert's, Church of Scotland

As I read the words, I could feel my excitement

growing. Mairi's marriage registration contained information I hadn't expected to be there: her father's name, his profession and her address in Edinburgh.

"We found it!" I whispered. "I can't believe it!" I hugged him. "We did it! We found it!"

"So, you'll be wanting to print a copy then?" he asked with a grin.

The first thing Ben and I did after we left the Register House was look for 24 Thistlewhite Road on Google maps.

When the map came up on his cellphone screen, Ben gave a low whistle. "Mairi Bain wasn't poor that's for certain."

"Why do you say that?" I asked, peeking at his phone.

"She lived in Murrayfield. Very Pricey neighborhood," he explained. "Here. Take a look." He changed to the Google earth image and showed me a row of Victorian houses, then zoomed in on number 24. It was a three-story house of red brick with bay windows, dormer windows in the attic, and a charming garden gate.

"Do you think it's the same house?" I asked.

"I don't know, but there's an easy enough way to find out," Ben said with a gleam in his eye.

"How?"

"We ask."

"You mean, drive over to the house and knock on the door?"

"Aye." He jangled his car keys under my nose.

I hesitated. "I'm sure the house was sold a long time ago. I mean, what are the chances that someone related to Mairi Bain still lives there?"

"Probably not much," Ben agreed. "But then, we won't know unless we go and ask."

I hesitated. "I don't know. What would we say?"

"We tell them we're looking for someone who used to

live in the house. Either they know the Bain family or they don't." He held up the copy of the marriage registration. "We can show them this if you like."

My heartbeat quickened at the thought of finding someone who could tell us about Mairi. I grinned at Ben. "Okay. Let's do it!"

We drove to Thistlewhite Road and found a place to park at the end of the street. We walked along the sidewalk, passing several other large homes as we searched for number 24.

"It looks like some of these houses have been converted into flats," Ben said, gesturing toward the number 18.

An intercom panel with four buttons was fixed to the front door. I assumed that meant that four apartments had been carved out of what had once been a large single-family dwelling.

My heart fell. "Oh. Do you think they did the same thing to Mairi's house?"

Ben shrugged. "We'll know soon enough."

We quickened our pace.

It turned out that 24 Thistlewhite Road had been converted into apartments. I was disappointed. There were four names listed by the front door, none of which was Bain.

"Well, it was a good try," I said to Ben and turned to walk back to the car.

"Where are you going?"

"Back to the car," I said. "The house has been converted to flats. The family doesn't live here anymore."

"You're probably right, but we've come all this way. We might as well ring them and ask."

"Why? The chances that anyone knows the Bain family are a million to one," I said.

Ben grinned. "A million to one is still a chance. Right? I say we ring them and ask. What have we got to lose?"

I shrugged. "You're right. Why not?"

I pushed the bell for the first flat. The name on the card said Dunbar. We waited for a few moments.

"It doesn't look like anyone is home," I said.

Ben pointed to the second name. "Onward and Upward."

I pushed the second button. After a few moments a harried woman's voice answered; we could hear a young child in the background. "Yes?"

On the drive to Thistlewhite Road, Ben and I had decided that I would do the talking, my American accent giving credibility to our story about looking for a distant relative.

Suddenly nervous, I stuttered. "H-h-hello."

"Yes?" she repeated impatiently. The child in the background started crying.

"My name is Lily Deene and I'm looking for the family who used to own this house. The Bain family," I said in a rush of words.

"I don't know anybody by the name of Bain." The intercom clicked off.

I made a face at Ben. "I told you this was a waste of time."

"You've only rung two of the flats." He grinned crookedly at me. "As we say in Scotland: in for a penny, in for a pound."

"Right," I said with a sigh. "Onward and upward." I pushed the button for the third apartment. The name Denison was affixed next to it.

"Yes?" It was an older woman's voice this time.

"Uhm," I took a quick look at the name on the door. "Mrs. Dennison? My name is Lily Deene and I'm looking for the family who used to own this house. The Bain family."

There was a moment of silence, as if she was thinking. "Hmm. What did you say your name was, luve?"

"Lily Deene."

"American are you?"

"Yes, ma'am," I answered, hoping I sounded like a trustworthy American.

"Well, you better come up then," she said and buzzed us in.

I looked questioningly at Ben, who shrugged.

"Onward and upward," he said, gesturing toward the front door.

We climbed the stairs to Mrs. Dennison's flat. She was waiting for us at the door. She was a large woman, somewhere in her mid-fifties. Her hair was dyed a bright red color that did not exist in the natural world. She wore a purple caftan.

"Oh, I didn't realize there were two of you," she said, looking us over doubtfully.

"Ben Hickman. I'm not American. I'm helping Lily with her search. My mum asked me to drive her around Edinburgh and give her a bit of a hand as she's visiting us from America," Ben explained helpfully with a disarming smile. At the mention of his mum, Mrs. Dennison seemed to relax her guard.

"We've just come from the Register House," Ben continued. "That's how we found the address. It was on the marriage registration." He held up our copy of Mairi's marriage registration for her to see. "Lily was hoping that someone in one of the flats might have information on the family that used to own this house."

"Oh, I see. Well, you best come in then." Mrs. Dennison toddled over to an upholstered armchair and eased into it, resting a bandaged right foot on its matching ottoman.

"Gout," she said by way of explanation. "I'd offer you some tea, but it's quite difficult for me to move about with my foot." She sighed. "There's nothing quite as pleasant as a nice cup of tea and biscuits when you are having a wee chat. Is there?" She looked at Ben brightly. "Perhaps you could manage the tea and biscuits for us?" she asked.

"I'd be delighted," he said with a small bow.

Mrs. Dennison called out directions to Ben as she watched him fill the kettle and arrange the tea tray from her armchair. I perched impatiently on the sofa. I had offered to help, but Mrs. Dennison, "Joan" as she insisted that I call her, wouldn't hear of it. "You're American, luve," she said by way of explanation.

Ben brought the tea tray out and set it on the coffee table before sitting next to me. Joan poured out for the three of us. "Do try the biscuits—they're really quite lovely," she suggested, taking two for herself.

She settled back into her armchair and smiled at us.

"May I?" she asked, holding out her free hand.

"We found the marriage registration for Mairi Bain at the Register House. Her father was Archibald Bain and her residence was listed as this house." I handed her the copy of the registration and she studied it.

"The two of you are quite the resourceful pair. And now you want to know about the family who owned this house?"

"Yes."

"Well, 1902. That was quite a long time ago."

"I know. I was just hoping that someone might know what happened to the family."

Joan sipped her tea thoughtfully. "I don't know if it will be of any help, but there was an older woman who came to the house about five years ago. She said that the house had once been her family home. She had to sell it once the upkeep was too much for her. Poor dear."

Joan returned the marriage certificate to me and took another slow sip of her tea as I tried to control my impatience. I could tell that Ben was making a similar effort.

"Would either of you care for another biscuit?" she asked as she peered at us over the edge of her teacup.

"No, thank you," we chorused.

"Well then. I'll just have one more, shall I?"

I inhaled sharply and opened my mouth, but before I

could say anything, Ben nudged me in the ribs with his elbow. I closed my mouth. He was right, it would be no use to try and hurry Joan. She was going to enjoy her tea and "wee chat." If we wanted information, we were going to have to grin and bear it.

"I do so enjoy these biscuits. Perhaps you could bring us a few more?" she asked, looking expectantly at Ben.

"With pleasure," Ben stood casting a meaningful look in my direction before returning to the kitchen to refill the plate with cookies.

"It is so tiresome for me to try and hobble about with my poor foot."

"*Is it* very painful?" I asked.

"Oh, my dear, you have no idea."

Ben returned with the biscuit plate replenished.

"Lovely. Such a dear," Joan said, sighing happily as she chose another biscuit.

"So, where were we? Yes. That's right. Now, if I remember correctly, I invited the poor old dear in to have a look around. The stairs were a bit much for her, as I recall, but she did manage. She said that this room had been the nursery and where the kitchen is now, the nanny's room. I think it put her off a bit to see the changes to the house."

My heart lurched with excitement. "Do you remember her name?" I asked eagerly.

Joan took a bite of her cookie. "Let me see. It was some five or so years back. Hmm. I don't think it was Bain. It was an old-fashioned name. Let me think. Agnes. Yes, I do believe her name was Agnes. Agnes Something. What was it? Agnes ... Agnes Something. I can't quite remember her last name. Never mind. It will come to me."

"Do you have an address or phone number for her?" I asked.

Joan shook her head. "I'm sorry, luve. I don't. Though I do remember she did say she had moved into one of those retirement villages. She said that she missed having young people around. Too many old people in those retirement villages." She shook her head. "I don't remember the name of it either." She sipped her tea. "Although I believe it did have something to do with kings."

As we finished our tea, Joan asked questions about me and why I was looking for the Bain family. I managed to keep things vague and mostly truthful.

"Agnes Sinclair," Joan said suddenly, nodding with satisfaction. "I knew it would come to me. Her name was Agnes Sinclair."

Ben and I looked at each other. We had a name!

Before we left Joan's flat, Ben and I washed up the tea things and left them drying on the rack. I asked Joan if the person in number four might know anything else about the building or the Bain family.

"I wouldn't think so, luve. He's a foreigner," she replied in a sotto voice.

We gave Joan our cell phone numbers, asking her to call us if she remembered anything else, and made out way back to the car.

"Back to the house then?" Ben asked.

I nodded. I was beginning to feel a bit discouraged. Sure, we'd found some information, but a marriage certificate, a woman's name, and a retirement village related to kings weren't much things to go on. For all we knew, Agnes Sinclair might not live in Edinburgh anymore. In fact, she might not even be alive. Five years was a long time.

While Ben drove, I started searching on my phone for retirement villages in Edinburgh. Surprisingly there weren't very many. None of them had the word king in their names. I told Ben. "Do you think she lived somewhere besides Edinburgh?" I asked.

Ben shrugged. "I wouldn't think so. If this was her home, why would she leave?"

"Maybe she had family somewhere else and she went to

live with them."

Ben nodded. "That's possible, I guess." We stopped at a red light and he turned to look at me. "So, what have you found so far?"

"What? You mean retirement villages?"

"Aye."

I began reading the list of names, "Corbenach, Tigh a'Chomainn, Beannacher ..."

Ben started laughing so hard at my pronunciation of the Scottish names that he missed the green light. The car behind us beeped impatiently.

He pressed on the accelerator and moved forward. "Sorry," he apologized. "I've just never heard Tigh a'Chomain pronounced quite that way before."

"If you don't like the way I pronounce them, we can always wait until you can read them."

"I didn't say I didn't like it." He grinned. "Go on. I promise I won't laugh."

"It doesn't matter anyway. There aren't any that have the word king in the name," I warned before continuing. "New Simeon, Loch Arthur ..."

"Wait! What was the last one?"

"Loch Arthur."

That's it!" Ben said excitedly.

"It is?"

He gave me a cocky grin. "A retirement village that has something to do with kings."

Suddenly came to me: *King Arthur and the Knights of the Round Table*. "Loch Arthur," I said excitedly. "Ben Hickman, you are positively brilliant!"

ANNIE GRACE ROBERTS

CHAPTER 12

21 September 1903

My Dear Friend Elizabeth,

Of news there is only one despicable particular that I can think of: Nancy our unworthy sootdrop of a servant is to be married to an aged Butcher, a drunken man with a grown-up family. It is surmised that she will increase it ere long by a kind of Into-the-Bargain. She will find her way no easier with that lout I dare say and with a child to boot! As to the children, I am sad to hear that Mairi lost the child, though I must admit that I am not surprised to learn that her impetuous behavior was the cause of the tragedy. You are correct to complain that it is long past time that she gave up her foolish pursuits and begin to behave as the grown woman she has become. As you say, she must learn to face the consequences of her actions or she will never temper her behavior. As for her lack of written correspondence, I suppose she is sulking. She will come to her senses eventually and see that you were correct to tell her to seek comfort in her marriage. I know that your long-suffering love of her has caused you no end of trouble. Perhaps she will learn from this most unfortunate episode.

In friendship and affection,

Agnes McDermott

***

Ben and I decided that it was too late to visit the Loch Arthur Retirement Village, so we returned home to his house, making plans to search out Agnes Sinclair first thing in the morning.

When I woke up the next day, I was practically vibrating with nervous excitement. Of course, I knew that I needed to temper my expectations. After all, Agnes Sinclair might not be any relation to the Bain family. She might not even live at Loch Arthur. I tried to keep my enthusiasm in check, but it was hard. Everything about it felt so right.

We ate a hurried breakfast, both of us grinning goofily at each other. Ben was as caught up in the exhilaration of the chase as I was. We were out of the house and in the car by nine a.m., both of us buzzing with excitement.

Loch Arthur Retirement Village turned out to be a series of tiny white cottages clustered around a three-story apartment building. We parked in the gravel lot and walked up to the front door of the main building. A tasteful brass plaque with the words Loch Arthur engraved on it directed us to ring the bell for service. A paper note was tacked below the intercom with instructions on how to use it. We read the instructions and I pushed the button.

After a few seconds a voice over the intercom answered. "Loch Arthur Retirement Village. How may we help you?"

Ben did the talking. We didn't want my American accent to complicate things.

"Good morning. We're here to visit Agnes Sinclair," he said, pressing the button as he spoke.

"Visiting hours begin at noon." The voice said crisply. "You'll need to come back then."

"Ask her if Agnes Sinclair lives here," I whispered to

Ben.

"Can you tell me if we've got the right address?" Ben asked into the intercom.

"This is Loch Arthur Retirement Village."

"Aye. We're just trying to confirm that Agnes Sinclair is in residence," Ben said.

The voice on the intercom turned suspicious. "Who did you say you were?"

"Friends of the Bain-Sinclair family," Ben chirped cheerfully into the microphone. "Have we got the right address?

"Yes," was the curt reply. "Come back at noon."

"Right, cheers," Ben said, though the voice had already clicked off by then.

"They're not exactly warm and welcoming at Loch Arthur, are they?" Ben said wryly.

"Well, we are a little early." I checked my phone: 10:12 a.m. "We've got two hours to wait. What should we do?"

"Find a coffee shop?"

"Sounds good to me."

Ben drove around until we found a shopping mall not too far from Loch Arthur. Lacking anything better to do with the two hours we had to wait, I decided to do a little shopping. I ended up buying a pair of pretty gardening gloves for Ben's mom and a T-shirt for Nick. I wanted to thank the Hickmans for their hospitality. Ben complained when I bought Nick the shirt, telling me that I shouldn't waste my money. I explained that since Nick had given up his room for me twice that he should get something for his trouble.

"What about me, then?" Ben joked. "I'm the one who has to share my bedroom with him."

"You get the pleasure of my company," I teased. "Which is much better than a T-shirt."

Ben snorted.

"Okay, how about a hug and coffee," I said, pointing to the coffee shop.

"Well, I guess if that's what you're offering, it'll have to do."

I bought our drinks and brought them back to the table. "Thanks for driving me around," I said, handing him his iced Frappuccino.

"No problem. I'm having a grand time. It's much better than helping my dad." He raised his cup. "Cheers," he said.

I touched my cup to his and slipped into the seat across from him.

We both drank.

"So, do you think Agnes will know anything about Mairi Bain?" I asked.

Ben shrugged. "We'll find out soon enough."

I toyed absentmindedly with the heart pendant around my neck as I thought about what I would ask Agnes, assuming she was related to the Bain family.

"Simon give that to you?" Ben asked, eyeing my pendant.

"Give what to me? Oh, this?" I asked, holding the necklace so he could see it better.

"Aye. Horseshoe nails, right?" Ben said. "I noticed it the other day."

"Yes," I said. "I mean, yes, they are horseshoe nails, but, no, Simon did not give it to me. I found it at Anchoret House," I confessed with a guilty smile. "I know I should have given it to Mr. McAfee, and I will, but at the time it seemed like it was a present for me. That I was meant to wear it. I guess that was part of Mairi's spirit …" I paused, searching for the right word. "Uhm, influencing me."

Ben gave me a knowing look. "Like what happened at the Broch, you mean."

The image of me throwing myself at poor Ben caused me to flush with embarrassment. "Yeah, like that." I looked down quickly and gave my full attention to drinking my iced mocha.

I liked Ben. He was easy to be around. He made me

laugh, and he was smart and nice. If he hadn't been Simon's cousin, who knows how things might have worked out?

Neither of us said anything for a few moments. We sat quietly sipping our drinks, each lost in our own thoughts.

Finally, Ben broke the silence. "So, what's going on between you and Simon?" he asked, his voice deliberately casual.

I looked up. "What do you mean?" I asked, stalling for time.

"It's pretty obvious there's something between you two. I just can't figure out what it is."

I gave him a rueful smile. "Me neither."

Ben nodded. "I've known Simon all my life. He's usually an easy-going bloke. Not much puts him out of temper. Then you show up and suddenly he's acting narky."

"Narky?" I asked with a lift of my eyebrows.

"Out of sorts. Bad-tempered. That's not like him. I can't remember the last time he threatened to break my nose. Oh, wait. I do remember. The last time he threatened to break my nose I was six."

"He threatened to break your nose when you were six?"

"Well, I can't say I didn't deserve it," he said, his mouth twitching at the corners. "I took Jenna's lolly. Made her cry."

I smiled at the thought of the three cousins as little kids.

"Simon can be quite fierce when he's protecting someone he cares about."

I sighed. "I don't think that's an issue. I mean. I guess he could feel like he needs to protect me, but I'm not sure how much he cares about me. He's made it pretty obvious that he doesn't want to see me."

Ben frowned thoughtfully. "I can see where that would be a bit confusing."

"Yeah," I agreed. "Our relationship is … complicated."

Ben nodded, a serious expression on his face. "Well, when you figure things out, let me know. Getting to know you might be worth a broken nose," he said.

I stared at him, open-mouthed, not sure how to respond.

Ben flushed, cleared his throat, and checked the time. "It's twelve-fifteen," he said, pushing his chair back and standing up. "Shall we go see what Agnes has to tell us?"

After speaking with the anonymous voice over the intercom a second time, we were buzzed into the reception area. A small love seat and armchair in matching blue upholstery sat near a coffee table offering a selection of outdated magazines and colorful brochures touting the benefits of Loch Arthur Retirement Village. Ben and I waited, unsure what to do.

After a few minutes, a side door opened and a woman appeared. She wore long pants, sensible shoes, and a shirt with the Loch Arthur logo tastefully stitched across the front pocket. Her long black hair was tied into a sleek bun.

"Good Afternoon. My name is Alana Singh," she said, introducing herself. "I'm one of the residential assistants at Loch Arthur."

Ben and I introduced ourselves.

"You've come to visit Agnes?" she asked.

We nodded.

"Are you family?"

I looked at Ben. "Not exactly," I said.

Ben launched into our story about how I was visiting from America and researching my family history.

Alana nodded. I was beginning to get the idea that researching family history is something people in Scotland expected from Americans.

She turned her attention to me. "How is it you've found this connection with Agnes?" she asked curiously.

"I only ask because she has so few family left."

I glanced at Ben "Uhm. Well, it's kind of a long story," I said uncomfortably.

Ben turned on the charm again. "Yes, we've no end of work tracing Lily's family roots. We spent most of our day yesterday at the Register House following the trail. The marriage registration led us to an address and a woman at the address gave us Agnes's name. From there we eliminated retirement villages until we found you." He smiled brightly at Alana. "I'm beginning to feel a bit like Sherlock Holmes."

"I imagine it is quite like detective work, isn't it?" Alana said to me.

"Uhm, yes. It is," I agreed.

"Well then, I'll just show you to Agnes's flat. I'm sure she will be thrilled to meet you."

"She has a flat?" Ben asked, looking around. "I thought she would live in a cottage. We saw them when we drove in."

"Some of our residents do live independently in cottages. Others prefer to live in our flats or rooms and have their meals in our dining room. It saves them the trouble of shopping and cooking. A few require a bit more assistance."

"And Agnes? Does she require assistance then?" Ben asked casting a quick glance my way.

"Agnes does have a bit of difficulty walking," Alana said. "Which keeps her from getting about as much as she would like, but that, I think, is to be expected when one reaches the age of ninety-four."

"She's ninety-four years old?" I asked, glancing uncomfortably at Ben. I had visions of meeting a feeble, bedridden old woman.

Alana nodded. "Yes, she may be a bit infirm, but you'll find that she is still as clever as they come. She's really quite a dear old thing. You'll enjoy meeting her."

Alana led us to room 216 and knocked on the door.

"Agnes," she called out. "I've brought you some visitors."

There was a muffled answer from behind the door, and Alana pushed it open.

A tiny old woman with a fluffy cap of white hair sat in an overstuffed armchair, knitting. Her face was wreathed in wrinkles but her dark eyes glittered with intelligence and curiosity.

"Oh my! Visitors." She smiled delightedly at us.

"I'll bring another chair, shall I?" Alana offered. "And perhaps some biscuits?"

"That would be lovely!" Agnes agreed.

Alana disappeared through the door.

There was a brief awkward moment as Agnes stared expectantly at us.

"I'm Ben Hickman and this is Lily Deene," Ben said, introducing us.

"How do you do?" I asked.

She clapped her hand together. "Oh, you're American. How lovely!"

I stood awkwardly while Agnes studied me with frank curiosity.

"Won't you have a seat, my dear," she said after a moment, gesturing toward the second chair. She turned to Ben. "I know it's frightfully old-fashioned of me, but do you mind terribly standing until Alana returns?"

"It would be my pleasure," Ben said with a courtly bow.

Agnes smiled and nodded. "A beautiful American and a charming and handsome young Scot. How mysterious!" Her dark eyes sparkled. "Perhaps you should tell me why you've come to visit."

Ben and I looked at each other.

"I'm helping Lily research her family background," Ben began. "We're hoping you might have some information for her. Mrs. Dennison gave us your name."

"Mrs. Dennison? I don't believe I know a Mrs. Dennison."

"She said you'd come to see her a few years ago. She lives at 24 Thistlewhite Road."

"Oh, yes. I remember now. She was quite lovely. Invited me in for tea."

"Yes," I said. "She mentioned that you used to live there and I was wondering if you might be related to the Bain family."

Agnes tilted her head and fixed her dark eyes on me, reminding me of a little bird. "What is it that you want to know?"

I held out the copy of Mairi's marriage registration. "I'm hoping you might be able to tell us something about Mairi Bain."

Agnes took the photocopy and studied it carefully before handing it back to me. "Why don't you tell me what this is all about then?"

"Well, like Ben said, I'm interested in finding out some family history and—"

"I'm an old woman and I've not much patience for foolishness, my dear," she said kindly but firmly. "You are not related to Mairi Bain. So, why don't you tell me what this is all about?"

Surprised, I glanced at Ben. He returned my look and gave me a little shrug. We'd been busted.

I turned back to Agnes. "Okay, but this is going to sound a little strange," I warned her.

"When you've lived as long as I have, you'd be surprised at how many things no longer seem strange," she said, settling back in her chair to listen.

I told her about visiting Anchoret and the portraits on the wall in the library. I told her about finding Mairi's trunk and the pearl necklace and her mysterious death. I mentioned that Mr. McAfee was going to open a bed-and-breakfast and knew everything about the colonel but nothing about Mairi. Finally, I mentioned that I didn't think it was fair that Mairi's story wasn't part of Anchoret also. I didn't tell her that Mairi's spirit was still roaming about Anchoret and the moors. Even if Agnes had lived for ninety-four years and "very little seemed strange to her," there were just some things better left unsaid.

Agnes listened intently to my story while I was speaking. She didn't ask any questions, just kept her bird-like eyes fixed on me the entire time. I finished just about the same time that Alana returned with the third chair and the cookies.

I looked at Ben. He gave me an approving nod. I have to admit, I sounded pretty convincing, even to myself.

Ben helped Alana bring in the other chair and thanked her. After she left, Agnes nodded to me. "Well, I suppose that's reason enough," she said. "Mairi Bain was my aunt. Or at least she would have been my aunt had she lived to see me born."

Ben and I exchanged glances.

"I think we best put the kettle on, don't you?" she asked. "Then we can have a proper chat."

Ben and I waited an agonizingly long time while Agnes made tea. She moved very slowly, as if it pained her. "I've a touch of arthritis," she explained. Ben and I offered to help, but she insisted on making the tea herself.

She did not begin talking about Mairi until she made sure that we each had a cup of tea and a biscuit.

"There were four in the family. Mairi was the eldest. Next came Alec. He was the only boy. Then Blaire. My mother Isobel was the youngest. She was ten years younger than Mairi, just a wee lass when Mairi wed.

"I never knew Mairi, but I knew of her, the way children do. I knew something terrible had happened to her, though it wasn't until I was much older that I learned that she'd drowned out on the moor. I've a photograph of my mother's family, if you'd like to have a look?"

"Yes," I said eagerly.

Agnes stood up and slowly, painfully made her way over to the small bureau, her cane clicking on the hardwood floor. She pulled a photo album from one of the drawers and hobbled back to us. Opening the album, she turned a few pages until she found the photo she wanted and handed it to Ben and me.

"Mairi is the one on the right, next to my grandmother."

I studied the photo. In the style of that time period, no one in the photograph was smiling. The girls and their mother wore long skirts and blouses with high collars. The father and son both wore dark suits, each one with a flower pinned to his lapel.

"This was taken in 1900. Mairi would have been sixteen. According to family stories, Mairi was a spoiled young girl with a rebellious streak. My mother told me that Mairi used to have terrible rows with her mother. I don't recall much about my grandfather, but my grandmother was a fierce woman with very set ideas on how proper young ladies should behave."

She tilted her head to one side, reminding me even more of a small bright-eyed bird. "Whenever I was feeling my oats, my grandmother would scold me and warn me that I would come to no good like my aunt Mairi. She would shake her finger at me and scold, 'You best mend your ways, lassie, or you'll end up dead and drowned on the moors like your aunt Mairi.' Aye, my grandmother was a force to be reckoned with. She had me so convinced that I was destined to drown that I never did learn to swim." Agnes chuckled. "Of course, back then, swimming wasn't something that proper young ladies were encouraged to do."

I handed the photo back to her.

"Mairi was a beautiful young girl," she said, looking again at the photo. "I believe there was a suggestion of an inappropriate friendship at one point. I always wondered if that was the reason they married her off so young, though perhaps she was just anxious to escape from her parent's house." Agnes shook her head. "It mustn't have been easy for her. To be intelligent, wealthy, and beautiful can be such a terrible burden for a young girl." She looked up at me. "Don't you agree, my dear?"

"I guess."

"Well, I suspect it is difficult for you to understand. You've grown up in a time where young women are encouraged to use their brains and develop careers, but back then it would have been very difficult. During Mairi's time, women were expected to do nothing more than to have children and support their husband's career." She sipped her tea.

"You said she had an inappropriate friendship?" I prompted eagerly.

Agnes smiled. "Aye. It was all rather hushed up, I'm afraid. I'm not sure how I learned of it. Perhaps in my grandmother's collection of letters. Yes. That must be it. I'm certain no one in the family would ever have mentioned it to me."

My heart rate quickened. "Letters?"

"Aye. Back in the day, one wrote and kept letters. I have quite a few from the family. I've kept them for sentimental reasons. I've been meaning to throw them out, but I just can't bring myself to do it. If you like, you're welcome to read through them. I'm almost certain that was where I learned of Mairi's friendship. As I recall, there are several from Mairi, written to her family after she married and moved away from Edinburgh."

"I would love to read them!" I said eagerly.

"You may borrow them if you like. There are far too many for you to read here. Why don't you finish your tea while I find them for you? If you promise to return them, you may take them with you."

"Thank you so much!"

Ben and I couldn't help but grin at each other after Agnes left the room.

When Agnes returned, she handed me a cardboard box tied with string. "Here they are, my dear. Some of the letters are quite fragile, so you'll need to take care."

I hugged the box to my chest. "I will, I promise! Thank you so much!"

Ben and I sat side by side on the sofa in his mother's house, the letters spread out in front of us on the coffee table.

"Why don't we divide and conquer," I suggested, dividing the stack of letters into two piles. "You start with those and I'll look at the ones in this pile, that way we can read them faster.

"Right."

I picked up the first one, realizing that it wasn't going to be easy. The elaborate cursive handwriting and faded ink made it difficult at times to decipher the writing.

The first letter I picked up was from Mairi's mother, Isobel, the date was 10 August 1916. I put it aside without reading it, knowing that there wouldn't be any information about Mairi in it.

I worked my way through six letters before I found one with a date of 1898. I read it but there was no mention of Mairi in it. I skimmed through two more letters before I found something.

"Listen to this!" I exclaimed. "It's from the grandmother's sister Jane."

I read the letter aloud to Ben.

10 July 1901
Dearest Liza,

I was much alarmed by your note of Wednesday last. I do hope that the situation you described with young Mairi has been resolved in a satisfactory way. Young girls can so easily be led astray by misguided sentiments. No doubt both you and Archibald will do your best: You must not be discouraged. Children it is said are the Bank into which we parents put our young industry, to be repaid in old age: Shame on us if we prove a failure. You and Archibald must do your utmost to remove Mairi from this young man's sphere of influence. Find some means to send him off. Once you do so, I am not without hope that Mairi's good sense and breeding will prevail. As you well know, young girls are extremely fickle; they bestow and rescind their affection as quickly as they change hair ribbons. Once the young man in question is removed from Edinburgh, I've no doubt that the situation will right itself without casting a stain on Mairi's reputation. Remember, dear sister, as the saying goes, "There is a dub at every town-end." You must bear steadfastly on in the hope all will turn out for the best and in another year, this unfortunate episode will be far behind you.

I stopped reading.

Ben wiggled his eyebrows suggestively. "Sounds like Mairi fancied a bloke and her mum didn't approve of him."

"Yeah," I agreed. "I think so, too. What does this mean?" I asked, pointing to the line about a dub at every town-end.

"A dub is a puddle. She's saying there's a puddle in every town." He wrinkled his forehead. "I think she's saying that everyone has some sort of trouble. It must be an old saying."

"Oh." I nodded. "Like this one." I said about children being a bank. I guess she means if they don't turn out so great, it's the parent's fault." I shook my head, feeling sympathy for Mairi. "I can't imagine what it would have been like to be raised in a family like that."

Ben shrugged. "It's the way it was back then. Spare the rod, spoil the child," he quoted.

"Rod? You mean like hitting them with a stick."

"Aye, it was common practice at that time."

"That's terrible."

"Oh, I don't know about that. Family picnics must have been grand. Instead of playing a round of croquet, imagine all those parents running about with mallets beating their children."

"Nice," I said laughing as I elbowed him in the ribs.

We continued with our reading. Ben found a passage in a letter signed, "Your affectionate friend, Agnes McDermott," describing Colonel Morris. "According to Warren, Colonel Morris is a man of resolute character, well respected by his peers, without any marked deficiency in intellect or temper. I believe he will make a satisfactory match for Mairi being a man of firm disposition and clear faculty."

"Gosh. Who could say no to that?" I commented sarcastically after Ben read the passage aloud. "I know I've always dreamed of marrying a man without any marked deficiency in intellect."

"No deficiency in intellect. Right. Good to know," Ben said. "So, what else do you look for in a bloke?" he asked, his expression only half-joking.

I felt myself growing uncomfortably warm. "Uhm. You know. The usual," I stammered.

He looked at me, one eyebrow raised. "The usual?"

The front door opened and Mrs. Hickman entered the house followed by Simon.

When he saw Ben and me sitting together on the sofa, his face stilled.

"Mum! Simon!" Ben said, jumping up quickly.

I flushed guiltily as Simon's gaze shifted between Ben and me. What was wrong with me? I had nothing to feel guilty about. I lifted my chin and returned his look.

"Simon, just give the box to Ben. He knows where it goes," Mrs. Hickman said.

Simon silently handed a box to Ben.

"Put them away in the shed, Ben, luve," she told him. "I'll just go and put these things in the kitchen." She turned. "Simon, you'll stay for dinner," she announced before the kitchen door swung closed behind her. It was a statement, not a question.

Simon and I stared at each other.

"When are you going back to Brynmoor?" he asked

after an awkward silence.

"I'm not," I told him with a defiant toss of my head.

The muscle in Simon's jaw jumped as he stared at me. "What do you mean?"

"I'm not going back to Brynmoor. I'm going back to Anchoret House."

"Are you daft?" he asked sharply. "Do you remember the state you were in when we brought you here?"

"I'm going back to Anchoret House," I repeated stubbornly.

"Not if I have anything to say about it, you're not!"

I smiled coldly at him. "But that's the point, isn't it? You don't have anything to say about it."

His eyes locked onto mine. "You're not going back."

I stood up and glared at him. "Yes. I. Am."

Simon stared at me silently for a moment, his look of frustration turning into angry resignation. "Fine," he said. "We'll leave tomorrow morning."

Simon joined us for dinner. I handed out the gifts I'd purchased earlier with Ben. Mrs. Hickman exclaimed over her gardening gloves. Nick gave me a thumbs-up on the T-shirt. Ben grumbled good-naturedly about his lack of a gift. Simon acknowledged the jokes with a tight smile. He joined in the dinner table conversation never speaking directly to me, although his eyes kept straying my way throughout the meal.

"Lily, luve, would you mind helping me with the clearing up?" Mrs. Hickman asked as we finished dinner.

Ben laughed. "You've become a member of the family now, Lily. Mum never asks guests to help in the kitchen."

Mrs. Hickman looked at Ben. "You lads can go help your father. He has a shipment of cement block that needs loading and I don't want him doing it himself."

Mr. Hickman stood. "Right, lads. Best get to it then. Mum's parceled out the chores for the evening," Mr.

Hickman announced with a wink and grin at Mrs. Hickman.

Simon, Ben, and Nick followed Mr. Hickman out of the house.

"There," she said as the door closed behind them. "Now you pick up those plates and bring them into the kitchen. We can enjoy a little girl talk while the lads are out from under us."

I brought the plates into the kitchen and laid them on the counter by the sink.

"I'll do the washing and you do the drying." Mrs. Hickman handed me a dishtowel. "And we can enjoy a wee chat while we work." She filled the sink with water and began soaping the dishes.

"Thank you so much for letting me stay here," I told her as she handed me a dish. "I really appreciate it."

"Oh, it's been our pleasure. I've heard so much about you from my brother and sister-in-law, I felt like I knew you before you even stepped through our door. They speak very highly of you and your mum."

"I think it's mutual. Mr. and Mrs. Fitzgibbon are really special people. I know my mom is always telling me how wonderful they are." I finished drying the plate. "Where do you want me to put these?" I asked.

"Just in that cabinet, over there to your right."

I found the cabinet and placed the dish inside.

Mrs. Hickman handed me another plate. "The poor lad is suffering, you know," she said giving me a sidelong glance.

"Uhm, sorry?"

She dipped her hands into the soapy water and began washing another plate. "I've known Simon since he was a bairn. He feels things deeply. He might not always show it, but he does. It's what makes him such a gifted healer. I am sorry to see him hurting so."

"Are you saying that you think I'm making Simon suffer?"

"Aye. I see the way he looks at you," she said as she rinsed another plate and placed it on the stack of plates waiting to be dried. "I'm not saying it's something you're doing on purpose, mind you." She gave me another long glance out of the corner of her eye. "No. I don't think you have that in you, but it might be best if you decide what it is you want and then, if it isn't Simon, it would be best if you leave him be."

I finished drying the plate I was holding and I laid it carefully on the counter before turning to look at her. "Mrs. Hickman," I began.

"Call me Nancy, dear, or Aunt Nancy, if you like."

"Aunt Nancy," I started again. "Simon is the one who decided that we were ..." I paused. "Simon was the one who decided not to spend time with me. Not me. I was in California when he stopped answering my phone calls and texts. When I came back to England, he'd left for Scotland without telling me."

"Ah. And then you followed him here."

"No, I didn't."

She looked at me, eyebrows lifted in gentle disbelief.

"I mean, I did, but not because I knew he was here. I came with Jenna. I didn't even know he was going to be here. I wouldn't have come if I had." My eyes filled with tears. "I don't know what I've done to make him hate me so much."

Mrs. Hickman clucked sympathetically. "Oh, now, now." She patted me on the back. "I know Simon, and it's not hate that's making him suffer, lass. It's love."

CHAPTER 13

31 October 1903

My dearest sister, Blaire,

　　You may see from the date on this letter that I am writing to you on All Hallows Eve. The weather is appropriately wet with a wild wind blowing across the moor. The noise is quite fearsome, almost as if the spirits of the dead were moaning and wailing as they rise from their graves tonight. Have I made you shiver with fright? Remember how we used to scare each other with terrible stories of ghoulies and ghosties and long-legged beasties. Oh, what fun we had! How I miss those days! I know you are too grown up to go guising, but perhaps you will take Isobel to beg for sweets from the shopkeepers tonight. I do hope so! Oh, but I am in a melancholy mood. I blame it on the terrible howling wind. It bays like a pack of hounds, so loudly that I can scarcely think. I am sending your Christmas scarves early this year since the fierce weather and poor roads make it difficult to know when the mail will be delivered to Edinburgh. The rose-colored scarf is for you. The peach is meant for Isobel and the green for Alec, though I suspect he will never wear it.

Your sister,

Mairi

***

Simon and I drove in silence, the tension snapping and crackling between us like a live electric wire.

Finally, I couldn't stand it any longer. "Why are you doing this?" I blurted out.

"Doing what?"

"Driving me back to Anchoret House."

"Because you insisted on going back to Anchoret House," he said, his eyes firmly fixed on the road ahead.

"You didn't need to drive me," I said petulantly. "Ben could have taken me."

Simon glanced at me but said nothing.

I sat back and crossed my arms in front of me. Why had I agreed to let Simon drive me back to Anchoret House? Now I was going to be stuck in a car with a silent and brooding driver for hours.

We traveled a few more miles in silence.

"Simon, I don't understand. What did I do to make you so mad at me?" I asked, once again unable to tolerate the silence between us.

"I'm not."

"You're not mad?"

"Mad, as in daft, or mad, as in angry?" he asked, flashing me a strange little smile.

"Mad, as in angry."

"No. I'm not."

"Then why are you acting like this?" I asked in exasperation.

"Like what?"

"Are you joking!" I huffed. Now it was my turn to be angry. "You can barely stand being in the same room with me, but here we are in a car together because you insisted on driving me. I don't get it! I don't understand what's going on with you! Why are you acting like this!"

Simon sighed deeply. He glanced over at me. He didn't say anything for a moment, and I thought he wasn't going to answer me, but then he said in a low voice, "Because I thought it was the right thing to do."

I stared at him, mouth agape. "What?"

"I thought it was the right thing to do," he repeated.

"You thought driving me was the right thing to do? Or did you think dumping me without telling me was the right thing to do?"

"Yes."

"Yes? You mean both?"

"Yes.

"Why?" I asked, my voice catching in my throat. "What did I do to make you hate me so much?"

Simon pulled over the side of the road and stopped the car. He stared out the windshield, his expression bleak. "You haven't done anything," he said finally. "And that's the problem."

I looked at him, feeling more confused by the moment. "I don't understand."

Simon leaned back and closed his eyes, sighing heavily. "My father is ten years older than my mum. He told me that he always felt bad because he had kept my mum from becoming the person she should have been. She's very intelligent, my mum. She could have gone to Cambridge, but she didn't. She married my dad instead. My dad said he had been a selfish bastard when he was younger because he hadn't wanted to lose my mum. He'd been afraid if she'd gone off to university, she'd meet some bloke and wouldn't want to marry him. So, he insisted on getting married, and now my mum works as a housekeeper when she could have had a university degree."

I looked at Simon, perplexed. "I still don't understand. What does that have to do with us?"

Simon turned to look at me. "You're eighteen. I'm twenty-five. Your mum said you had been accepted to some universities in the states, but you didn't want to go."

He looked away. "I didn't want to be a selfish bastard."

"Are you saying that you dumped me for my own good?" I asked in disbelief.

He nodded. "I thought if I didn't have to see you it would be easier. So, I took the job in Edinburgh."

I stared at Simon in astonishment. I couldn't believe what I was hearing. "Are you joking! You decided to dump me, without telling me, because you thought I wanted to get married instead of going to college?"

"Yes," he said.

"You arrogant, arrogant sod!"

Simon flinched. "I guess I deserve that."

I started laughing. It was all so ridiculous. "Yes. You do! I can't believe it! I can't believe you actually thought that I was planning on marrying you."

Simon stared at me. I could see the hurt in his eyes and tugging at the corners of his mouth before he turned away. "I see," he said.

I hadn't meant to hurt him. Okay, maybe I had, just a little. I mean, the guy put me through hell, but I couldn't keep it up. Yes, he was arrogant and thought that because he was older and wiser he knew what was best for me, but he was still Simon. My Simon.

"Simon," I said when I'd caught my breath. "I may be eighteen, but I'm not stupid. The reason I'm not sure about going to college in the states has nothing to do with wanting to marry you."

"Yes, you made that quite clear," he said stiffly. He turned the key in the ignition.

I placed my hand on his arm. "I just graduated from high school," I said gently. "I don't want to marry anybody right now."

He stilled, but he didn't look at me.

"The reason I'm not sure about going to those universities is because I'm thinking about studying theology," I said quietly.

Simon turned off the car and slowly turned to look at

me, a shocked expression on his face. I'm not sure I could have said anything that could have surprised him more than that.

"Theology? You want to be a priest?"

"I don't know about being a priest," I said with a little smile. "Like you said, I'm young and I need to figure things out. I don't know exactly what I want to do, but what I do know is that I want to understand more about what happens after we die. About what happens to our souls or spirits or whatever you want to call them. I have so many questions and I want to find answers about life and about death." I paused. "And life after death."

He regarded me silently.

"After last winter break, I started thinking about things. Where does our life energy go after we die? Why is it that some spirits stay with us in this world and others don't? I thought theology might be a good place to start to find some of those answers." I gazed intently at him. "I would have told you, if you had given me the chance."

Simon raked his fingers through his hair. "I guess I am an arrogant sod," he said with a ghost of a smile.

I didn't deny it.

"I'm not going to argue with you about that." I smiled to take the sting out of my words.

"So, what are you planning on doing then?" he asked.

He looked so miserable; I took pity on him. "I've written to Kings Cross College in London. I missed the application deadline, but I'm hoping they'll accept me for the next term."

"That sounds like a good plan," he said, his voice tight and unnatural. "I hope that works out for you."

I leaned toward him, a sly smile on my lips. "You may be an arrogant sod," I whispered. "But I love you anyway."

It was as if someone had suddenly released a bowstring. All the tension in his face and posture disappeared. His eyes locked onto mine, then he gathered me in a crushing embrace. "Lily, I've missed you," he said, his voice husky with emotion.

We eventually got back on the road to Balairie. The day was gray and overcast, but I was glowing so brightly I could have lit up all of London. I kept glancing over at Simon as he drove. He would catch my eye and his mouth would curve into that slow, lazy smile that I loved.

Of course, he still wasn't pleased about my returning to Anchoret House, but when I explained that I had to help Mairi, he relented.

"Just because she's dead doesn't mean she's a good person or that she won't harm you in some way. Look at what happened last time you were there."

"I know, but last time I wasn't prepared. I didn't know what was happening to me. Now I do."

Simon looked at me doubtfully. "What will you do if she gets in your head again?"

"Listen."

Simon frowned unhappily.

"Simon, I know her now," I reassured him. "I will handle it. I promise you. I'm the only chance she has to find peace. She is suffering. I can't leave without trying to help her, any more than you could walk away from an injured animal."

He sighed resignedly, knowing that there was no use arguing with me. "Fine," he said. "But you promise me that you'll ask for help if you need it."

I held up my right hand and looked solemnly at him. "I promise."

"Good." He turned his attention back to the road.

I leaned over and kissed him on the cheek. He glanced my way, smiling contentedly.

As soon as we crested the hill leading to Anchoret House, I could feel the familiar pressure building behind my eyes. Mrs. Hickman explained to me that my headaches were likely caused by a conflict between my subconscious and Mairi. She said that the trick for me would be to open myself to communicating with her without allowing her to influence me. Easier said than done, but I leaned back and quietly tried to open my mind to her. Mairi was trying to tell me something and I needed to find out what it was.

Simon parked the car in front of the house and we got out. When Jenna saw us, her face broke out into a huge smile. I don't know how she knew, but she did. Perhaps my expression gave me away. I must have looked as happy and contented as I felt.

"Lily! Simon!" She hurried over to us. She gave me a hug and whispered, "You've patched things up?"

I nodded.

"I'm so glad!" She gave me another fierce hug.

"Well, Simon," she teased. "You look like the cat who got the cream."

"Never mind that, Jenna," he said, but he couldn't keep the pleased smile from his face.

Katie, needless to say, was less than enthused about the change in our relationship. Simon tried to soften the blow by being kind to her. He wasn't oblivious to the fact that she had a schoolgirl crush on him.

"Katie, I brought you some herbs for your garden," he told her. He opened the back of the car to get the two plants Ben's mother had sent with us as Katie stared sullenly at me. It wasn't going to be easy, but given time, I hoped I would be able to smooth things over with her.

"You'll never guess what Ben and I discovered," I said, directing a bright smile Katie's way.

"What?" Jenna asked for her when Katie didn't respond to my question.

Before I could answer, Simon came around to the front of the car. "Here you go, Katie. My aunt said to be sure to plant the mint in a container so that it doesn't take over the herb garden." He handed the herbs to her with a gentle smile.

Katie gazed up at him, her eyes suddenly filling with tears. "Thanks," she whispered before turning away quickly and hurrying to the garden, sobbing.

Simon turned to look at me, a troubled expression on his face. "Perhaps I'd better go talk to her."

Jenna put a restraining hand on his chest. "No. I think it would be best if I go talk to her."

"But—" Simon began.

Jenna shook her head. "I'll go talk to her," she said firmly. "You'll only make it worse if you try to be nice to her."

Simon looked at me.

"She's right. There's nothing you can do to make her feel better, except to get rid of me." I stepped closer to him. "And I'm not planning on going anywhere."

Jenna grinned at us. "Right. I'll go talk with Katie. Why don't you two take a walk on the moor while I see what I can do to patch things up with her."

"That's a great idea." I hooked my arm through Simon's. "Shall we?" I asked.

The gray morning had given way to afternoon sunshine, a rare occurrence in the Highlands. We hiked across the moor, batting away the swarming midges as the sun above us burned a yellow hole in the cloudless blue sky.

"I think I like it better when it rains," I said, swatting at the cloud of flimsy insects.

Simon laughed. They seemed to be more attracted to me than to him.

"Why aren't they bothering you?" I asked a little grouchily.

"Must be my manly scent," he said with a smirk.

"Oh. please." I leaned into him and sniffed.

"What are you doing?" he asked with a laugh.

I sniffed again. "Testing your manly scent," I replied.

"Perhaps if you walk closer to me, it will help keep the midges away," he offered.

"Like this?" I said, snuggling next to him.

"Hmm." He pulled me closer, wrapping his arms around me and leaning down to nuzzle my neck.

"What are you doing?"

"Trying to help," he said with a sly grin.

Laughing, I pushed him away. "I don't see how that's going to help."

He assumed an expression of mock indignation. "Right. Well, if you don't want me to share my manly scent with you, I'll keep it to myself then."

I rolled my eyes. "Yeah, I think you'd better do that." I flailed my arms at the cloud of annoying insects.

"Suit yourself," he said, grinning.

We walked to the broch side by side. He, relatively unmolested by the pesky insects; me, waving my arms about my head like a crazy person.

When we reached the ruins, I saw his face tighten momentarily. I knew he was remembering the incident with Ben.

"Hey, you," I said to distract him. "Come with me." I grabbed his hand and tugged him gently into the stone circle. The midges mysteriously disappeared.

"They're gone," I said, surprised. I turned to look at Simon. "This is a magical place."

"It's a haunted place," he countered, looking around warily.

"Yes. But it's haunted by good memories." I pulled him into the center of the circle and held his hand.

"What are you doing?"

"Trust me," I told him. "Now, close your eyes," I ordered. I held onto his hand and did the same, tilting my face toward the sky. "Just relax and open yourself to it."

"To what?"

"You'll see."

As we stood there, my skin began to hum. Simon's hand tightened around mine. It was as if some kind of current was flowing through us, binding us together. It was the most amazing feeling. I felt as if a warm, liquid happiness was coursing through my veins. I turned toward Simon and the warm glow I was feeling turned into a heat of a different kind.

We lay tangled together on a bed of lichen in the center of the broch.

"Lily, we need to stop," Simon said, his voice hoarse.

"Why?" I asked nuzzling him, my fingers tracing circles on his chest.

"Because ..."

I rolled on top of him and planted a series of kisses along his jawline. "Because ..." I teased.

He groaned. "Lily. Please."

I trailed kisses down his neck.

He sat up abruptly, causing me to roll off him.

"What's wrong?" I asked.

"What's wrong is you might not have any choice but to marry me if we don't stop now."

I smiled seductively at him. "Okay," I whispered, reaching for him.

He pushed me away and gave me a hard stare.

I reached for him again, my lips curving upward. "I'm not afraid."

Simon's expression darkened. "We need to leave this place." He grabbed my hand, jumped up, yanking me to my feet with him.

"Simon!"

"Let's go! Now!"

I dug my heels in, but I was no match for him. He pulled me out of the stone circle and dragged me away from the ruins.

After we'd gone about twenty feet, I jerked my arm free. "What is wrong with you!"

He stopped and looked at me, one eyebrow raised.

"Lily? Or is it Mairi?"

I stared back at him. "What?"

He gazed at me for a moment, studying me. "Right. Maybe you should tell me what just happened in there. Mairi," he said, gesturing toward the broch with a lift of his chin.

I turned to look at the broch before slowly shifting my gaze back to Simon. I took a deep breath. "Oh," I said, only now realizing what had happened. "I guess she used to meet Robbie at the broch."

"I'd say that is a definite possibility," he replied dryly.

I gave him a crooked grin. "Well, you can't fault a girl for trying."

He looked at me, one eyebrow raised. "I think it's best we head back before Mairi gets us both in trouble."

Simon and I walked hand in hand back to Anchoret House. We didn't say much. We were each lost in our own thoughts.

I had thought that since I was aware that Mairi was influencing, I would be able to control things better. Apparently not. I loved Simon, but in my normal state of mind, I would never let my feelings for him overrule my common sense, not like that anyway.

It was probably easy for Mairi to influence me. I suspect I hadn't needed much persuasion. It wasn't as if I hadn't thought about what it would be like at least a million times. Though I have to admit, I'd never quite imagined a broch, in the middle of the open moor. I knew I was lucky that Simon had figured things out before we both did something we would regret. What if I had gotten pregnant? What if Mairi had gotten pregnant?

With sudden clarity, I knew.

She had.

Dinner at Anchoret was interesting. We sat around the table: Katie, red-eyed and unhappy, Jenna sympathetic, Mr.

McAfee polite but not overly thrilled to see me, Simon looking and feeling guilty, and me.

I single-handedly kept the conversation going. I showed Mr. McAfee the copy of the marriage registry and regaled everyone with details of Ben's detective skills. When I told them that I still had hundreds of letters to review, everyone offered to help, even Katie. Although I think she offered mostly so that she could sit next to Simon.

After dinner, while everyone cleared the plates, I retrieved the box of letters from the car. I hadn't brought all of them with me. Simon had made it very clear to Ben that he was not invited to join us on our drive back to Anchoret. Ben had looked so forlorn at being left behind that I left a stack of letters with him. Now I regretted it. With five of us sorting through the letters, we would be able to get through them much more quickly than Ben would.

I put the box on the table.

"The letters are not in any order. They're just kind of jumbled together. Because there are so many, Ben and I skipped any letter that had a date after 1904, but since all of us are reading them now, maybe we should skim those, too," I said, looking around the table.

Mr. McAfee nodded, his excitement palpable. "Right you are, lass. Why don't you pass round the box and we'll each take a few."

I snagged half a dozen of the letters and piled them in front of me, then passed the box down the table.

The five of us read letters for about two hours. Katie struggled the most with the difficult handwriting, but she stuck it out. In fact, she was the one who found the letter about Mairi's wedding.

"Listen to this," she said eagerly. "I was very gratified to read your last letter. It is indeed good news that Mairi has been wed. You should be quite pleased with yourself for having made such a fine match for her under the circumstances. I wish her marriage all prosperity and hope that a dose of Colonel Morris's good sense will aid her in curbing her more impetuous nature. I must admit that I much prefer our sensible, modest Scottish weddings to such vulgar spectacles. To my mind the binding of man and woman before God should be a solemn occasion, not one of excess frippery. I recently attended the wedding of a distant English cousin who had in attendance eight garlanded bridesmaids all flopping on their knees at the appropriate moment and two clergymen parading about the altar reading by turns from gigantic prayer books in front of great masses of gaping spectators as the poor bride stood affixed between her father and her husband. It resembled something between a religious ceremony and a pantomime!' What a perfectly horrid woman. I would never invite her to my wedding," Katie declared incensed.

"Let me guess," I said. "The letter was written by someone named Agnes McDermott."

Katie turned the paper over and read the signature. "You're right. How did you know?"

"I've read quite a few of her letters," I said.

"She doesn't appear to be one to mince words," Mr. McAfee commented.

"Oh no. Agnes tells it like it is," I agreed.

We managed to make quite a dent in the box of letters. It went a little more slowly than I had anticipated. Once you started reading and began to know the people writing them, it became more difficult to skim. Each letter was like a window to another time and place.

"Here's our Agnes again." Jenna passed me the letter she'd been reading. "You'll enjoy this one. She complains about uninvited guests tumbling into tea and making pigs and whistles of the whole heart of her day. Then she says that she's had a moral shock from the hair on her head to the soles of her feet," she quoted. She grinned. "Agnes really is the most frightful old gossip, isn't she?"

It went on like that for more than an hour. Anytime someone found an interesting letter, they would read it to the rest of us. We would laugh or make comments about it before returning to reading our stack of correspondence.

"This is better than a reality show on the tele," Jenna commented, leering at us. "Here is a letter from Mairi's aunt to Mairi's mother. She's talking about how she had to fire a servant. I'll pass it around if you like. It's long but worth reading.

"Read it aloud," Katie insisted.

Jenna glanced around the table. "All right. If you insist." She read a passage aloud, "'I cannot believe I was so deceived by Helen, our serving girl. She is the worst of girls! She brought an illegitimate child in my house, in my very own dining room, while John was taking tea in the next room with Mr. Russell. Can you imagine! Only one thin door between! Apparently, Helen had been keeping company in my kitchen and frightening our other girl into silence by threats of poisoning her and cutting her throat! Need one ask where all my fine linen napkins went.'"

When she finished reading, we all laughed, except Mr. McAfee, whose ears had gone bright red. He cleared his throat and went back to reading the letter in front of him.

Because the letters we were reading were not in chronological order, it was kind of like reading a book out of order. At first, things didn't make sense, but the more you read the more everything started falling into place. You started figuring out the relationships between people and piecing together a timeline of events.

Katie found a letter written by Mairi to her sister about love. Mr. McAfee found a letter from Mairi written, appropriately enough, to her father. Jenna found two letters written to her mother asking permission to go home to Edinburgh to visit.

I knew Mairi was listening to the letters with me. Every time I listened to someone read one of her letters aloud, I experienced the same emotions Mairi had felt when she wrote them. One moment I was sad and lonely, the next giddy with love. It was a strange and exhausting experience to be reading the letters through someone else's eyes. It took its toll on me. My head felt as if it had an iron band around it squeezing tighter and tighter with every letter we read. I wasn't sure how much longer I was going to be able to last before I needed to take a break.

Then I found a letter from Mairi. As I read it silently to myself, the blood suddenly drained from my head. I broke out in a cold clammy sweat, my vision narrowing to a pinpoint. I think I gasped or moaned as I clutched my stomach. I felt as if I was the one who had lost the baby, not Mairi.

Simon reached over and clasped my arm. "What's wrong?"

With shaking hands, I passed the letter over to him.

He skimmed it and looked over at me, his forehead furrowed with worry. "Are you all right?"

I shook my head.

"Right, then. We're done for now. Let's get you upstairs."

He stood up and everyone looked over at him. "Lily and I are going to take a bit of a breather."

"Are you all right?" Jenna asked, her expression mimicking Simon's.

"I've got a headache, again."

"No wonder," Mr. McAfee said heartily. "It's reading all this small handwriting. Why don't we finish up tomorrow?"

Simon walked me up the stairs and fetched me a glass of water so I could take two more paracetamol pills. "Are you sure you're all right?"

I was feeling better. I still felt that familiar throbbing behind my eyes, but I no longer felt like I was going to faint. "I'm fine. I just need to rest. It was the letter. It was a surprise."

"To you or to her?"

I smiled wanly. "It's a little hard to tell right now."

He looked me over, his eyes narrowing speculatively.

"I'm fine. Really. I just need to rest."

"I'll check back in a little while." He gave me a gentle kiss on the cheek before I shut the door.

I changed into my pajamas and brushed my teeth. There was a knock on my door. I opened it. Jenna stood there, grinning at me like a red-haired Cheshire cat.

"Are you feeling up for a chat?"

I mustered a smile. "Sure."

She waltzed over to my bed and sat on it, watching while I put away my hairbrush and earrings. "Thanks for talking to Katie," I said. "She seems better."

"She'll be all right. So ..." She gave me a cheeky grin. "Are you going to tell me?"

"Tell you what?"

She looked at me, both eyebrows raised.

"We talked."

"And?"

"And things are good between us now."

"Good." She flopped back on my bed. "So, what happened downstairs just now?"

"I'll tell you, but this is going to sound weird."

Jenna waited, eyes wide with curiosity.

"Uhm, I think I was sharing some of Mairi's memories when we were reading the letters. It's a little hard to explain, but for some reason, she's identified with me and is kind of, uhm, in my head sometimes."

Jenna flicked a hand in the air dismissively. "I know all about that. I called Simon after you went to Edinburgh. He told me all about how Mairi was making you do things." She propped herself up on her elbows and grinned. "Don't worry. I forgive you for being so snarky, since it wasn't really you."

"Snarky?"

"Snarky," she said with a smirk. "Definitely, snarky."

"I guess I'll have to work on that."

"Don't worry about it. Now I'll know to be cross with Mairi if it happens again." Jenna tilted her head staring at me. "So, what does it feel like having her inside your head?"

"You mean aside from the headaches?"

"Yeah."

I shrugged. "It's the same. I wish it weren't. I thought that since I now know she's influencing me that I would be able to tell the difference, but it isn't that easy."

"You don't hear her voice whispering to you, telling you to do things?"

"No. And my head isn't going to start spinning around either," I said crossly. "I'm not possessed by some evil demon."

"Sorry. I didn't mean it like that."

I walked over to the bed and sat next to her. "I know. It kind of freaks me out, too. I don't hear her or see her. I just feel what she feels. It's like if I want to go right and she wants to go left, then sometimes I go right and sometimes I go left, but I don't know who is making the decision. It might be me or it might be her."

Jenna shivered. "So she can control your thoughts and make you do things?"

"Kind of. Your aunt said she can influence me, but if I am careful and aware, I should be able to keep things under control. It's like if you had a really good friend you trusted, and she wanted you to do something you weren't sure was the right thing to do, you might do it even if you knew it was wrong. So now I'm going to have to stop and figure out what it is I really want to do or say and make sure that it's me making the decision."

"It kind of gives me the willies."

"You? What about me? I'm the one with another person inside my head."

Jenna wrinkled her nose. "Am I talking to you or to Mairi right now?"

"Me. Her. Both of us, I guess. I don't know."

"Spooky." She cocked her head and stared at me thoughtfully. "Does that mean she feels what you're feeling?"

"I don't know. That would make sense, wouldn't it?" I thought about how I had thrown myself at Ben, not to mention Simon.

"That is definitely spooky. So," she said with a sly grin. "Does she like Simon?"

Laughing, I picked up my pillow and threw it at her.

There was another knock on my door.

"Who is it?"

"Me," responded a familiar voice.

"Simon?"

"Speaking of Simon," Jenna said with a giggle. She hopped off the bed and scurried over to the door, opening it.

Simon flushed when he saw his sister standing there grinning at him.

"Looking for me?" she teased.

"I just popped by to see how Lily was doing," he explained stiffly.

Jenna's smile widened. "Me, too. Fancy that." She turned toward me and winked. "I'll be off then. See you in the morning. Both of you," she added.

Simon waited until Jenna had closed the door behind her. He walked over to me and stood looking down at me as I sat on the bed.

I tilted my head to him coquettishly. "Did you come to kiss me goodnight?"

Simon cupped my chin in his hands as he gazed into my eyes. "No," he said firmly. "I did not. I came to see if you were feeling better."

"I am," I said, tugging him toward me.

Simon leaned forward and kissed me lightly on my forehead. "Goodnight, Lily." He took a step back while I stared at him confused.

"I'm not touching you again until we leave this place," he said firmly.

"Why?"

He stared at me for a moment before answering. "Because I'm not sure who you are."

"What are you talking about?"

"I don't know how to act with you. Are you Lily? Are you Mairi? I'm willing to accept the idea that ghosts exist, but I'm not willing to … to do things with them. When we were out on the moor, at the broch …" He stopped and started again. "I just can't get it out of my mind. I wasn't kissing you. I was kissing a dead person. That she was inside of you like some kind of alien being, making you do things, making you say things." He shook his head. "I don't even know if I'm talking to you or to her right now."

"You're talking to me," I told him.

"How am I supposed to know that?" he said, frustrated. "I'm sorry, Lily, I'm trying, but this supernatural stuff is new to me and it's going to take me time to get used to it."

"It's pretty new to me, too," I said.

"Right. Well, it's different for me. He paused and sighed. "You can see them and feel them. So maybe they're real to you. To me they're something I've grown up fearing or not believing in. I know you want to help her, that's fine. I'll do what I can to help you. I'll be here to keep you safe, but I can't do more than that."

He crossed the room, pausing at the door. "I've waited six months for you to come back to Brynmoor. I can wait a little longer until she is out of your head," he said lightly. "Though you might want to tell her hurry things up a bit." He smiled, but I noticed that his smile didn't quite reach his eyes.

CHAPTER 14

7 January 1904

Dear Mr. Bain,

    Colonel Morris has bid me write to you regarding a most terrible tragedy. I am saddened to inform you that your daughter Mairi met with a fatal accident Wednesday last. As I suspect your family will want the particulars, I will relate the details to you as I know them to be. Last Wednesday, Mairi left the house in the morning to take her usual stroll alone on the moor. When she did not return home at her accustomed time, Colonel Morris and one of the servants went to search for her. They were unable to find her and the next morning rallied several men from Balairie to form a search party. Fearing the worst, we set out across the moor. We searched until darkness forced us to stop our efforts. We found her scarf and hat near the loch but found no sign of her. The only conclusion that I can draw from our findings is that Mairi met with an accident near the loch and drowned. It is with heavy heart and pen that I write this letter to you. Please accept my condolences on the loss of your daughter. I suspect the colonel will write to you himself as soon as he has recovered sufficiently from his grief to do so.

Most Sincerely,
Dr. Joseph Hunter

***

I guess I hadn't thought about how difficult dealing with the paranormal might be for Simon. He was used to dealing with sick animals and science, so this kind of thing was pretty far out of his normal comfort zone. It was one thing to admit that ghosts might exist, a whole different thing to ask someone to interact with them. The idea that Mairi was able to influence me still made me uncomfortable; I could see where it would be really creepy to him.

With Simon's words about hurrying things up ringing in my ears, I removed Mrs. Hickman's sachet from under my pillow. He was right. We needed to finish this business for Mairi as quickly as possible. Mrs. Hickman had told me that she thought ghosts spoke to me in my dreams because that's when my defenses were at their lowest and I was most open to listening to them. I wasn't keen on the thought of waking up choking again, but I was willing to take the chance if it meant that I would find out what it was Mairi needed from me.

Of course, I was so tense and nervous about what I might dream or feel that I couldn't fall asleep. I had been really frightened last time and the worry that it might happen again kept me staring at the ceiling for several hours. Finally, I gave up and turned on the light.

If I couldn't sleep, I reasoned, I could at least accomplish something useful by reading more of Agnes Sinclair's family letters. Maybe I would get lucky and find something.

I padded down to the dining room where we had left the box of letters and noticed that the door to the library was open and the light was on. I paused and peeked inside the room.

Simon stood with his back to me studying Mairi's portrait.

"Simon?" I said softly.

He turned.

I stepped over the threshold, that same feeling of icy dread rippled through me as I entered the room. "What are you doing here?"

"I couldn't sleep," he said. "So I thought I would read some more of the letters and see if I could find something. What about you? Another headache?"

I walked over and stood next to him. "Not any worse than usual," I said. I rubbed my eyes and stared up at Mairi. I could feel the intense sadness and grief inside this room almost as if it was in the very air and I was breathing it in like incense. I also sensed that it was mixed with anger. No. Something more than anger. Rage. I felt the heat of it radiating from the stone wall as if there were a fire behind it.

"What is it?" Simon asked.

"I don't know. I don't like this room," I said.

Simon gave me a sidelong glance. "You? Or Mairi?"

"I don't know," I said in frustration. "I can feel something, but I don't know what it is." I closed my eyes and tried to let my mind relax. An image flashed before me. I saw the chimney and Ben. No, I corrected myself. Not Ben, Robbie and me. No. Not me, Mairi. Robbie and Mairi. Something about Robbie. Dark stains on the floor. Intense shock and grief and anger! The image was gone! I opened my eyes and stared at the hardwood floor beneath my feet.

"What is it?"

I shook my head. I couldn't be sure about what I had seen. "Something terrible happened here," I said. "I think there was blood on the floor."

"You saw blood?"

I pressed my hands to my head. "I don't know. I can't be sure. I saw dark spots on the floor." The pounding in my head was growing worse. "She's trying to tell me something, but I don't know what it is." I pressed my fingers into my temples, hoping to clear my thoughts.

Simon put his arm around me. "You need to leave this room. Let's go."

I looked up at him. "I have to figure out what she wants me to do. I want to try again."

Simon's expression darkened. "Not if trying to figure out what she wants hurts you." He glanced up at Mairi's portrait.

"I have to help her, Simon."

"Lily, she's dead. There's nothing you can do for her. Come on, let's go." He pulled me toward the door.

"I can help her. She's hurting. I have to help her," I argued. The pressure behind my eyes was growing intolerable. I pressed my hands to my forehead.

Simon sighed wearily. "Fine, but you can't help her if you get another migraine. So, let's get you out of this room and see if that helps with your headache."

He had mentioned the magic word, migraine. His comment about the migraine was all the convincing I needed. I didn't want to experience that again. I looped my arm around his waist, leaning in to feel the warmth of him as he curled his arm around my shoulders and led me from the library.

We ended up in the dining room.

"Sit here," Simon said, pulling out a chair for me. "I'll make us some tea. Perhaps that will help your headache."

I nodded. I pulled the box of unread letters toward me after Simon went to the kitchen. He was right. Leaving the library had helped. My headache was slowly dissipating. I grabbed the first letter in the box and opened it.

When Simon returned with the tea, he found me sitting at the table, tears streaming down my cheeks.

"Are you all right?" he asked alarmed.

I handed him the letter I'd found from Dr. Hunter. "I want to go to the loch."

Simon skimmed the letter. "We can go first thing tomorrow," he said gently.

Simon and I both woke up late. No surprise, given that we didn't go to bed until sometime after three a.m.

Because of my headache, I chickened out about dreaming and replaced Mrs. Hickman's sachet under my pillow. Her sachet didn't seem to help much. I was tormented by nightmares. I tossed and turned, dreaming of kelpies and dead babies floating in cold, dark water. I sat up in bed letting the sunshine erase the last remnants of my terrible dreams. Catching sight of myself in the vanity mirror, I made a face at my pale reflection.

"Got to work on my beauty sleep," I said aloud.

Glancing over at Robbie's photograph, I picked it up. I was getting closer to finding out what had happened to him. This was the reason Mairi's spirit was lingering at Anchoret House. She wanted me to find Robbie. I was certain of it. I hung his pendant around my neck and stumbled downstairs.

Katie and Jenna were already at the dining room table reading letters. Jenna's welcoming smile faded when she saw me.

"Another bad headache?" she asked.

I shook my head. "No. Bad night."

"Dreams?"

I nodded.

"Were they bad?"

"Bad enough."

"Did you find out anything?"

"No, they weren't that kind."

Katie's eyes flicked from me to Jenna and back again, unsure what to make of our conversation.

"We saw the letter," Jenna said, a small frown appearing between her eyebrows. "About her drowning."

"It's very sad, isn't it?" Katie interjected. "To read

about her dying, I mean."

Jenna gave me a knowing look.

"Yeah," I agreed. "I'm going to walk to the loch today," I told them. "I need to see it."

"It's quite far," Katie said. "It will take you hours to walk there."

"I'm okay with that. Can you give me some insect repellent and maybe loan me a hat and a backpack?"

"You're not going by yourself," Jenna said firmly. She glanced at Katie. "We'll go with you."

Katie pursed her lips, looking unhappy at Jenna's offer, though she perked up quite a bit when she realized that Simon was going with us.

Mr. McAfee had confirmed Katie's warning that the loch was a "fair distance" from the house. We packed water, insect repellent, and lunch in two backpacks before leaving on our hike.

As we started out across the moor, Katie was filled with bubbly good cheer. She walked next to Simon, happily chatting with him. Jenna and I trailed behind. The day was clear and uncharacteristically warm. It wasn't long before we had all stripped off our sweatshirts and tied them around our waists. Unfortunately, the midges were also enjoying the good weather. In spite of using liberal amounts of repellent, we found ourselves relentlessly pursued by clouds of the vicious insects as we walked.

Katie's enthusiasm for our trek began waning after about forty-five minutes. "How much farther?" she asked Simon.

"At this rate, a couple of hours or so."

Katie didn't say anything. She didn't have to, her expression said it all. I bit back a smile. I wasn't sure that her enthusiasm for walking with Simon was going to be enough to last the entire trek.

"I'm thirsty," she whined five minutes later.

"Right. I'll get your water bottle for you," Simon said patiently. We stopped and Simon unzipped the backpack he was carrying, pulled out a water bottle, and handed it to her. "Here you go. Anyone else?"

"I've got mine," I said, holding it up.

"Jenna?"

She reached her hand out and Simon handed a water bottle to her.

We drank. Katie gave her bottle back to Simon.

"Right then. Off we go," he said cheerfully.

We walked another ten minutes before Katie asked to stop because her foot was bothering her.

We stopped. I rolled my eyes at Jenna, who turned away to hide her smile.

"Let me take a look at it," Simon offered kindly.

Katie removed her boot and sock, sighing happily when Simon crouched down and gently examined it.

"Hmmm," he said, catching Jenna's eye. "It looks like you're developing a bit of a blister. I don't think you'll be able to make it to the loch. "Perhaps we should divide up. You can walk back to Anchoret House with one of us while the other two head out to the loch."

"Good idea," Jenna agreed with a brief nod. "We can manage."

Katie smiled prettily at me. "I'm sorry, Lily," she apologized.

I shrugged. "That's okay. Blisters happen."

She put her shoe and sock back on while we waited then stood, smiling expectantly at Simon.

"You'll need to carry your own water bottle. Do you think you can manage?" he asked her.

Her head bobbed up and down enthusiastically.

He handed her the water bottle. "Right. Then we'll see you two back at the house in a few hours," he told Jenna and Katie cheerfully.

Katie's face fell. "You're not walking back with me?"

"No. Jenna will walk back with you while Lily and I go to the loch."

"But I thought you were going to go with me. What if

211

my foot hurts so badly, I can't make it all the way back?"

"You'll be fine. Just take it slowly." He gave her a gentle pat on the shoulder. "Jenna will take good care of you."

She looked so crestfallen. I winced. Simon meant well, but the poor kid didn't want to be treated, well, like a kid.

I smiled sympathetically at Katie, but she turned abruptly without returning my smile. I watched her walk away with Jenna, her shoulders slumping dejectedly.

I felt for her. There was nothing more miserable than being in love with someone who didn't love you back, as I knew from my recent experience with Simon.

Simon and I turned in the opposite direction and began walking toward Loch Shufte. The soft thud of our boots accompanied only by the gentle sighing of the wind as it swept through the water-soaked bracken surrounding us. Things were not quite as comfortable and easy between us as they had been, but we walked together in companionable silence. The quiet and scenery of the empty moor cast a peaceful spell over me, and I found that I enjoyed our hike more than I thought I would.

We caught our first sight of the loch as we crested a small hill. We stopped at the top and I held up my hand, shielding my eyes from the glare of the sun as it bounced off the surface of the water. In spite of the warm day, I shivered, suddenly feeling cold.

We carefully picked our way down the rocky hill. I kept my eyes fixed on the loch. The closer I drew to the water, the colder I felt. My field of vision slowly narrowed until all I could see was the dark, still waters of the loch beckoning to me. I walked toward the water as if I was being pulled by some invisible force.

I was cold, incredibly cold. An icy numbness seemed to travel up my body, beginning with my feet and legs and slowly rising. My muscles became more and more lethargic as the freezing cold sapped their strength. I felt as if I was walking in slow motion.

Everything slowed down and it became hard to move. Cold. So cold. It became hard to breathe. The icy numbness stole over my chest. So ... hard ... to ... breathe ...

I gasped and coughed, sucking air deep into my lungs, spluttering with the shock. My eyelids fluttered opened and I stared in surprise at Simon, his face hovering inches from mine.

I gazed at him, dazed and confused. His eyes blazed with intensity.

"Breathe, damnit!" he shouted.

"Breathe?" My thoughts were growing fuzzy.

"Breathe!" he shouted at me.

Frightened, I gasped.

"Again!"

I inhaled again.

"Again!"

Each time I inhaled, it became easier, and the freezing sensation that had weighed down my body slowly receded.

Simon hovered over me, his eyes fixed intently on mine, crowding me. I noticed idly that he was perspiring. Damp curls plastered his forehead. It didn't make sense to me. How could he be perspiring when I was so cold?

"Keep breathing," he said. His eyes still locked on my face, though he was no longer shouting. "In. Out. In. Out," he commanded.

I feebly pushed him away. "What are you doing?" I asked him irritably as I struggled to sit up. The cold, numb feeling had left my body and I discovered that everything hurt. I felt as if a two-hundred-pound gorilla had landed on my chest.

A look of profound relief crossed Simon's face. He gathered me into his arms and pulled me tightly against him, shuddering as he buried his face in my hair.

I let him hold me for a moment as I tried to figure out what was going on. Something must have happened. I just didn't know what it was. The last thing I remembered was walking to the loch.

"Simon," I said softly. "You're squashing me."

He let go of me.

I stared at him, frowning. "What's wrong?" I asked.

He sat back and stared at me for a moment before letting loose a short bark of laughter.

"Are you okay?"

"You're asking if I'm all right?" He shook his head in disbelief then reached over and cupped my chin in his hands, fixing his eyes on mine. "We are leaving this place and you are never coming back here," he said, voice harsh. "Let's go. Now!"

He tried to tug me to my feet, but I resisted. "What is wrong with you?" I asked irritably.

"What is wrong with me?" He gave another short bark of laughter.

I glared at him. "Yes! Why are so angry?"

His face stilled, and he exhaled slowly. Something he always did when he was struggling to maintain his composure. "I am angry," he said in a slow deliberate voice, his eyes burning into mine like lasers. "Because you almost died. Because I watched you drown right before my eyes and there was nothing that I could do to stop it."

I stared at him confused. I had no memory of going into the water.

I looked down at my clothes. They were dry.

Simon had revived me with artificial respiration. At first, he hadn't understood what was happening to me. I had walked toward the water's edge. He wondered why I was moving so slowly, but he thought I was reluctant to see where she had drowned. It wasn't until I fell to the ground and started turning blue that he realized I was actually reliving her death.

"I think I need a drink of water," I said slowly after he explained everything to me.

When he handed me my water bottle, I couldn't help but notice that his hand shook slightly. I was surprised at how calm I was about what had happened. Maybe it was because I had experienced the same drowning sensation earlier, or maybe it was because I just couldn't take it all in. But, for whatever reason, I just wasn't worried about it.

"We are leaving this place now," Simon said firmly after I finished drinking. I didn't argue. There was nothing more that I needed to see at the loch. I knew now that Mairi had definitely drowned. I also knew that she had been alone when it happened.

The walk back across the moor was hard and long. My whole body hurt: my lungs, my chest, my legs. The only good thing was that for some mysterious reason the midges left me alone. They continued to plague Simon, swarming in clouds about him, but they did not come near me. I wasn't sure what it was that attracted the insects to humans. Body heat? Scent? I had no idea, but whatever it was something had changed. Maybe I smelled different after my near-drowning experience, or maybe Mairi, feeling guilty about almost killing me, was keeping them away. Whatever the reason, I was grateful for the relief.

We walked silently and slowly back to Anchoret House as stray thoughts bumped around inside my head. I knew Simon believed that because I'd left the loch willingly, that I was also going to leave Anchoret House. If he had his way, he was going to pack me in the car and drive away as soon as we got back to the house, but I couldn't leave. Not now. I was so close to finding out what had happened here. To finding out why Mairi was haunting Anchoret House. I couldn't stop now.

Simon's eyes kept straying to me as we hiked, as if to reassure himself that I was okay, but he didn't say anything. I knew he was afraid for me. He had thought I was going to die, but I wasn't so sure. I didn't think Mairi would have let that happen to me. After all, I wouldn't be able to help her if I was dead. It was possible that she might hurt me by mistake, but I didn't think that she would intentionally harm me. Maybe, because she was a spirit, she simply "forgot" how important it was for living people to breathe.

When Anchoret House finally came into view, Simon sighed with relief. "How long will it take you to pack?" he asked.

I inhaled deeply. "Simon, I'm not leaving."

His eyes narrowed dangerously. "Yes, you are. If I have to throw you over my shoulders and carry you away from here, you are leaving."

I lifted my chin and met his gaze. "No. I'm not ready to go yet."

"What is wrong with you?" he blurted. "You could have died. If I hadn't been there, you would have died!" Simon's face was hard and angry. I'd never seen him this upset before.

Even though I knew he was worried because he was afraid for me, I wasn't going to back down. "You're wrong," I said firmly. "I wasn't going to die."

"You didn't see yourself! You were turning blue! She was killing you!" His voice was rising, his eyes blazing.

I shook my head and tried to reason with him. "I don't think she was trying to kill me. I think she made a mistake."

"A mistake? Is that what you call almost killing you?"

"I'm sorry, Simon, but I'm not leaving. Not yet."

I watched a mix of emotions parade across his face: anger, frustration, fear. "Why are you doing this?" he demanded.

"Because I have to help her."

"No, you don't!"

I took a breath and placed my hand on his arm. "I'm so

216

sorry I scared you, but I have to stay. I understand if you want to leave, but I can't. I have to help her. I can't turn away from her. I'm the only one who can help her. I have to stay and try."

Simon studied me, his face immobile.

"I promise you I will be all right."

We stared at each other silently for a moment.

"I don't know if I can do this," he said finally, then turned and began walking back to Anchoret House.

"Do what?"

"This." He gestured vaguely. "All of this. You. Ghosts. Me."

CHAPTER 15

06 August 1901

Dear Mr. Bain,

I am writing to you to inform you that I have dismissed Robert Cameron from my employ. Furthermore, I have advised him that he should not seek further employment in Edinburgh. I have offered him a position with my brother-in-law who is in need of a hostler on the understanding that he shall have no further contact with your daughter. He is a reasonable lad whose family relies on his wages for support, so he quickly agreed to the terms of employment and leaves for Perth tonight. I hope this arrangement is to your liking. I look forward to your continued patronage.

Yours cordially,
James Logan

***

Simon didn't leave Anchoret that night, though he probably should have. He was not in the best of moods.

He left it up to me to tell Jenna and Katie what had happened at the loch. I gave them an abbreviated version of the events, downplaying the drowning incident. I avoided looking at Simon while I was talking. Although, I cast a quick glance his way after I finished. He didn't say anything, just looked at me, his face shuttered of all expression. In fact, the only one enjoying herself that evening was Katie, who, noting the increased tension between Simon and me, was restored to bubbly good humor.

After dinner, I went to bed early. I couldn't remember the last time I'd been so exhausted physically and emotionally.

The next morning, Simon again tried to talk me into leaving Anchoret with him. I refused.

"I am leaving today. I have to go back to work."

"I know. It's okay."

"I want you to come with me."

"I can't," I said apologetically. "I just can't leave yet."

"Why?" he asked, frustrated. "You can come with me and we'll drive back to Anchoret next week."

I shook my head. "I'm sorry, Simon. I need to be here. I have to stay. It's the only way. Besides, weren't you the one who said you wanted this finished as quickly as possible," I teased.

Simon did not return my smile. He exhaled sharply. "There's no reasoning with you."

Please, Simon," I wheedled. "I don't want to argue with you."

"Then don't. Come with me."

I shook my head.

Simon raked his hands through his hair. "God, you're stubborn."

I shrugged. "And I'm not even a redhead," I joked.

He gave me a half-hearted smile and I knew I had been forgiven. He wasn't happy about it, but he grudgingly accepted my decision. "I've promised Mr. McAfee to help him this morning. I'll be leaving after lunch, if you change your mind."

"Thanks for understanding," I said, giving him a hug.

He held me tightly. "Just be careful," he whispered before releasing me.

I finished reading the letters that Katie and Jenna had set aside while Simon and I were hiking back from the loch. We now had quite a large pile of letters relating to Mairi and Anchoret House.

"I think we should put them in order," Jenna suggested. "We can build a timeline and maybe that will help us figure out what happened to her and to Robbie."

"Good idea," I agreed. "We began placing the letters in order from earliest to latest on the dining room table. There were more than three dozen. They covered the entire length of the table.

"Okay, now what?" I asked as we looked over our timeline.

Jenna grinned. "You're the psychic, you tell us."

I gave her a scathing look. "I'm not a psychic."

She shrugged unfazed. "Close enough."

I sighed and glanced over the letters trailing across the tabletop. "This one I think talks about Robbie," I said, pointing to the letter of February 1903 that she had written to her sister about being in love.

"How do you know? She never says his name," Katie pointed out.

"No," I agreed. "But why would she write about falling in love with her husband almost a year after she was married?"

Katie pointed to the letter. "But she says richer and poorer and in sickness and in health, that's what you say at weddings," she argued.

"I know, but I don't think she was talking about the colonel. Look." I pointed to the letter to her father dated

December 1902. The colonel gave her the horse in December. Robbie started working at Anchoret the same month. Most likely, he was hired to help take care of her horse, right? She's riding Biscuit." I showed her the letter to her father of February 1902. "We know she's riding Biscuit, right? That same month she writes to her sister about how she's found love. She's also spending a lot of time in the stable with Robbie." I looked up. "She was in love with Robbie. I know that. This just confirms it."

"She's pregnant in March," Jenna said with a suggestive lift of her eyebrows. "What do you think? Robbie?"

I nodded. "That would be my guess, though I don't know for sure."

Jenna pursed her lips thoughtfully. "Wow. At that time that would have been quite the scandal, not just because she was cheating on her husband, that would have been bad enough, but she was cheating on him with a servant. This would have ruined her completely, if other people found out about it. I don't know what she was thinking."

Remembering what had happened when Simon and I were at the broch, I said, "I'm pretty sure she wasn't thinking. She was too busy doing."

Jenna and I both giggled.

"That's horrible!" Katie burst out. "I don't know why you two think it's so funny!"

I turned to look at Katie, surprised to see tears in her eyes. "Katie, we're just joking around. It's no big deal."

Jenna caught my eye and gave me a little shake of her head. I belatedly remembered about her parents' divorce. I didn't know the particulars of the divorce, but I suspected there might be some reason Katie was at Anchoret with her dad instead of staying with her mom.

"Sometimes it just happens, I guess," I said gently. "The heart wants what it wants, and there's no telling it to be reasonable."

Katie glared at me. "I don't want to do this anymore!" She spun around and stormed out of the room.

Jenna and I looked at each other.

"I'd better go talk to her," Jenna said. "It's been rough for her. Her mum's left her dad and sent her up here, and now you've shown up and stolen Simon away. It's never easy when the person you love loves someone else." She gave me a crooked smile.

I nodded. "You're a good friend, Jenna."

After Jenna left to console Katie, I stood contemplating the letters on the table, trying to decide what I should do. I was vaguely aware of the sound of the front door opening and closing, but I assumed it was Mr. McAfee or Simon, and so I didn't pay it much attention.

"Hullo? Anyone home?" A voice called.

I hurried out into the hallway. "Ben? What are you doing here?"

His face broke into a wide grin when he saw me. "Nice way to welcome someone who just drove all the way up from Edinburgh to see you."

"Sorry, you surprised me." I paused. "But what are you doing here?"

Ben's face creased into a Cheshire cat-like grin. "I've something for you."

"For me?"

"Aye." He opened a large manila envelope. "I finished the packet of letters you left down in Edinburgh and I have something you need to see." He pulled a sheet of paper out of the envelope. "She knew him," he said, handing the letter to me.

I reached for the letter, my eyebrows drawing together. "She knew him? What are you talking about?"

"Read it. You'll see," he said cheerfully.

I quickly scanned the letter. It was written to Mr. Bain, Mairi's father. When I saw the name Robert Cameron, my heart started skipping in my chest. I checked the date on the letter: August 1901. I walked to the end of the table and checked the date on the first letter in our timeline. July 1901 was when Jane had written to Mairi's mother advising her to remove Mairi from the "young man's sphere of influence." Robbie must have been that young man.

You're right," I said excitedly. "She knew Robbie Cameron in Edinburgh and he followed her up here! You are a genius!" I wrapped my arms around him, giving him a big hug.

Of course, Simon chose that exact moment to walk into the dining room. Ben and I jumped apart, although we had no reason to feel guilty.

"Simon, look who's here," I said stupidly.

Simon gazed steadily at the two of us. "Hullo, Ben," he said, his voice cool.

"He found a letter about Robbie," I said quickly, holding out the letter to him. "He drove up here to give it to me."

Simon pinned Ben with a sharp look. He took the letter from my hand and glanced at it.

"Uhm, she knew him before," I said uncomfortably. "Mairi. She knew Robbie Cameron before she was married and I think he followed her up here."

Simon's eyes flickered between Ben and me.

"I think the colonel hired him when he bought her horse and Robbie was working in the stable and ..." My sentence trailed off. "Well, you can read the letters if you want." I gestured to the letters on the table.

"I think I have the general idea," Simon said dryly. Turning toward Ben, he asked, "You drove all the way up here just to deliver a letter?"

Ben shrugged amiably. "Two letters actually. I found another, though it's not much of a letter. More like a short note, but I thought Lily should see it." He turned to look at me. "It's from the colonel. You were right. He was an old bastard. Didn't even go to Mairi's funeral service."

Simon looked at Ben, one eyebrow lifted. "Perhaps that's because she cheated on him."

Ben smiled coolly and held Simon's gaze. "Aye. Perhaps if he had treated her better, she wouldn't have gone looking elsewhere."

I felt my face flush, not entirely sure we were still talking about Mairi. "Uhm," I interjected loudly. They both turned to look at me.

"Can I see the other letter?" I asked, directing my question to Ben.

Ben flashed me a wide smile. "Absolutely." He pulled a second letter out of the manila envelope and handed it to me.

Colonel Morris had written the note on stationery that bore the crest of his Royal Scots Dragoon Guards, but I knew as soon as I saw it who it was from. I recognized the handwriting. Dark slashing lines in rigid formation marched across the page. I read the one-line letter. Ben was right; it was not really a letter, more like a curt note of dismissal.

18 February 1904

Dear Mr. Bain,

I regret to inform you I will be unable to attend the memorial service for Mairi.

Colonel George Morris

"He didn't go." I looked up. "You're right. He didn't even go to her funeral." I glanced down at the letter again, reading the Latin words encircling the thistle on the crest: *Nemo me impune lacessit.* "No one harms me without punishment," I said softly to myself. Suddenly everything made sense. I looked up at Simon and Ben. "I think he killed her."

CHAPTER 16

1 March 1903

Dearest Liza,

Please forgive my tardy response to your last letter. Unfortunately, my poor health continues to keep me from traveling to Edinburgh. Molly has written to say that the service was both beautiful and touching. How terribly distressing the entire affaire must have been for you. I am much aggrieved that I was unable to attend, though perhaps it is for the best, as I find myself shocked and dispirited to hear of the atrocious behavior of so many of our friends and acquaintances with their overeager letters and calls of condolences. It does not require any particular acuteness to detect more impertinent curiosity than genuine sympathy, especially when so many came to ask about the particulars of Mairi's death. Poor Mairi. I fear I cannot help but think that the end of her life was much like the course of it. She was always headstrong and impetuous. Yet we should remember she was also a pious young woman. Take comfort, my dear sister, from the knowledge that our Lord in Heaven will hold no good thing from those that love him. Keep this in your heart and know that Mairi is at peace.

Yours,
Jane

***

We sat around the dining room table after lunch talking about the letters that Ben had brought with him. I was convinced that Colonel Morris had killed Mairi in a fit of jealousy. I didn't know how he had found out about Robbie, but I knew he had.

"But she drowned, right?" Jenna asked. "How did he manage that?"

I had to admit that was the one weak point in my argument. I answered honestly. "I don't know."

"Are you certain she drowned?"

"Yes," Simon said, shooting a look my way.

I nodded in agreement. "She definitely drowned."

"Maybe he dragged her out there and threw her in the loch?" Ben suggested.

"Maybe," I said tentatively. I thought about Mairi slowly walking into the water. She hadn't struggled. It seemed to me that I would have known if something like that had happened. "I guess he could have threatened her and made her walk out to the loch."

"I don't believe it. I don't believe he killed her," Simon said. "If he knew about her affair, he might have been angry enough to come to blows with Robbie." He let his gaze rest on Ben for a moment before continuing. "But he wouldn't hurt her. Besides, we don't even know if he knew about the two of them. For that matter, we don't even know if this is the same Robert Cameron or if this letter has anything to do with Mairi at all."

"Are you joking?" I asked incredulously. "That's ridiculous. Of course, they're the same person!"

He shrugged. "There's no proof of the connection, and Robert Cameron is a common enough name. We don't even know why this James Logan dismissed him. It could have been for anything."

Katie sat next to Simon, gazing at him with adoring eyes. "Simon's right, there's no proof," she echoed.

"You are just being difficult," I said to Simon, ignoring Katie. "She was in love with Robbie Cameron. You read the letters, and I'm sure even you can see that."

"She never says his name, not once," he said, glancing around the table.

"Fine. She doesn't say his name. She just took photographs of him and saved them. Something you would do if you loved someone."

Simon shrugged. "She might have, but that doesn't prove anything. It doesn't prove that they were having a love affair. Besides, we don't even know for certain that she was the one who took the photographs."

"Her father sent her a camera!" I said with exasperation. "Why are you being so stubborn?"

He leaned back in his chair. "I'm not being stubborn. I just want you to admit that most of what you are saying can be interpreted another way." He cocked his head a little to the side and looked at me as if he had just thought of something. "What does Mairi say about this?"

I glowered at him. "That's what I'm telling you. I *know* she was in love with Robbie. I *know* she took those photos. I *know* she drowned."

"But do you *know* that the colonel was involved with her death?" he asked, mimicking my emphasis on the word know.

I paused, thinking. "I think he had something to do with it," I answered finally. "But I don't know what exactly."

"Maybe," Katie jumped in, "you could put your hand on the library wall again."

I stared at her.

"That's how you found out in the first place, right? When you started crying, that was because of her, right?"

"Hmm, that's not a bad idea," Ben commented. "Do

you think that would work?" he asked me.

"I don't know."

"Maybe you should try," Jenna said. "Mairi might be able to show you what happened to her."

"We know what happened to her—she drowned," Simon said sharply.

"Yes," I agreed. "But something terrible happened in the library. Maybe Katie's right. Maybe I should try again."

"No," Simon said, a mulish expression on his face. "You might get hurt."

"Simon," I said gently. "She didn't drown in the library." I glanced around the table. "Something had happened in the library. Something terrible. I think it's the key to this whole thing."

I stood up. "I want to try."

As we filed out of the dining room, Simon caught my arm. "I don't think this is a good idea. Remember what happened last time?"

I shrugged. "You can't have it both ways. You're the one who wants proof."

"Not if it's going to hurt you," he said.

I smiled up at him. "I'll be okay."

"And if you're not?"

"You'll be there to give me mouth to mouth again."

His eyes narrowed. "That is not funny," he growled.

I had made him angry. "Simon, she didn't drown in the library," I said soothingly. "It'll be okay."

We gathered around Mairi's portrait. In spite of my assurances to Simon, my heart skipped nervously at the thought of touching the stone wall again. I stepped toward the wall. My stomach clenched with anxiety as a familiar feeling of dread stole over me. This time I wasn't sure if it was coming from me or Mairi.

I was aware of Simon's eyes burning a hole between my shoulder blades. I was nervous, but I had complete confidence that he wouldn't let anything happen to me. I squared my shoulders and lifted my hand, placing it on the cool rough stones.

I felt an immediate physical shock, like jumping into ice water. A wave of raw grief washed over me, but this time I was prepared for it. I kept my hand on the stone. Once again, I was enveloped in bleak, wintry darkness. So vivid was the image that for a moment I was afraid that I was drowning again. I gasped.

From some other part of my brain, I was vaguely aware that Simon had moved closer to me. He placed an arm around me, and I could feel the heat from his body warming me. I focused on my breathing. I wasn't drowning. I was in the library, I told myself.

Inhaling deeply, I tried to see past the sadness and pain to what was beyond. My eyes were open, but it was as if I was somewhere else. Blurred, disjointed images appeared before me, as if I was watching something through shattered glass.

There was a fire in the fireplace. Someone was in the room with me. I tried to concentrate, but I couldn't see very clearly.

A man. A boy. Robbie, I think. Yes, it is Robbie I see. He wants me to do something. What? I can't understand what it is he wants. I am impatient. I want him to leave. Why is he still here? Someone new appears and I am suddenly afraid. My body starts shaking. I don't want to watch anymore, but I can't allow myself to look away.

They are arguing. Voices are loud, but it is as if I am listening to them underwater. I can't understand what they are saying. I am so afraid. Why won't he leave? Robbie looks at me and holds out his hand. I stare at him. I do not move. I cannot move.

There is a sudden sharp explosion. I flinch at the loud noise. Robbie's body jerks, then folds, collapsing like a puppet without strings. Dark stains appear on the floor. I stare at the dark liquid pooling at my feet. With sudden clarity, I know this is my fault. My fault!

A tsunami of pain and sorrow slams into me, knocking

me to my knees. I am now the one who has collapsed as wave after wave of deep, raw pain surges over me, dragging me under the cold, black water.

Apparently, I let out a scream before crumbling to the floor, though I have no memory of doing either of those things. Jenna told me that Simon picked me up and carried me to one of the library chairs. She said I was deathly pale and cold to the touch, but still breathing. Simon hovered over me worriedly, checking my pulse until my eyelids began to flutter. In fact, his anxious face was the first thing I saw when I finally managed to open my eyes again.

I sat up, feeling exhausted and hollowed out from the experience. "I know what happened," I said softly.

Simon's worried expression turned to one of relief. I knew he had been frightened for me. I reached out and touched his arm. "It's okay. I'm okay," I reassured him.

He closed his eyes as if he was in pain. "I can't do this," he said in a heartbreakingly quiet voice. "I'm sorry." He turned away from me without saying another word and walked out of the library.

I watched him leave, aching for him and me, and Mairi.

Simon left Anchoret House. I had hoped I would have time to talk to him, to explain, but he didn't give me the chance.

Katie spoke to her dad about the stone wall in the library. I wasn't sure that Mr. McAfee truly believed that I'd been channeling Mairi's spirit, but since removing the wall was part of his long-term renovation plans, he was willing to humor Katie. Ben offered to stay and help.

They started dismantling the wall the next morning and found Robbie's skeleton before lunch.

Mr. McAfee drove to Balairie and called the police to report what they had found. The police came out to

Anchoret House that evening to investigate. We were all interviewed multiple times by various people in uniform, all of whom looked at me peculiarly when I explained that the skeleton was named Robert Cameron and he had been shot and killed in 1903 by Colonel Morris. Finally, after hours of people coming and going, the Medical Examiner and the police finished.

"It looks like Simon was right. The colonel shot and killed Robbie," Ben said as we watched the police van leave with Robbie's skeleton. "Then stuffed him in the fireplace."

"Why didn't he just bury him?" Katie asked.

"It was winter. The ground was frozen," Ben answered.

"But why did he put him in the fireplace?"

"Well, he couldn't very well stuff him and hang him on the wall, could he?" Ben said with a wicked grin.

"Nice, Ben," Jenna said, giving him a frosty look.

I turned to Katie. "I think the colonel suspected that something was going on between the two of them. That was why he sent Biscuit away and fired Robbie. Robbie came back to Mairi. He really loved her and wanted her to leave with him. I think that's when she gave him the pearl brooch.

"Why?"

"Money. He needed money."

"Then they were running away together," Jenna said.

I shook my head. "No. He came back for her, but Mairi understood more than he did what would happen to her if she left with him. You were right, Jenna. It would have been an unforgivable scandal for her to run away with a servant. Can you imagine how her family would have treated her? I think she realized how much it would cost her and her family. She made the choice to stay at Anchoret House. Robbie came back to plead with her."

"And he ended up dead," Ben said. "The colonel shot him when he came back for her."

I nodded. "Yes. I think guilt is what has kept Mairi at

Anchoret House."

"But she loved him," Jenna said. "You said she loved him."

"She did, but not enough to risk losing everything for him. She knew that if she left with him, she would be poor, cut off from her family and friends. She wasn't meant to live the life of a servant. She knew that. She loved Robbie, but not enough to make those kinds of sacrifices for him.

"No one forced her to marry the colonel. She was excited on her wedding day. I felt it. She wanted to have a wedding at St. Cuthberts and a big house and an important husband. Unfortunately, none of those things turned out the way she wanted them. She was unhappy and lonely. When Robbie came here to work, she thought she could have everything that she wanted and love."

"She did, until the colonel found out," Ben said ironically.

"But Mairi drowned," Katie said. "Did the colonel kill her, too?"

I shook my head. "No. Simon was right. The colonel didn't lift a finger to harm Mairi. He didn't have to. She walked into that loch of her own free will."

Ben caught my eye. "*Nemo me impune lacessit*," he said.

"Exactly. She was punishing the colonel the only way she knew how."

"What a horrible love story," Katie said. "There isn't a happy ending."

"No," I agreed, thinking of Simon leaving Anchoret House earlier. "Not all love stories have happy endings."

CHAPTER 17

30 June

Dear Mr. Fitzgibbon,

I hope you will forgive a meddling old woman for interfering, but I am nearing the end of a very long life and perhaps because of this I feel free to dispense unsolicited advice. I have recently made the acquaintance of a most remarkable young woman and I hope that by writing to you I might repay her for the kindness she has shown me.

Lily has spoken quite highly of you. She is in love with you as I am certain you are aware. Love is a terrible thing, is it not? For it is by loving that we make ourselves most vulnerable. When we allow ourselves to love, we open ourselves to the risk of loss and that can be frightening to even the most stalwart of hearts. However, it is important to remember that while love is a terrible thing, it is also a beautiful gift. One that should not be cast away lightly. You will agree, I think, that without love, death has little meaning, but alas neither does life.

Lily tells me that you are a young man of great courage and character. I hope that you will find within yourself the courage to risk love.

Sincerely,
Agnes Sinclair

***

Ben drove me back to Edinburgh. I called Simon and left a message on his cell phone, letting him know that I was leaving Anchoret House and asking him to call me. Ben's eyes slid in my direction while I spoke on the phone, but he didn't comment.

Our first stop, once we arrived in the city, was the retirement community of Loch Arthur. I wanted to return the letters to Agnes and fill her in on what we discovered.

We parked the car and walked up to the main building. I pressed the intercom button.

"Good afternoon, Loch Arthur Retirement Village. How may we help you?"

I spoke into the microphone. "Hi. This is Lily Deene and Ben Hickman. We're here to see Agnes Sinclair." I heard a faint electronic buzz.

"The front door is open. Please make yourself comfortable in the waiting area. Someone will be with you shortly."

I pushed open the door and we walked inside. Almost immediately, the side door opened and Alana greeted us with a welcoming smile.

"How lovely to see you again. Agnes so enjoyed your last visit." Her smile dimmed. "Though I'm afraid you'll find her a bit under the weather. She's had a turn for the worse, I'm afraid."

"What's wrong?" Ben asked.

"It's becoming more difficult for her to manage the pain," she said with a little shake of her head, but then her smile brightened. "This is so wonderful that you are able to visit. It will be good for her to have a happy diversion."

Ben and I exchanged glances. "Is there anything we can do to help?" I asked.

"I think your visit will be just what she needs. She's brave about it, but I know she gets a bit lonely, especially now, as she's unable to move about much. Do you remember how to get to her room?"

We both nodded, answering her at the same time.

Then you two can go on up. I'll bring some biscuits and the three of you can enjoy a nice chat."

Ben and I made our way to the second floor and found her room. I knocked on the door. We heard something that might have been a feeble "come in," though the words weren't clear.

I looked at Ben and he shrugged. We pushed open the door expecting to see Agnes sitting and knitting. Unlike last time, the living area was empty.

"Agnes?" I called out.

"I'm afraid I'm still abed today." Her voice came from the bedroom.

"Would you like us to wait out here?"

"Is that you, Lily?"

"Yes. Ben's is with me."

"Oh, how lovely, do come in. Both of you."

The door to her bedroom was ajar and we pushed it open. Agnes was propped up in bed, her face pale and drawn. She looked even smaller and frailer than our last visit, though her eyes were still lively. She welcomed us with a warm smile.

"How lovely to see you both again."

"We've brought the letters back," I said, showing her the box.

"Have you now? I hope they were helpful."

"Yes. They were. Where should I put them?"

"Anywhere will do."

"Why don't I put the box in the dining room," Ben suggested. "I'll get us a couple of chairs."

Ben brought in a chair for me. "I can make us some tea while you two young lassies enjoy a wee natter," he said with a wink at Agnes.

She laughed. "Oh my. That would be lovely."

I pulled my chair closer to the bed. "How are you?"

Her hand fluttered in the air dismissively. "Don't bother about me. I want to hear all about your adventures."

I started telling her about Mairi and Robbie and the colonel. Ben came in at one point with the biscuits and tea. We made her a tray and fluffed her pillows for her. She listened eagerly to our stories, though her tea and biscuits remained untouched. Alana was right, she did tire easily. At one point, she leaned back on her pillows and closed her eyes.

"Never mind, dear. You keep talking. I'm listening. I just need a little rest."

When Ben and I left, she was sleeping lightly.

We found Alana and let her know that we had left the biscuits and tea things in Agnes's room.

"How was she?" she asked.

"Okay, I guess. You were right though, she seemed tired. She fell asleep."

Alana nodded. "The morphine makes her tired. She doesn't like to take it, but it does help her manage the pain."

Ben's eyebrows rose in surprise. "Morphine? She's taking morphine for arthritis?"

"Arthritis? Oh. It's not for her arthritis. No. She's taking morphine to help manage the pain for her cancer."

Ben and I exchanged glances.

"She has cancer?" I asked.

"Yes. Poor dear. She's been on pain management for five months now. It does seem to help, though not as much as it used to."

"Pain management?" I asked.

Alana nodded, her eyes shadowed. "Yes. There really isn't much else that can be done, except keep her as comfortable as possible."

I felt hot tears pricking the back of my eyelids. "Does

that mean she's dying?" I asked, blinking rapidly.

Alana gave me a sympathetic look. "Yes, I'm afraid so."

I walked back to the car with Ben, my throat felt tight and hot. I swallowed with difficulty.

"I feel so bad for her," I said.

Ben nodded. "I know. It's sad, but she is ninety-four. She's had a long life."

"But she's so alone. She's stuck in that room all by herself."

"I'm sure the staff come in and visit her."

I shook my head. "No. They have so many people in there. It's not enough." My eyes filled with tears. "No one should die alone like that."

"No," Ben agreed. "They shouldn't."

We got into the car. I fastened my seatbelt, glancing out the window at the Loch Arthur building.

"Ben," I said. "I know you were supposed to drive me back to Brynmoor, but do you think your mother would mind if I stayed a little longer, so I could visit Agnes?"

Ben's mouth curved into a soft, sad smile. "I know she wouldn't."

I stayed in Edinburgh for two more weeks. I called my mom: still no baby. I called Simon: still no answer. I visited Agnes every day. My visits with her were a welcome distraction from the fact that Simon wasn't responding to my texts or phone calls. I kept thinking about what he said before he left Anchoret House. Maybe it was too much to ask of him. If Ben's mother was right and I did have "the sight," then there was no way of knowing if or when something like what happened with Mairi might happen again, and I could see how that could be difficult for Simon. I knew he cared for me, but I think the situation by the loch really frightened him. No one wants to watch someone they love die.

During our visits, Agnes and I talked about everything. Actually, to be honest, I did most of the talking.

I told her that I wanted to study theology.

"A serious subject for such a young girl," she'd commented.

"I want to learn more about life after death. I know our energy goes somewhere after we die. I want to understand why it sometimes lingers."

"Lingers?"

"Stays here. With us."

"Ghosts?"

"Ghosts, spirits, souls. Some people can see that energy can hear their voices and ..." I faltered. "I think they stay behind because they need to understand what happened to them, or maybe they're lost. Or, sometimes, if they have something they need to do or someone they need to save or a wrong to right. I think they stay with us. If someone can see that energy, then they can help them, but I want to know how."

Agnes looked at me, her eyes sharp. "Ah, I see," she said. "You want to know how to help them."

"Yes."

I ended up telling her about my experiences with spirits, something I rarely shared with people. I told her about what happened at Brynmoor last summer and what had happened at Anchoret. I think it soothed her to know there was something after death. We talked about life and death and, of course, because I couldn't talk about all those things without mentioning Simon, I told her about Simon.

I ended up telling her everything about him: How I loved him. How I didn't blame him for avoiding me. How I was hurt and lonely, but I understood why he didn't want to be around me. Dealing with the supernatural was unnerving for me, I couldn't imagine what it would be like to watch it happen to someone else.

"I love him so much, but I think I've scared him off," I told her tearfully one morning during a visit.

She patted my hand. "Don't you worry, dear. I am certain he'll come around. Your young man does love you. He's just frightened of things he can't control. It's the price of love, isn't it?" she said with a small sigh. "Love makes' us vulnerable. That can be very frightening, especially to a strapping young laddie like yours. They do so like to be in control. Don't they?"

"He can be a bit bossy," I agreed, smiling through my tears.

"There you have it, then," she said confidently. "He'll come 'round. Give him time."

I shook my head sorrowfully. "I don't think so. I think it's just too much for him. He's scientific and, well, practical. This is something he can't control or understand, and it scares him. It scares me, too," I said with a rueful smile. "But I don't have much of a choice. I can't walk away."

"Well, if I was to lay a bet, I would say that if your young man will come to his senses before too long."

I didn't have much hope, but her confidence in Simon comforted me.

Our visits fell into a kind of routine. I would show up and Alana would bring us biscuits. I knew she wasn't feeling well, because even when she managed to sit in the living room, she allowed me to make the tea and pour out, despite the fact that I was American. Although, I noticed that she hardly ever drank it. When I teased her about it, she managed a small sip and pronounced it quite respectable.

She was always happy to see me. We would talk and sometimes she told me things about her childhood or family. Small bright memories that brought her joy to share with someone. She would grow tired after a while and then I would clear the tea things and hold her hand, keeping her company until she fell asleep.

Alana said she was in a great deal of pain, though I never would have guessed it from our visits. Apparently, my visits helped soothe her and it was the only time she slept well. It made me feel good to know I was doing something nice for her.

One morning on my way to visit Agnes, Jenna called me on my cell phone to tell me that the police had found the pearl brooch inside the tattered cloth of Robbie's jacket pocket.

"You were right. She did give it to him."

"You doubted me?" I asked, knowing she would hear the smile in my voice.

"No. Not me."

I heard someone say something in the background.

"We're driving down to Edinburgh to get the set appraised at the jewelers. Apparently, Hamilton and Inches is still in business. Katie wants to know if we can meet the woman who gave you the letters."

"I think she'd like that." I told her about Agnes and the cancer.

"Wait a minute," I heard her repeating what I'd said on the phone to Katie and her dad. They had a short conversation.

Mr. McAfee will drive us down to Edinburgh tomorrow. We can bring the photos and the pearl necklace and brooch to show her. What do you think?"

"I think she'll love it," I said enthusiastically. "You probably won't be able to stay too long; she gets tired pretty quickly, but I think that's a great idea."

"Right. We'll see you tomorrow then. Cheers."

I was happy to have some exciting news for Agnes. After I got off the phone with Jenna, I caught the bus to Loch Arthur.

Alana met me in the waiting room. I could tell from her expression that something had happened.

"Is Agnes all right?" I asked anxiously.

She gave me a sad little smile. "Agnes passed in the night."

My throat closed up. "Passed?"

"Yes," she said gently.

I felt myself growing unaccountably angry. I should have known. Shouldn't I? She was a friend and I didn't even know that she had died. What was the point of hearing dead people if you couldn't hear the ones that mattered?

"When did it happen?"

Alana gave me a sympathetic look. I supposed working in a retirement home meant that she was used to people she knew dying. "Last night sometime. She went peacefully in her sleep. She left a box for you. Would you like to visit her room, or if you prefer I can bring it to you and you may wait here?"

I'd like to go to her room, if that's okay," I said stiffly.

"Of course."

I followed Alana to the second floor. I knew I was being unreasonable, but I felt as if I had been cheated. Agnes should have told me. She should have said good-bye. Why didn't she tell me good-bye? The logical point of my brain pointed out that she might not have been able to. Maybe it took time to learn how to do those things once you were dead, or maybe only unhappy people lingered. Logically I knew I was being unreasonable, but that didn't keep the emotional part of my brain from feeling hurt and angry.

Alana unlocked the door to Agnes's room. "Take all the time you need," she said. "Just close the door behind you when you leave."

I nodded, unable to speak. I looked around the room. Someone had already started packing her belongings. There was a large cardboard box on the floor with the words "Clothing for Donation" scrawled in black marker across the top of it.

"Why didn't you say good-bye?" I asked aloud.

Then I felt it. Something touched the back of my hand, soft as a whisper, and I knew she had waited for me to come for one last visit before leaving. She was there for a brief moment. I felt her.

"Good-bye, Agnes," I told her. Then I sat on a chair and cried. I wasn't crying for her. She was at peace. I was crying for me because I had lost a friend.

Agnes left the letters and photos to me. In her note, she asked me to find a good home for them.

When Jenna and the McAfee's arrived at the Hickmans the next day, I told them about Agnes. I gave Mr. McAfee the letters and photographs. He promised to display them as part of the history of Anchoret House. We had dinner with the Hickman's at an Italian restaurant. Simon did not join us.

Before the McAfee's began their drive back to Balairie, I removed Robbie's necklace and handed it to him.

"No, lass, it's yours to keep. I've no doubt it was meant as a gift for you."

"Thank you," I said, slipping it back over my head.

The next day, Ben drove Jenna and me to the train station and we boarded a train back to Brynmoor.

Jenna and I arrived at Brynmoor on the same day that William Patrick Randall, the 10th Earl of Yarlbury, decided to make his appearance. It was amazing to me how one tiny baby could create so much chaos. Eventually things settled down. Although perhaps settled wasn't really an accurate description of life at Brynmoor Manor post-baby. Will, as the 10th Earl of Yarlbury was known, kept things hopping in new and unexpected ways.

The rest of July passed quickly. When I wasn't crooning over my new baby brother, I spent time at the stable or on long rides with Posy and sometimes with Jenna. I was still waiting to hear from Kings Cross College.

I decided that if I didn't hear anything, I would go to California, start college there, and reapply to Kings Cross for the following term.

One afternoon in August, I went to the stable to saddle Posy for a trail ride. Jenna had said she would join me, but she was late.

I held out a slice of apple for Posy.

She sniffed the apple, snorting unhappily at me.

"Sorry, girl. Old Joseph says no more sugar cubes."

She looked balefully at me.

"I would if I could," I told her, offering her the apple slice once more.

This time, realizing this was the best she could hope for, she nibbled at it.

I gave her a pat on the neck. "See. That's not so bad." Her head bobbed up suddenly, her ears pricking forward eagerly. She gave a little happy nicker and my heart froze. There was only one other person she greeted like that.

I turned to look, my heart bumping in my chest.

"I hope you're not feeding her sugar cubes," he said. "Old Joseph will have your hide if he catches you."

I shook my head, not trusting my voice.

He walked toward me. "How have you been?"

I inhaled deeply as I tried to keep my feelings in check. "Fine."

He stopped beside me and reached up to rub Posy behind her ears. Posy nickered again and bumped her head impatiently against Simon's hand, excited to see him.

"You heard about the baby?" I asked, working hard to keep my voice casual.

He nodded. "My mum called."

"I'm sure she told you how crazy things have been around here lately." I managed a little smile. "Crazy in a good way," I added.

"I can imagine," he said, his eyes crinkling at the

corners.

We stared at each other as an awkward silence fell between us. We both started speaking at the same time.

"You first," I said.

"I called Dr. Eames last week. I'm coming back the end of summer. I'll be working with him in Shawbury."

"That's great, Simon."

"And you? Have you heard from Kings Cross?"

"No. If I don't hear from them, I'll leave for California the end of August."

"Right. Well ..." He sighed and combed his hand through his hair. "Lily, I'm sorry."

"Hey. It's okay. I understand. It's weird for me. I can only imagine how hard it is for you."

"Yes, but that doesn't make it right. I acted like a selfish bastard."

"And an arrogant sod," I teased him.

"And an arrogant sod," he agreed, giving me a quick glimpse of the Fitzgibbon dimples. "I've no excuse. I should have rung you when you were in Edinburgh, but I needed time to sort things out."

"I'm sorry if I made you angry."

He shook his head. "I wasn't angry at you. Well, not too much. I was mostly angry at ..." He gave a little laugh. "At a ghost and at myself."

"I know. It's okay. It freaks me out, too, and I'm the one doing it. I don't think most people are very comfortable with talking to the dead."

A little line appeared between his eyebrows. "It's not that so much, though it does take getting used to. No. It was watching you die." His voice caught. "It was the worst thing I've ever experienced. Worse than the fire, because at least then I didn't have time to think about it and I knew what to do. This was something else. I was helpless. There was nothing I could do to stop it."

"But you weren't helpless," I interrupted him. "You gave me mouth to mouth."

He shook his head as a gesture of his frustration. "I had no idea what to do. How do you fight a ghost? I was just hoping that if I got you breathing whatever it was would stop and I could bring you back. I didn't know if it would work." He grinned crookedly at me. "They don't exactly cover treatment for spirit possessions at the R.V.C."

I stared at him, not quite trusting myself to speak. So, this was it. I was getting the "Let's be friends" speech, I thought.

"When that happened at the loch and you wouldn't leave Anchoret, I was angry. Then in the library, I thought it was happening all over again. I was angry at you, at myself, and angry at the damn ghost. That's why I left. That's why I didn't ring you back. I'm sorry. I treated you badly. Again."

I stared at him, my heart breaking, but I understood. If our positions had been reversed, I knew that I wouldn't be able to stand by helplessly and watch someone I loved suffer. I decided that as hard as it would be for me, I'd rather have Simon as a friend than nothing at all.

"It's okay. I understand." I fished another slice of apple out of my pocket and offered it to Posy.

"I got a letter after you left Edinburgh."

I looked at him blankly. "A letter?"

He smiled faintly. "From your friend Agnes."

"Agnes Sinclair?"

He nodded.

"She died," I said softly.

"I know. Ben told me."

"But why would she send you a letter?"

He took the letter out of his pocket and handed it to me.

I read the letter. When I finished reading it, I looked up at Simon.

Simon's mouth twitched at the corners. "She's called me a coward."

"It was nicely done," I said. "And you have been called worse."

"Yes, I have."

I held his gaze.

"If you're willing to take on an arrogant sod like me, I'd like another chance."

"Absolutely, you arrogant sod," I said as I folded myself into his arms.

***

Mairi,

I pledge to ye with my body and my spirit that I will not forsake ye. I will come for ye, tho' it were ten thousand miles.

Robbie

SNEAK PEEK AT THE NEXT LILY DEENE NOVEL...

Something was wrong with me. My head ached and throbbed. My mouth was dry. I tried to lick my lips, but my tongue felt abnormally thick and heavy in my mouth and I couldn't quite manage it.

I opened my eyes cautiously, feeling confused and disoriented. The dark was so complete that for a moment I wasn't sure if I was awake or dreaming? I blinked. I blinked again and I slowly became aware of sensations. Cold. I was very cold.

I struggled to sit up. My arms and legs felt like stone weights. I managed to lift myself a little, but my stomach heaved, and I had to lie down quickly to keep from throwing up.

What was wrong with me? I breathed deeply, drinking in the cold and dark in large gulping breaths as I tried to snag the half-formed thoughts that floated past like drifting clouds. Why was it so dark? Was I sick? Where was my pillow? My comforter? Where was I?

Gingerly, I moved my fingers testing the area around me. I lay on a hard surface, stone or brick. I wasn't in my bed. I should have been in my bed. My head swam with the effort as I tried to figure out what was happening to me. My mind was in a fog. I had no recollection of coming to this place.

Again, I tried to sit up. This time I managed to raise myself up on my elbows before I felt a sudden saltiness in the back of my throat. Once more, my stomach heaved and roiled. I quickly rolled over and retched, the hot sour smell of vomit permeating the air, worsening my nausea. I lay on my back, too dizzy and disoriented to move. Closing my eyes, I surrendered to the darkness.

DON'T MISS THE FIRST LILY DEENE NOVEL

Lily Deene has a new dream guy. There's just one small problem. He's dead.

Seventeen-year-old Lily Deene has no choice but to spend her summer at Brynmoor Manor in England where there are more sheep than people. She isn't thrilled, but after her mother enlists Simon, the housekeeper's son, to give her horseback riding lessons, Lily decides to make the best of a bad situation. It turns out that it's not all tea and crumpets at the manor house. Long buried secrets are stirring. Secrets that are haunting her dreams and Lily quickly finds herself galloping straight into danger.

AVAILABLE WHERE BOOKS ARE SOLD....

ACKNOWLEDGEMENTS

I would like to acknowledge The Carlyle Letters Online collection, a digital archive of the Thomas and Jane Welsh Carlyle letters found at Duke University. I have borrowed from these letters making changes to better fit the story of Mairi and Robbie.

I encourage readers interested in reviewing these fascinating letters to visit

https://carlyleletters.dukeupress.edu/home

ABOUT THE AUTHOR

(photo from 2004)

Annie Grace Roberts is a mother-daughter writing team from California. They share a love of adventure and happy endings. Neither has ever met a ghost they didn't like.

www. AnnieGraceRoberts.com
AnnieGracebooks@gmail.com
AGRoberts_books twitter
AnnieGraceRoberts instagram
facebook: /www.facebook.com/Annie-Grace-Roberts